HOW IT

Dan Collins is the author of *Cannibals*. He lives in
West Cork, Ireland.

ALSO BY DAN COLLINS

Cannibals

Dan Collins

HOW IT ENDS

V

VINTAGE

Published by Vintage 2004

2 4 6 8 10 9 7 5 3 1

First published in Great Britain in 2003 by
Jonathan Cape

Vintage
Random House, 20 Vauxhall Bridge Road,
London SW1V 2SA

Random House Australia (Pty) Limited
20 Alfred Street, Milsons Point, Sydney
New South Wales 2061, Australia

Random House New Zealand Limited
18 Poland Road, Glenfield,
Auckland 10, New Zealand

Random House (Pty) Limited
Endulini, 5A Jubilee Road, Parktown 2193,
South Africa

The Random House Group Limited Reg. No. 954009
www.randomhouse.co.uk/vintage

A CIP catalogue record for this book
is available from the British Library

ISBN 0 099 44514 X

Papers used by Random House are natural, recyclable products made from wood grown in sustainable forests. The manufacturing processes conform to the environmental regulations of the country of origin

Printed and bound in Great Britain by
Bookmarque Ltd, Croydon, Surrey

To Jason Arthur

how it ends

crushed

Billy and Alessia had been together fifteen months, when, without much prompting, I decided to fuck him when Alessia went in the hospital overnight to have her nose fixed. I didn't understand that, neither did Billy, Alessia wanting to have her nose done. So far as either of us knew, Alessia had lived with the same nose for twenty-five years and never previously uttered a word against it. Neither had anyone else commented on or complained about that part of her appearance. Now, suddenly, she couldn't live with it any more. When I ran into Billy at the hospital, he claimed Alessia's decision was making him a little anxious about other areas, other issues, what else Alessia might be unhappy with, what else she might want fixed.

I said, 'What're you saying, Billy?'

He looked directly at me, spoke deliberately, 'You know what I'm saying.'

That was the start of it.

A taller, leaner version of me, a year younger, pale and dark haired, his skin smelling of soap, his tongue tasting of coffee, his prick cut and salty. I stayed the night with him, fucking and talking, mostly talking; the sex, or rather the penetrative element, was over

3

and done with in a watery pea-sized emission. He told me he had been afflicted for weeks with a strange, strangling, somehow portentous, case of dry ejaculation, so pea-size was quite a triumph for him, for both of us; reversely, its meagerness and insipid appearance was even more critically reassuring given our failure to deploy any prophylactic due to the unplanned, impetuous nature of the encounter. OK, due as much to a prudent desire to establish, at least in our own minds, an absence of premeditation, lay down some proof against the horrors of remorse.

In the morning, he stripped the bed even as I was dressing. How indelicate of him, I thought, not waiting for me to leave before starting on the clean-up. As I walked up the hill toward home, I considered what a good friend I was to Alessia and Billy. I had visited her in the hospital, refrained from criticising her choice of rhinoplasty as the way to mark her birthday. And I had kept a sisterly, watchful eye on Billy the one night he had to forgo what passed in his commitment-phobic fashion for conjugal coitus. Better me than some noxious streetwalker, I reasoned; not that I would ever express such a view to Alessia. And Billy got to put it in me. A sort of one-off bonus following on almost four years of relentless touring.

He wasn't that different to the range of men I usually tolerated in my bed, all taking out their little revenge on me, their stilted little intrusions into my sex, their greedy hot breath in my ear, punishing me for whatever life had denied them – beauty, talent, wealth, celebrity, hair, a sympathetic wife, a tolerant accommodating mistress – calling me darling, doll, bird, bitch – worse – cunt, whore, and lying about love, until I came to believe that's what you get out on the edge or wherever it was I was dissipating my life. And I had to absorb it all without showing a trace of true emotion or affect. I had to play the part their desire decreed, I had to feign arousal and moan a cocktail of delight and terror as they unzipped and flourished, if you could call it that, their average domestic puniness. Such dribbled insignificance was partially how I tolerated them. Their sad pathetic in-adequacies, their so-called manliness, simply made me want to roar with glee and continue the endless search for the surely mythical 'something better'.

The day after we'd slept together, the day after Alessia went to have her nose done, Billy tells me he's getting married to someone else, someone other than Alessia, someone certainly not me. The shock is enhanced because I never expected I was so vulnerable, but it's the same as if he's driven an axe without warning deep into my chest and worked it there, his foot one moment on my hip for leverage, then on my throat, pushing and pulling on the handle, prising apart the bone cage until my heart is exposed, and then he reaches in and rips it out, holds it high, a crimson spouting prize with ribbons of vein and artery trailing, dripping and sigh-ing, a gory spectacle in the chatter and tinkle of the terrace bar where we've agreed to meet, the sigh of the breeze through the trees, high umbrellas of pine, deep skirts of willow, swaying and billowing, the cry of an outboard on the streaming tide below, like it's another estuary entirely and nothing to do with me and my life or what he's telling me. For the first time in years I'm homesick for the past, the landlocked interior of my childhood when all was uncompromised and life unsullied, and now I'm forlorn, a mess, and no one so much as bats an eye, sees anything amiss, all these placid featured effigies, day-trippers, foreigners, locals, a smattering of saints and martyrs by the look of some, looking, not looking, tears searing in my eyes, a veil of smoke, and tremulous choking in my throat, so much that I believe I'm drowning, half drowned already, unable to comprehend why no one comes to my aid, merely persist with sipping their drinks and smoking their poison and voicing their own inflated inanities, and right then I know that I'm done for. Three days later I'm in LA, staying with Pearl Mundy, where a vestigial shard of vanity mixed up with a whole trailer-load of atavistic fantasy, along with Pearl's gentle wheedling, suggests there's a better than fair chance I'm going to run into Brad Pitt, or Russell Crowe, or George Clooney, or, let's face it and fuck it – which according to several people I could mention has always been my preferred mode of blitzing seduction – Robert Downey Jr. But I'm feeling older than life, and frankly, if I had a father worthy of the name he would take a gun and shoot Billy through the quick for my sake, and as it seems, here I am, fairly bereft where fathers and romantic delusions are concerned, why should I be surprised or act surprised, and this seems to ensure that I don't run into anyone even vaguely famous, or wealthy, or talented, or cute enough to want to sleep with them and prove some important things to myself, other people.

★ ★ ★

Pearl lives in Venice, which is sometimes fifteen or so degrees cooler than it is ten miles away on that part of the strip around Tower Records and Book Soup and the Viper Room, which I've always regarded as the heart of LA. One night, Pearl takes me up to the Chateau Marmont for drinks in the great sunken room off the lobby and to look at the men there. After an uneventful hour – the place is hushed, a few couples, smug souls – we go on to a concert at The Vynyl to check out this singer that Pearl knows.

Eddie Pope plays this enormous accordion, swings his mane of blond hair, showering the stage with his sweat, is this compelling force-field. Pearl describes the music as Gothic Christian Country, but that doesn't bother me, the sweep of the sound gets me past all that, and I hardly register the lyrics or the fact that Eddie Pope doesn't look my way even once. No one cares enough to let us see that anyone here tonight might be interested. At one point, this dark-suited kid leans between us but it's only to light his cigarette from the tea light burning on our table. He looks in both our faces, and he's tall and lean, and there's something strained in the tightness around his fierce blue eyes, and after he takes a drag he moves away back into the shelter of the crowded floor, and immediately he's pursued by three, four bouncers who surround him, make him put out his cigarette on the sole of his shoe, and pocket the butt.

Which is the moment when Pearl recognises him, saying, 'That's Scott Weaver.'

'No,' I say, trying to sound impressed.

It all seems so exciting, to be in this club, like I

belong here, like no one cares that I'm not at home here, that without Billy by my side I'm unfocused, lacking identity or purpose. After the show, Pearl leads me backstage, introduces me to Eddie Pope, who, towelling his chest and neck, asks how long I'm going to be in town, dimly expresses a wish to meet up sometime. Someone else is here, poised in the shadows, whispering, just as we're about to leave, echoing my name, his hand reaching for me, brushing the unflattering softness of my hip as I pass.

Another night we boldly go to The Smog Cutter, this karaoke bar in a less than savoury part of Echo Park, where a blanket covers the upper half of the doorway leading to the street, and this Thai, or Vietnamese, bargirl, I can't tell which, Asian anyhow, dark and sleek, who's called Rainbow, cries, 'Awesome,' after I take a shot at 'Bette Davis Eyes', and the applause gives me a boost but it doesn't take long before I discover that Rainbow cries 'Awesome' whenever anyone sings. Apparently everyone is awesome in Rainbow's eyes. And even here, on the wall, in a clutter of unframed photos – there's no escape – I find a picture of Billy, looking wasted, his arms around Clive and Will, guys from the band, all three of them leering at Rainbow.

Pearl works hard at keeping me distracted. She drives me up the coast. She drives me down the coast. She drives me into the desert. She drives me out to Zabriskie Point where we encounter pilgrim Italians who avert their eyes and fail to clamour for my number, or a date, or even to have their picture taken with me. Mostly Pearl brings me shopping. And one day, having called ahead and booked a parking space, we drive to the Getty which is strangely disappointing, a museum after all is what it is, crowded with old art, and scarcely ambulatory aged people. Some sign of life would not go amiss, some toxic antics, sumo wrestlers in the courtyard, fly-fishing instruction by the ornamental brook, rubbers in the washrooms to cater for those visitors improbably impassioned by the surroundings.

In a bookstore on Sunset I buy Pearl a book of Araki photographs. Women with love in their eyes. Knickerless women. Women bleeding from thimbleberry nipples. Women beset by toy plastic dinosaurs. Women bound and suspended from trees, from roof beams. Pregnant women with garden hoses snaking from their painted vulvas. Hirsute women. Sad women. Baby women. Hopeless women. Dead women. I suspect there's a significant lesson somewhere in Araki but as of now it escapes me.

Neither of us speak about why I left London in such a rush, nor about me and Alessia, about me and Billy, about the abrupt demise of Anaconda, about Billy's plans to forge a solo career, marry some faceless creature – *why marry for Heaven's sake?* – or why I precipitously chose to come out here, or what I might find to do with the rest of my life, or why I insist on returning to London at all; and through all of this, all this glum toing and froing, Pearl never lets on to be the least burdened by my presence.

The night before I'm due to fly out, we eat tuna at Chez Ray's on Ocean Avenue in Santa Monica, and Ray joins us for a moment, informs us how he's seventy-something, has a forty-something daughter, a thirty-something wife, a twelve-year-old son. He looks fifty-something, agreeable, charming, reminds me a little of what Billy possesses. Even so, he's hardly what I'm looking for. Afterwards we go down the street for drinks at two adjacent hotels – Shutters on the Beach and the Casa del Mar. Pearl confesses there's a slight chance the inscrutable, fabulously talented, elusive Eddie Pope is going to drop by. As soon as we arrive at each hotel, she insists we go up on the roof to look at the swimming pools, beautiful, deserted, calming, tiny, lit like jewels, the out of doors balmy, seductive. No one stops us as we make our way along hotel corridors, no one asks us where we think we're going, or comments on how we wear our unease, our need, our hurt, like ill-fitting basques. Downstairs, we take in the lounges, one larger than the other, one with a real fireplace burning real logs, the other with live piano music which somehow reminds me of the Hotel Quisisana on Capri where we visited with Alessia's family, and Billy upset the piano player by drawing attention to the melancholy woman who lingered so needily after her friends had gone to their rooms for the night.

There are plenty of men sitting around here but again none of them cares enough to make a move despite the clarion signals of availability we seem to be broadcasting. I begin to suspect my aura has acquired this damaged, aggrieved air which deters them, never mind renders Pearl miserable. So, I excuse myself, make my way to the restroom, conscious all the way of striving to appear decorous, in keeping with the ambience.

I check my reflection, see that I no longer look like myself but someone bloated, tired and vanquished, and

I have no idea what I'm doing in LA, no idea why I'm still alive. I admire the neat pyramid of rolled white cotton hand towels arranged by the basin, another flatter greyer stack of paper towels beyond. The light in here is sepulchral, seems to slow time, invite appraisal of my predicament. For all I know there might be gnomes, swift tiny feral creatures secreted in the stalls behind me, poised to leap on me and quiz, probe, judge, diminish, infect, dismiss me, just the way a husband or a traitorous lover does. And there's a faint noise from the shadows, and I turn, certain that someone is there, and I whisper, 'Billy?' and a stall door creaks and slowly swings open to reveal a gleaming ceramic perch, unoccupied, and I wonder what Pearl might have heard from London as regards my behaviour, my troubles, my plight, and I wonder why she never made any effort while I was out here to encourage and facilitate a proper meeting with the much-hyped Eddie Pope. From which it's only another small step to realising that Pearl has been bringing me to all the wrong sorts of place if finding a man is what you're interested in, all you're interested in, apart from vindication, validation, some tortured variation on justice, a blind lunge at secret self-annihilating revenge.

I touch up my eyes, adding shadow a little hastily; gaze overlong at the suddenly regrettable magenta lipgloss; my cheeks burning of their own accord, no need to pinch or burnish, apply anything; turn on my heel, precariously enough – five-inch pencil heels, a Corona with dinner, three daiquiris on top of that; and reaching the door, haul it open only to step into an overwhelming cloud of Cuban bluey grey darkness

11

and the waiting, easeful arms and chest of . . .

'I know you,' I snaffle, trying to keep myself from falling into his blue eyes, bluest blue, lit it seems from inside and out. 'You're . . .'

And he says, 'Serge.'

Something wrong here, the name, the cigar, the beautiful boy in his gleaming white T-shirt and faded chinos, the daiquiris catching up, the fact I know I look tired, this is the wrong time for something like this, but it seems like I don't have any other choice, all the optimism gone from my heart, the confidence from my manner, the elasticity from my skin, my pores exposed, and still he lingers. Maybe he's not Scott Weaver. Maybe he really is someone called Serge. Maybe all Californians now look alike to me. These beautiful children with their serenity, their teeth, their flawless profiles, their refusal to countenance anything other than light and innocence. I look around to see who else is here in this tiled passageway, manipulating this cutesy encounter. No one. Just the two of us. And he's in no rush to release me.

I try again. 'Sergio, you said?'

And he says, 'It's Serge.'

And I say, 'I'm sorry.'

'Serge,' he says, repeating himself, a languid instructive air, phoney as the scuffed heavy work boots he wears. This one definitely never hewed lumber, hauled rock, poured patio, dug ditch in his young pampered life.

'What've you got,' I say, 'with the cigar, some sort of death wish?'

'Only for humankind,' he says.

And I say, 'Such, what's the word, morbidity in one so young.'

And he says, 'You're intrigued.'

And I say, 'Isn't it against the . . .'

And he says, 'Law?'

And I say, 'Isn't it?'

And he says, 'So far as I know.'

And I try again, saying, 'You're Scott Weaver.'

And he sticks to his guns, showing his teeth, saying in this drawl, 'I'm Serge.'

'Aw,' I go, disappointed now he won't come clean, although recognising it's some part of the celebrity game, and accepting it's possibly a critical element of the prelude to whatever lies ahead for both of us.

'And you remind me of someone,' he says.

And I persist, 'Aren't you?'

And he says, 'You're not going to tell me?'

And I say, 'Lee Annis.'

And he says, 'Who?'

And I say, 'That's what they tell me.'

And he says, 'You're not from Texas? Why do I think you're from Texas?'

And I say, 'Some people think I'm Danish.'

And he says, 'So, tell me.'

And I say, 'You are Scott Weaver, aren't you?'

And he says, 'Look, why don't we step outside so I can finish with this over-priced stogie, and I'll tell all if you promise to come clean and explain who you are, what you're doing here, why I've never seen you here before.'

And I say, 'I'm afraid my friend is waiting for me at the bar.'

And he says, 'He'll keep a couple more minutes, won't he. Even lousy cigars cost money. It'd be a shame to waste it, don't you think?'

'Sinful,' I say, faltering, neither indifferent nor brave enough to correct him as to who's waiting at the bar for me; increasingly anxious that Pearl will appear at any moment and not just ruin the illusion he at least lets on to bear regarding my companion but disrupt the easy dynamic we've established. So I allow him to escort me to a little alcove which leads through a glass door out onto a flagged walkway, and then onto the beach where the night rumbles easily, with the ocean battering the shore, all part of the deal.

Two steps into the deep, soft sand, and I need to crouch to undo my shoes. He watches as I unbuckle the tiny straps, and when I straighten, the shoes dangling from one hand, my purse in the other, a smile glides easily onto my face, the skirt of the blue and grey dress swirling now, billowing, and I'm ambushed by images from that recent afternoon meeting with Billy on the river – why the river? – where did he think we could go and fail to be discovered, recognised, billowing, that horrible feeling in my stomach, calling for my hands to press it against my thighs, the relentless way he got through all that he had to say, battening it down as best I can, the front rising, cold-hearted, like a stone, now the back, and he walks on, turning once to face me, the rich wake of cigar smoke, wanting to luxuriate in it, before hurrying toward the foaming line of water, intoxicated, compelled, this annihilating need to be held, vaguely aware of the off-shore phosphorescence, wondering if that's his voice saying something to me lost in the roar, walking after him, no longer Billy, his T-shirts, his jeans, so like this Californian with his casual way, all the occasions when I followed him, attended him and Alessia, the others, all the stories in the papers of his ambition, his talent, his professional ferocity, his unremitting focus, the saga, the reports and rumours of his dalliances, countless infidelities, pitching his lean body forward a little as if the wind decrees it, hurrying now to catch up to him, trying to keep my step light on the sand even as he turns goofy, labouring clownishly, exaggerating the cloying heaviness of the beach the closer we get to the ocean. And when I catch up to him, conscious of all my exposed flesh, stippled with goose bumps, teeth chattering lightly, he faces me, quickly leans into me, kisses my neck, sucking until he knows he's marked me, and I pull away, laughing, breathless like, what else, a schoolgirl, revitalised, aching to let him know everything there is to know about me, silly, giggling, crouching, fending off imaginary chill, acknowledging his eyes, amused, my hands busy, pressing shoes and purse against my kiting skirt, then throwing myself to my knees, and he joins me, his hands slapping at my dress, pushing me all the way to the ground, rolling me over, palming sand onto me as if I'm in flames.

Lying here, side by side, the dark sky over the ocean before us; the glow of the city behind us; our heels, our backs, our shoulders, all planted on sand; our fingers, our hips, touching.

Without looking at me, he says, 'Can I tell you something?'

'You can talk to me,' I say, 'say anything you like.'

'You know you've got a pretty smile.'

'Thank you.'

'You should smile more.'

'I try my best.'

'Oh, I didn't mean to . . .'

'That's OK. What, what did you want to say? You wanted to tell me something.'

'It's nothing.'

'Tell me.'

'You remind me of someone.'

'I do?'

'You know who you look like?'

'Tell me.'

'Libby Elapida.'

'Who?'

'Libby, Libby Elapida, movies, she's, used to be, she's, you know . . .'

'The actress?'

'Yes.'

'You think I look like an actress?'

'Yeah.'

'Oh.'

Games, all these games, like I doubt there's anyone out there doesn't know who Libby Elapida is, doesn't know who he is, this boy, the reason why he's come onto me in the first place, because I know, everyone knows, everyone keeps telling me, in fact, OK, I even used to cultivate years ago a sort of Libby Elapida impression, a look, down to once going so far as to buying the colour to brighten my quim a whole mess of shades, the other end of the spectrum in fact, in order to match that golden honey coiffured slick Libby showed the world when she spilled juice, preserves, paint – blood, was it? – on her skirt and simply took it off to rinse it out, standing there, bare beauty, doing her soliloquy in what was the name of that, was it an Altman picture, no, that was redhead Julianne Moore in, that was a different picture, but the bold detail was virtually the same, yet I know what he means, I've always known everyone is someone else, maybe more, so that he mightn't be who he says or thinks he is, any more than who I think or say he is, but other people entirely, all together, and at once.

There's a wall of tape here in his Wonderland Avenue house, looks like he's a voracious video fiend, seems like he must have jacked off to his mother's entire '80s oeuvre of lame video-bin features, OK, soft-porn mostly, but presented in the classic three-act structure which, according to my avid readings of trash movie magazines, comfort-seeking nitwits claim Aristotle bequeathed for them to cling to – ah, those over-plotted stories, oh, those klaxon resolutions, uh, that universal neatness – what morbid compulsion that particular demi-fucking-aesthetic proved to be. They should have stuck with the money-shots, gleaming jism shooting nearly parabolic through the air, which was all the audience ever expected, pearly salsa on her tits and face, her coy mannerisms, the flash of her crooked smile, the shiny pink plumbing of her gullet, her latently wayward thighs, her incipiently slack boobs. All, it must be admitted, were a little off, a little quirky, to begin with, the charm of her appeal back then the modest flaws which played off and compounded her beauty, the intervening years have only profoundly exaggerated until it's getting to be a sort of merciless self-parody though there are still some twisted parties, fairies mostly, who remain devoted fans, read poignancy and human vulnerability in the slight cast of her nose, the pouty, bruised occlusion of her lips, the crushed bias of her face.

Of course I wake just as she's about to tongue me – part of a rococo scenario involving gold-digging lesbian vampires – to find the room flared, distorted by noise, floors and walls reverberating, easing now, inflating again, waves of sound from outside, music, voices, tyres squealing, motors shrieking, seems to be coming from not much further up the narrow canyon. A party exporting its heaving message. Wonderland Avenue choked at this point like a railway cutting, houses higgledy-piggledy, a tunnel roofed with trees and eaves and overhanging rock-face causing sound to reverberate, booming, percussive. The boy, Serge, or Scott, or whoever he is, naked, pacing the floor, gesturing vividly, talking on the phone. I try to remember how old he is – I must have read it somewhere, *Movieline*, *Premiere* – eighteen? twenty-one? somewhere in that range. After a while it's all the same to me, I can't take my eyes off him, so like a child, jutting hip bones, pale skinny legs, hairless chest. I can barely make out what he's saying, his voice so small beneath the backdrop of noise, his words dopplering against my drowsiness as he strides back and forth, something about he needs his sleep, how he's got a big day to-morrow, early start flying out of state on location, the

18

house in question, the source of all this unwelcome bedlam, is unoccupied, he knows for certain his neighbours are in Europe on culture safari, no one told him they're back ahead of schedule, besides they live like mice, not a squeak out of them, and now there's some sort of orgy going on over there, even a slaying for all he knows, full blood, involving animal sacrifice, children at risk maybe, and why does he pay taxes, why, so he needn't have it on his conscience come morning should it transpire something demonic in fact occurred right next door, so do something about it, won't you, before it's too damn late for some mother out there can't afford to lose another child to whatever horrible excess, OK.

Nothing about me, not a word about having a guest stay over, a bona fide guest, more or less, not a whisper about me, the far from restful sleep I'm being denied. That's how it is. I know the score. Time to move. I stretch, noticeably pale flanked, relieved it's not that easy working up a tan, even after a week in California, forever trying to dodge the sun, now attempting to ease all these diffuse aches, telling myself I'm too sad, too old, for this type of fleeting encounter. At this stage I need, deserve, some degree of finesse, meaning, significance. These sheets I notice too could do with laundering. He's no clean sleeper. Some mothering nerve-tail has me twitching, instantly compiling a list of what needs doing, a roster to straighten out his domestic situation, guide his life toward some minimal equilibrium. The effort of rousing myself from the comfortable bed, finding my clothes, dressing, the prospect of the long drive back to Pearl's house, all make me wish I could lie on, stay here, but apart from his having an early start, I appreciate how ravaged I will seem to him come morning, how my presence must disturb his seamless self-devotional household.

He throws himself violently onto a chair, shudders as cold leather hits warm skin, then stretching his hands over the sides, one empty, the fingers curled, the phone balanced on the fingertips of the other. From this angle, in that pose, his tummy a little sprung, nothing off-putting, simply heartrending, cute, an actor after all and not an athlete. Wondering whether he's eating the right kind of food, nutritional fruit, greens, none of that comforting tasty high-fat junk, knowing he must live his life chasing his own tail, can't be good for him. Looking at him, it's possible he might still be growing. What is he? Six-one? Six-two? Where's his mother? Where's Libby? What kind of . . . ? Why doesn't she . . . ?

He says, 'You're leaving?'

And I say, 'Would you call me a taxi?'

'There are no taxis,' he explains with a thin smile, watching me shake out my dress and underwear before fitting them on.

Not caring whether there are no taxis, I can walk, can't I. All the way back to Venice Beach? I can tell he'd like to see me try that at one in the morning through this sick metropolis. Shaking the dress, scattering microscopic traces of sand we can neither hear nor see as it peppers the boards of the floor.

'I'd like you to stay,' he says.

And I say, 'You're sweet but I've this early flight, I really have to go.'

'It was something, wasn't it?'

'Oh, yeah,' I say, and as soon as I finish adjusting straps, smoothening my skirt with the archetypal mom gesture, brow furrowed, leaning forward, swiping from opposite hip to knee, the back of my hand to the back of the skirt, a thumb flicking at the bodice, he pops to his feet, drags on chinos, buttons, not all, no more than two from five, searches for and finds car keys, stands there barefoot, bare-chested, hair-tussled, while I finger-brush the insole of each shoe before slipping them on, nails painted damson carefully, thinking of my mother's six toes on each foot, the sign of a witch she used to say, though few noticed or commented, part of her ineluctable magic. I wonder whether he's going to put on a T-shirt, a sweater, something to ward against the night air. I lean low, close into a mirror, catch a flash of someone else's sex-blanched skin, a stranger's muddy eyes, and searching for neatness, run fingers through hair all sticky and stubbornly wrong shaped, an aura of struggle, a hint of salt, thinking how awful, conjuring up, flashing this flip thumbnail of some sort of primitive priestess figure, Etruscan, pre-Etruscan, what do I know about that, murky outlined Ur-witch, cursed, sorry to have put him through this whole ordeal.

He starts to say something, 'Listen,' he says.

And as I wait for him to say what he has to say, something, anything, even if it's just my name, an offer to drop me off, a request to see me again, I realise how much I wish there were some men in the world that are not the men I always meet.

utah

East of here, earlier, eight, almost nine years ago, before I underwent that extravagant reinvention which supposedly leaves a large portion of the world guessing who I really am, where I come from, abstractions out of life-given flesh and pain, the green pyre of history, the miasmic rot of dreams . . . I – or Mrs Edward Pirie as I was then – lie stretched behind the three men as they stand in line, rapid-firing at the paper silhouettes they've set up, seven, fifteen, twenty-five yards downrange. A smoke-haired woman of nineteen sunning myself on this weathered tangerine recliner someone months before had brought to the range for his woman of the moment to laze decoratively upon, and had at the end of that particular day forgotten to carry away, no doubt distracted by such as impending coitus. My shorts a similar citrusy, reddish hue to that of the recliner. The brassiere, what I'm wearing topside, having shucked the lime-coloured Sands T-shirt, a startling, snowy, direct from the wrapper, white. Skin coated creamy this side of merging with the honey-coloured desert. Nails, twenty, I've counted day after day for as long as I can remember, a scandalous scarlet, what else, a little localized, monochrome bunting registering my recent semi-exotic past.

Of course I need not lie and wait in the background in the manner of some minor appendage. I could as easily go stand alongside the boys or some distance down line, and blast away contentedly like some of the women are tolerated to do so long as they don't happen to outperform their men or anyone at all owns a peenie. But Edward doesn't like for me to butt in when he's gunning competitively with his buddies. Not that Edward is some throwback ignoramus same as you'd find plenty of on any one of a thousand ranges throughout the West. He's a surgeon, a registered, upstanding Republican, with plastics his game and Vegas the stage. He likes to remind me, there is nowhere better to play that particular game. Money in the bank and all that carpetbagging twaddle.

Now, this moment, on impulse, feeling the sun warming my inner thighs, I shuck those shorts, and pinch these high-cut briefs, also utterly white, though merely freshly laundered as opposed to fresh from the store, until they lie modestly, comfortably enough about those various orifices, generative and voidive, which men spend so much of their lives in blind devotional pursuit of. I close my eyes, demurely cock one knee halfway over the other, relax, proceed to toast. I picture myself going in Neiman's and the haughty birdlike women working there flocking and trotting in my wake, nodding and agreeing for once with all my selections, squealing, 'Yes, Mrs Pirie. Good choice, Mrs Pirie. You're a paragon, Mrs Pirie.' And now I'm having that flying dream that leaves you with a sinking feeling all the way from your eyeballs to the pit of your tummy, making you want to gasp and shriek at the same moment, and my foot flicks out, Ellesse tennis shoe and all, finding nothing but dry Nevada air, and I'm certain I'm falling, plummeting, mile after mile, but it's only Edward, his fist on my arm, hurting me, yanking me awake.

'Hey,' he says, 'it's time. We're going.'

And I sit up too quickly, wipe a hand over my face, dislodging my shades so they dangle a moment from my ear. My mother always told me I'd these dainty pert ears, and so far as I know they haven't altered that much over the intervening years. Now my mouth's dry and the sun's in my eyes. I'm confused, drowsy, like it's post-op recovery, asking croakily, 'What time's it?'

Edward doesn't even look at me. He's gripey, standing off by the towel-draped tailgate of the truck, speed-packing his Colts in their hard plastic carry cases, like, I'm guessing, Les or Calvin must have had better figures on their targets. He just whines in the baleful way he thinks women sound, imitating me, going, '*What time's it?*'

I allow him that much for his shooting eye being off, tell him I've had the strangest dream.

'Swear it, Lee,' he says, 'I'm not the least interested in hearing your dreams right now, OK.'

Sure. OK. But I wish he'd keep it down a little. Maybe hiss at me. Instead of this barking and bawling like a rabid dog. It's not proper or gentlemanly. Not for a doctor. Not for my husband.

'And put some clothes on,' he says, 'for Christ's sake, flashing your bonus like this is *Girls Girls Girls*, and

25

Les and Calvin're paying clientele. You're a mother, you need to start acting like one.'

I suck on my bottom lip as I tug up those shorts, and believe I must cry. Of course I understand what he's telling me and realise that he's partly right. So I drag myself, all arms and hair akimbo, into the T-shirt, and trot over to climb in the truck. Here, in the warm, green-tinted air, sitting, waiting for him, it comes to me, one of those uninvited thoughts you could scarcely deny – if Edward is partly right then he also has to be partly wrong. This is a cataclysmic realisation for any adoring young wife to make. So much so that I immediately put it to one side for later consideration.

Neither of us say much on the drive back to town. I'm busy thinking some about the baby, and more about what having one has meant to me. Almost a year since the mite popped out, without my needing an epidural or even a Tylenol, much to the astonishment of the delivery-room nurses, and to this day you can't tell, just by looking, nor even by touching, unless of course your specialty's obstetrics, that I've ever had a child. Belly's unmarked, bosoms push out straight like boobies on sweater parade same as when I was fifteen with boys and men ogling me till I felt my blushing cheeks could start scrub fires all the way the other end of the valley. I'm guessing I was lucky. On some women it shows big time. Sallow skin, poor veins, stretch marks, dimpled butts, lopsided bosoms, retracted nipples, lax muscled vestibules. Not me. It was the same with my mother and aunts. None of them showed up that much worse for having kids. Least not until they were in their early forties and then it had been the same unmentionable cancer had ravaged their looks and swept them all away in the space of a very fast, very cruel, two and a half or so years, all three sisters gone from this life like they'd always been fated. These tall, rangy women, strong features, good bones, could have been professional athletes except they were ladies from a time and place when ladies didn't go running around, sweating and grunting like porkers in a sinkhole, chasing after tennis balls, showing their lacy derrières on the television to the whole world bar blind folk. Those were the genes, I guess, got to my becoming a dancer, finding my way out here when I was too young to know better. And those were the same genes brought various men, Edward among them, to sniffing at my feet. And since he was the first one of my beaux to propose to me who also suggested I should give up working and live like the lady I evidently was, I'd felt it was my mother and her sisters were behind that particular proposal, so I'd happily plumped for becoming Mrs Dr Edward Pirie. Married him right off, hung up those dumb G-strings, never danced another set, never looked back, never regretted leaving that glitzy stage-bound life behind.

The baby's name is Serge. It was Edward's notion to call him that, and believe me I'd have been happy to name him Milhous Nixon and run the risk of his becoming a small-time liar with overactive sweat glands so long as he was happy and healthy, my very own Sergio little creature. If I'd had a girl I'd have liked to call her Olga, not for any particular reason only I liked the name, it sounded so Russian, and there were lots of famous dancers who were Russians. But I didn't have a girl, so the Olga didn't come into play, and anyhow I suspect Edward would have had some suggestions of his own if he'd fathered a daughter instead of a son, though lately, lying awake next to him while he sleeps and dreams his secret life, I've had an inkling how this man I've married would never condescend to fathering mere daughters.

Looking at Serge, all wrinkled, pink and powdered after his bath with Shimako, the Jap girl Edward picked out to be our nanny, I can't help doubting Serge will ever make it as an athlete or a dancer, he's so puny, puny from the first moment I laid eyes on him and he'd stolen my heart. Maybe that'll be for the best since all the athletes I know from high school were brainless, muscle-bound, no-neck bozos with nothing on their minds more interesting than getting you to blow them in the back seats of their mothers' Hondas, and the boy dancers I know, though sweet and caring human beings with a lot of good taste when it comes to dressing up and eating out and shopping for home furnishings, well, so far as I can tell, they're all of them avid homosexualists. No, my Serge will be something regular like a park ranger, or a deep-sea diver, or a race-car mechanic, or maybe a faro dealer.

Soon as he drops me, Edward drives off to visit the clinic where, according to what he tells me, his specialty's mainly structural – noses, chins, boobs and butts. Lipo he leaves to his partner, Henry, the suction-meister. Henry's forever teasing me about my accepting some of the fat he routinely vacuums from his patients. I could carry a couple of extra pounds easy, he keeps telling me, a shame to see perfectly good lard going to waste. Henry's a tonic. But then he goes the wrong way. It often seems to me that most of the nicest folk I know are fairies. Not a particularly original or startling thought but nonetheless one which starts me crying. It's good to cry, but not too often, too often and you'd have to rush see what pharmaceuticals there are in the house.

Soon as the tears dry up I go take a shower, don't dawdle, and still drying myself, steal back in the baby's room, kiss him on his soft downy head and watch him move in his sleep. My little baby, I think, more than impressed, bewildered, so full of awe. My very own sweet baby.

Back in my room I climb into bed, lie there, staring at the water from the pool which somehow manages to get reflected onto the ceiling, thinking maybe I should go outside for a swim but it feels like I daren't move so I don't, and the sheet which covers me rises and falls as I breathe, and even this seems to be too much movement, so I hold my breath for an age, staying the sheet, deciding a little more of this life and I will go out of my mind.

Tuesday a.m., I shop for a mobile for Serge's room at this small store I've had recommended by Henry, called Kites'n'Stuff, where apparently I should find something that'll stimulate a baby's brain in important ways I know absolutely nothing about. As I push open the door, I notice a sign behind the glass informing me the proprietor's one Evan Sutter. I see him right off, way at the back, working on what looks like some kind of undersized parachute, can hear what sounds like a sewing machine humming. He leaves me to myself which is how I prefer it. Gradually though, as I move through the store, I come closer and find I can get a good look at him by peeking through sheaves of hanging kites, which display of nylon produce reminds me of nothing so much as brightly coloured tobacco leaves hung to dry.

He's about my age, maybe a year or so older, has this wispy blond goatee beard, sun-bleached bangs, silver rings in his ears. I like looking at people, new people. It's one of the things I miss about working. Once I'd gotten married there weren't all that many new people in my life. Freddie Metzzer, the gynecologist; a friend or two of Edward's; Shimako, the nanny; Rose, who cleans and cooks for us; Chester, who tends the garden, details the cars, runs errands.

'How are you today?'

The voice startles me, it's so close. His eyes are in my face, blue eyes, the same blue as Edward's. 'Just fine, thank you.'

'If you need any help, you be sure and ask.'

I see he has a real smile so I reward him with one of my own. 'I'm looking for something for my baby's room.'

'You're kidding me.'

'Excuse me?'

'You're a mom?'

I smile again, show him my perfect teeth.

'Oh, man,' he says, 'I don't believe it.'

'Are you hitting on me?'

'I'm Evan,' he says, offering his hand.

'Mrs Pirie,' I say, taking it.

Wednesday a.m., Evan drives over, hangs one of his more elaborate mobiles from the ceiling directly over the baby's crib. Naturally the baby's not around while he's setting it up, but out of the way, safe in a playpen on the floor in about a virtual menagerie of stuffed animals, Serge's favourite being a small cheerful-seeming burro in Mexico's national colours, red, white and green. I stand in the doorway, arms folded close, watching Evan's every move, as if he might steal away my baby, or run off with the twisty Oriental nanny. It's obvious from the way his eyes search for her and linger that Orientals are a big turn-on for him. Though I know there's something about me also hooks him. He probably decides for sure I'm ready to be amenable the moment I lean over to write him out his cheque. Aside from noting the generous gratuity I'm including in my loopy upside-down figures, he's certainly helping himself to a terrific scope of what lies in the gape of my shirt, and I've known since for ever it's most guys' belief no woman ever grants such a view unconsciously. I tear out the cheque, hand it to him, and we both step aside as Shimako comes, takes the baby away for a change of diaper.

He stares openly at her low-slung hips, says, 'Ca-ca,' grinning stupidly, sniffing as if he knows it's time to change the baby, which he doesn't.

'Thank you so much,' I say, 'for your time, Evan,' making it sound like he's my kid brother's goofy pal

31

from way down the block whom I'm plain obliged to be polite to if I don't expect frog spawn spread between my sheets.

'My pleasure,' he drawls.

He gathers up his gear, goes to move past me, but hesitates, starts at inhaling my scent, something expensive I guess he's deciding, and letting some devil take hold of him, blunders into me, grabbing at hips, planting this wild, wet kiss on my lips.

I'm stepping away, slapping him hard across the face just like we've both seen legions of offended, well-bred ladies do in innumerable movies and TV shows, and whispering, 'My husband will kill you.'

He just stands there, waiting for what I can't imagine.

'Silly,' I say, gently, and right then and there I can tell he thinks he's in with a shot.

I kill off the afternoon watching MTV, trying to crib some of the better dance routines, talking to myself; low-grade talk, mostly elementary pep; the TV ditto, grade-wise; the cribbing, careless. I don't even raise a sweat on the dance. I decide to try something novel, talking to the Jap. Her door's open so I don't knock, I just stand in the hallway, watching her lying on her bed, face down, arms flung out, napping in these silky white jammies, with my Serge, cutie Serge, gurgling wide-awake by her side, wearing this fresh pair of Huggies, sucking away on his big toe, quite full of himself. Wondering whether she ever pleasures herself while Serge is around. Certainly doesn't go out much. Has no known beaux, other than Serge of course. It's evident she dotes on him. Choosing her is one thing Edward hasn't fouled up on.

He wakes me, howling and stomping around like a bee-stung bear. He's fucking poked his fucking eye on the fucking mobile in the fucking baby's fucking room, why hadn't fucking no one fucking warned him. 'Fuck, fuck, fuck.'

I'm rolling out of bed, trying to baby him, but he swings away from me, all flailing arms and jigging feet, not even heeding my proffered breast which foolishly I think he might be inclined to nurse on, the same way Serge instinctively keeps a hand there whenever I have him in my arms.

'What was that hell-blasted thing doing in there?'

I feel myself wince, and shrivel deep inside, as if I've been caught out, exposed, as if he knows how I'm playing at being a mother, as if I'm playing at life, and so am prone to take the wrong step, get myself lost. 'It's a mobile,' I explain, 'supposed to stimulate the baby's eye-hand coordination as well as improve depth perception among other things I don't remember exactly.'

'It almost took my fucking eye out.'

'Let me see.'

He tries to swat me away but I persevere the way I think wives are supposed to do when their men need wiving, or mothering, or whatever. He submits in the end as I shushshush away in the soothing, sibilant way my own mother used on me when I'd had my child-hood scrapes, as well as on my full-grown interim daddies, when those strangers in her bed had been weighed down by unimaginable adult terrors. Now a wife and mother myself, I'm shuffling into the outsize role, stepping close to a husband to plant cool fingers on his temples and steady his head for closer scrutiny, which in itself, I already understand, should ease most minor annoyance and affliction.

'Let me see now,' I'm whispering, moving my body the last inches toward him until my hips touch his, and his hands move to my waist, securing our balance. Eyeball to eyeball, I can't avoid noticing a smidgen of unspecific shiftiness in his. Enough to make me lose interest in advancing any further unsecured succour for the moment. 'You're fine,' I say, breaking the embrace and walking stiffly to the door. 'I'm just going check on Serge.'

'Serge's sleeping,' he says.

'This whole rumpus must have woke him for sure,' I insist, and as if on cue here comes the quickening call.

'Let Shimmy see to him.'

'I want to do it.'

'Whatever you like,' he says and throws himself backwards across the bed.

In Serge's room, I lower the side rail of the crib and hoist him out. I'm walking barefoot, round and round on the powder-blue carpet, holding a son upright in my arms, humming and singing showtunes to him, getting him to clap along with his little pudgy hands. He misses nearly every other clap, showing he needs some work on his eye-hand coordination OK, but I guess he's advanced enough for his age. I can't help looking ahead a couple of years and wondering whether he'll be too young at three or four to start dance, thinking I should enquire around town, until I realise I could always instruct the little honey myself.

The mobile lies in a tattered pile on the floor. I step around it, avoid looking at it, until, minutes later, I feel Serge slump heavier in my arms, finally asleep. As I lay him down again, I'm thinking Edward must have pulled the contraption from the ceiling in some sort of fit. It certainly doesn't look like it can be fixed.

There follows a fog of days during which Edward attends the Safari Club International Convention, thinks long and hard about laying out $80,000 on a bespoke pair of Holland & Holland shotguns he'd have to wait a year to get his mitts on. Not that he can't afford that kind of money, especially for something he reasons he would get a lifetime's use and satisfaction from. Only, he feels he has to be fiscally responsible now he's a husband and father. This at least is the line he feeds me. As if I should feel honoured and some-way select by his deciding against spending more money than I've seen in my entire life, on something which to me is so banal. After all you could walk in any K-Mart, head straight to the firearms counter, lay down $200, walk right out again with a legally held, perfectly good Remington pumpaction. Anyone can tell you double-ought buck doesn't much discrimi-nate what price barrel it comes roaring out of. Not that I voice such opinions to Edward. He would only have sneered at my ignorance and lack of appreciation for the finer things.

It's getting so there's not an hour goes by that I don't speculate as to what Edward's getting up to. At least in his mind. I need to talk to someone. Someone who might have something useful to say, something which might be used to address the mysterious malaise I've suddenly decided afflicts my marriage. I call Henry and he takes me to lunch at this new place, Ton Ton Macoute, and I blab over the entrée, both of us having ordered blackened crab, how Edward has ceased being affectionate toward me.

'He loves you,' says Henry.

'I know that,' I say with more conviction than I feel, 'only he doesn't like doing it to me anymore.'

Nothing bothers Henry, he just wades right in, dead-pan, 'Some men have periods, intervals rather, often occurring in the post-parturition term, though the condition is more commonly observed among the female of the species, where the inclination to, shall we say, conjugally diddle, atrophies to varying degrees.'

'Well, Edward has it bad. He used to think I was irresistible. Now he doesn't find me even remotely attractive.'

'You're attractive, honey,' he says, all thumbs, show-ing he's an inlander, comically soldiering with his obdurate crab.

'You're a lilac-scented fag, Henry. To you, attractive is a butt twenty times tighter than mine, preferably welded fast on an imported white-bread, seventh-grader boy-scout type, out of one of those blond Scandinavian countries like, what're they called?'

He laughs at the notion, though I suspect he's not at all amused by my vulgar rejoinder.

'The simple truth,' I say, 'is he doesn't find me desira-ble.'

'God, what is it with you, you always need compli-
ments. I'll say it again. You are the most desirable. And
again. You are the most desirable. Happy? Happy?'

'I thought you could tell me what I ought to do.'

'You want him to resume intimate relations?'

'Of course, silly.'

I'm waiting for the key to getting Edward to jump
my bones like he used to before the baby came, but
Henry seems to lose the train.

'He's crazy not to love you,' is all he ventures.

'You're telling me you think he needs psychiatric
care?'

'You're very funny. No, pamper him, make him little
gifts, bless his mornings with some tenderness. There's
nothing like a little head before breakfast to set a guy
up for the day.'

'He doesn't like me to get that close to him any
more. And besides, I'm a lady, and ladies don't go down
on nobody, especially not their own spouses.'

'Where'd you hear that? Sally Whup'me? That
Springer person? You still sleep in the same bed, don't
you?'

'Barely. He's just lost interest in me that way.'

'So, get him interested.'

'I could make him jealous,' I say, hopefully.

Henry doesn't seem to think that's such a great idea,
suggests instead I buy Edward a necktie, gets all caught
up in this whole idea of hunting the most suitable
gift, insists on prolonging his lunch hour in order to
take me shopping, drives me out to this gun and knife
dealer works from home, you almost have to make an
appointment to get in there, but Henry charms us in

past these totally vicious, misbegotten poodles patrolling the front yard, and seeing as how Henry and Edward are professional knife-wielders, we quickly decide a samurai sword, this genuine replica, hand-forged in Montana of all places, and priced at a little over $3,000, would make an appropriate gift for Edward. Only I don't have $3,000, not on my person nor anyplace else outside my quarterly dress allowance. Henry promptly declares he'll loan it to me. I throw my arms around his neck, hug him tight, kiss him a dozen times, even once on the lips. I'm walking over to the dealer, asking him nicely whether he'll gift-wrap the sword I've been looking at earlier.

'Certainly,' he says.

So I smile at him, feeling this is all going to work out fine. Henry's a darling. The sword will do the trick.

'How will you be paying, Miss?'

'It's Mrs, and I'll be paying with lard,' I say, shrieking with laughter. So much laughter that Henry comes and drapes his arm around my shoulder, and pulls me close to muffle my mouth against his precious linen jacket.

Edward adores the sword but still doesn't want to touch me, never mind sleep with me. He doesn't even ask where I got the money from. I ache to enquire aren't I good enough for his peeder any more, but don't have the nerve to confront him with his vanished passion.

Everyone's happy, save me. Edward with his new toy, the expensive sword, which in no time at all he's ceased associating with me so that I don't even get the faintest credit for being at the source of his present contentment. Shimako seems fulfilled with the baby that's not hers, and which she guards so jealously there doesn't seem to be any unchallenged ground left for me to mother in. And Henry's consumed overnight with another lithe young college tennis star he's decided to bankroll, who's about to drop out of Stanford, turn pro, race up the WTA rankings, and conquer the universe.

Edward has Chester order up $150 worth of watermelons from his lady-friend, Gigi, at the farmers' market, giving Chester, in the process, credits toward an endurable interlude in Gigi's preheated boudoir, and the two men spend hour upon hour out in the yard, hanging those melons from poles, racing around, stabbing, and chopping, and slashing the soft pink flesh with the Japanese sword, all the while yelping in a juvenile catty way that's more John Belushi than Bruce Lee. Evidently they derive as much satisfaction from pulping those defenceless globes as if they were butchering hordes of vicious, night-stalking assailants. Even Shimako joins in the fun, taking a turn at the heedless carvery. Their partying voices crowding the bright outdoors challenge me to do something about it. In my experience, unhappiness has a way of congealing into a petulant glut where nothing will console only ambushing the fun-mongers by changing the rules and shutting down the party.

Sunday, a little after four, I call him, seeking directions how to get to his house, something urgent on my mind, and find him broiling in his yard, watching the spray from the sprinkler cast about with a gentle soothing haze, and he admits he's a little wasted, after all it's a Sunday and he's put in six straight days at the store and out most evenings on house calls tutoring pesky rich kids in the ancient subtleties of aggressive kite-flying. And though he bears no devotion to any deity there is in his bones some impulse to mark the so-called Lord's day with some special treat, in this instance grass rather than pot roast, and perhaps he's right to do so, for here I am, maybe only a faux angel but doubtless by his current book an angel nonetheless, wearing this dark blue tennis outfit which involves a sleeveless top and short swirling softly pleated skirts that combine to give him an immediate pup tent he makes no attempt at suppressing.

'Evan,' I say right off, 'how would you like to take me to Utah?'

'Now?'

'First thing in the morning.'

'There and back?'

'A couple of days at the most.'

'Sure,' he says without further hesitation, adding how business has been good, he can afford a little break, hell, he deserves it. He grins at me, happily picturing the delights which taking someone to Utah surely entails.

'Naturally I'll pay you,' I say, extracting the folded cheque from my little purse, and handing it to him.

He doesn't bother to look at it, puzzled as he is as to why I'm introducing money into what had, only moments before, promised to be such a diverting trip.

'I want,' I'm saying, 'to keep this entire deal on a business level.'

'I'm a kite-maker, I make kites, there are plenty people who'd drive you to Utah whose business it is to drive other people to Utah.'

'But I'd like you to do it.'

'I don't know.'

'Why don't you take a look at the cheque.'

He sees it's been made out for $500. No doubt he hadn't known driving a babe, even a faintly cooky one, to Utah could pay so well. And for him the whole idea here has to be who knows what might happen between us once we're out there on the road together. He lies back on his lounger, considers the possibilities. A breeze pulls at my skirt, informs him what's underneath is matching, faithfully blue. Closing his eyes, probably picturing me smiling down there. The way their little minds work, transparent, twisting and turning through the same restricted options.

'Well?' I'm asking.

He opens his eyes, seems astonished to find the actual Mrs Pirie still here. Looking as though I don't like to be kept waiting.

'Why not,' he says.

Next morning, bright and not so early, Evan sweeps into our driveway, and I beckon him inside, knowing he can't fail to be distracted by how I look, hair lying in wet strands on nurtured creamy shoulders, half-dressed, wearing this satiny, light slip like my mother used to wear, maybe his as well, that almost comes to my knees, this brassiere edging into view, four straps, two on each shoulder, fouled under one another, clumping around in a pair of scuffed black cowgirl boots that come to mid-calf on stockingless legs, all of it calculated to inflate his desire. I toss him a lazy smile, mention the ill-fated mobile, ask if he'd mind taking a look, seeing whether it's repairable. I assure him I only need to throw a few things in a bag for myself and the baby, and we'll be ready to leave in a matter of minutes.

It hits him pretty hard when I mention the baby. A baby must limit the opportunity for what's so obviously on his mind, what he's travelling for, that special Grail. Men have little interest in the small change of companionship, particularly if it looks like dragging them into the scrub for a bout of soul-baring, which activity usually leaves them with flu-like symptoms, feeling wizened and out of sorts.

Of course he finds the mobile's beyond repair, comes looking for me. The housekeeper steers him in the den. It's got this wet bar, walls hung with diplomas, framed photographs, mostly men in the act of hunting, shooting, fishing, a small collection of worn-down Colt revolvers inside a glass display case, cavalry sabres in pitted scabbards on a wall rack. No doubt he likes kids' stuff as much as the next guy, decides Mr Pirie must have some good qualities to have gathered as neat a collection as this, indeed to have opted for Mrs Pirie as a life-partner marks the fellow out as fairly astute. On another wall, metal- and stone-tipped arrows, the wooden shafts brown and aged, the feather flights faded and cracked, a stone-headed battle-axe with a couple of dozen long reddish hairs bound to the shaft with bright beading, which hairs, Edward never tires of telling me, must have been scored off a white woman from an ill-fated homestead or wagon-train.

By the time I show up, Evan's discovered a pail of golf balls along with a club, and is putting away contentedly, herding those balls into a corner. I step close, take the putter from his hand, toss it on the sofa. I know how I look, slim, this twisted rope I've made of my hair, now dressed for the outdoors in hiking boots, heavy socks, khaki shorts, a T-shirt with a picture of a fish, a trout it may look like to him, a Yellowstone Cutthroat in fact, front and back.

'Who'd have believed it,' he goes, clownishly, 'Vince Lombardi's lucky putter, in my humble hands.'

'Don't be stupid,' I'm saying, turning on my no-nonsense heel, walking out of the room.

'What?' he asks, following me.

'Why do guys always presume women don't know from boondoggles who Vince Lombardi was.'

'Boondoggles?'

'My daddy was a scoutmaster, and Vince Lombardi coached the Packers to six, no, five NFL championships and two Super Bowls.'

'Your daddy was a scoutmaster?'

'Before he went to jail,' I say, and laugh a strange, roiling laugh, that surely leaves him wishing he knew all about me, could see the true facts roosting inside my head.

Evan's face fairly crumbles when he encounters the quantity of luggage I'm expecting him to load in the back of his pickup. He stands there, mulish and mumbling, and I know what he's thinking, suspects his passengers are up to no good, leaving town for ever, but all it takes is another instant, brings moronic relief, the way his face floods brighter, no doubt dredging back the prejudice how culturally, even genetically, women are inclined to pack everything they can carry though they're only embarked on an overnight.

I direct him across town, and we drive by Edward's building where a large sign, like those you see out on the highway advertising mortuaries, reads, *Bodyworks Inc – Compare Our Prices*. He parks in a space reserved for staff, and I tell him I'll just be a minute, and leave him holding the talc-scented baby.

The heat shocks me as soon as I step down from the truck. It has to be touching a hundred, and for the first time I question the wisdom of leaving the comforts of home to go wandering off in the desert in search of something so ethereal and elusive, so corrupt and misjudged as a husband's original love.

I hurry to the door and wade into the cool relief of the air-conditioned interior. I know Edward has surgery scheduled and Henry should be in his office. I wave to Tori, Henry's receptionist, a bulimic First Person with Navajo features, barge on through to his office, just as he finishes injecting himself in his thigh. His insulin shot, he explains while pulling up his trousers. Without hesitation or query, he writes out the cheque I ask for, and after I hug him, I confide I'm off to Utah for a few days' break with a very old, very dear friend of mine, and he should under no circumstances tell Edward who would surely be insanely jealous.

After this breathless encounter, I direct Evan to drive by the bank where I deposit Henry's cheque for $2,000 in my Visa account. And after stopping off at Taco Bell for some fatfree nourishment, we head northeast on 15 toward Utah.

Evan claims not to know any songs, not even show-tunes, and it's not much fun singing by myself, no matter how much Evan seems entranced by my voice. I catch him looking at me out of the corner of his eye, and trust he finds me stunningly mysterious and alluring. I like to think there's no accounting for anything about me unless you're an idle-minded barfly or a college psychology professor awash with overly plausible theories. It's already evident to me this past century's craze for psychology is just a passing fad, a deceit appeals most compellingly to the spiritually bereft and the intellectually challenged. Hawking answers, when any fool can tell there are none worth having in all creation. A bleak but inescapable observation wrapped defensively around itself. Evan has questions though.

'Where we going?'
'Utah, dummy.'
'Is a big place.'
'That's why.'
'Mr Pirie know you're going?'
'It's Dr Pirie.'
'Does he?'
'What do you think.'
'He knows where to contact you?'
'That works both ways, don't it.'
'It's none of my business.'
'Really.'

'You can tell me.'

'Loose lips sink ships.'

'Lake Powell?'

'Save your breath, Evan.'

'Lake Mead?'

'That's not in Utah, sir, now is it?'

'He's not a jealous guy?'

'Absolutely.'

'Not or is?'

'Got any gum?'

'You're not supposed to carry firearms over the state line.'

'Gum. I said gum, smarty-pants.'

'When we stop for gas.'

'OK.'

'OK.'

By five in the afternoon we're in Utah, have lost an hour to the different time zone, are sitting down in this high desert town, St George, to an early dinner of cheeseburgers, fries, one side order of onion rings to be shared, colas all round. I take a tub of baby food from my tote bag, spoon the truck-warmed goo past the baby's lips.

'How you doing, Sergio?' I coo.

Serge makes a flatulatory noise with his tongue and lips, projecting some of that hyacinth-coloured mush I'm feeding him. His demeanour indicates contempt and derision. It's difficult to ascertain how much his having his father's physical features, nose and lips, the way his blue eyes sit so starkly arrogant above sheer cheekbones, causes me to ascribe to him those adult qualities, how much it's a case of him trying to tell me it's time I renewed that diaper.

'Serge,' says Evan, 'you're a hell-raiser.'

I ignore Evan's effort at insinuating himself into the family unit, and tilt the plastic capped beaker of cola toward Serge's lips. Evan burps, and Serge gurgles appreciatively.

'Don't do that,' I say.

'Serge likes it. Don't you, Serge?'

Evan burps again, and Serge does seem to relish the sound.

'It's vile and pointless,' I say.

'I agree.'

Directly, I'm disturbed by a raised voice from two booths away, the voice of a very tall, sun-mottled, middle-aged man with grizzled hair sprouting from his nose and ears, and whose teeth seem to cause him some bother. I've earlier categorised him as belonging to the RV in the lot, whose stickers calling attention to the mystery of the UFO crash at Roswell and the consequent government conspiracy at Groom Lake, signal his woolly terminus to be Pod Central. An observation consolidated by his plaid jacket and camo fatigue pants. A livid scar across his bald pate indicates he has one time been lightning-struck. I can picture him striding bullishly with ball and driver to the tee, refusing to give way to the thunderstorm bellowing around him. The caddy I'm allowing him in this projection has fine, static-ridden hair that stands on end, the familiar stance of someone near and departed – the only way my father ever materializes for me, skittish, about to bolt.

Instantly I'm scrambling the sliding banks of sense, seeking purchase, my spine tingling, more perturbing than a foot on your grave, or a stunning smack of déjà vu, praying for a tree root to latch onto, or a friendly hand to appear from the mire, or any physical, or psychic extension whatever of a saviour might assist my escape from this gripeyness, all this morbidity, boost me back to where I need to be. My prayers abruptly answered – I leave it at that, as quickly it seems as I had thought to utter them – I manage a breath.

Evan notices nothing, is wagging his fingers too close to the baby's eyes. Somewhere in my ill-ordered memory there's an injunction to report all psychotic incidents to your nearest druggist. I don't need to strain to catch the stranger's words so maybe, just maybe, they're intended for my ears as much as his companion's.

'Say the SEC allege you're attempting to corner the Tabasco market. They're going to put wet-behind-the-ears, crotch-itching, kirsch-stinking kids on your case? They got more sense than to waste their time and yours. They're going to play hardball. They're going to attempt to go ballistic, suborn your associates, plant bugs in your office, your car, your home, your polyp-speckled rectum . . .' the fire-struck fellow leans low for a slurp of his coffee, and sticks it to us, his buddy and me, 'maybe even in your Titleists.'

'Huh?'

'Your golf balls, Sonny.'

'God almighty, Tom,' slurs his captivated buddy.

'And when they discover what it is they want to discover about you, which is after all never going to be any more or any less than what you want them to know, they're going to decide it'd be more prudent all round if instead of persecuting you they befriended you, recruited you. So, after a while, word gets out, and everyone, except maybe your Missus, hears what a persuasive son of a twister you are. And, well, from then on, you coast.'

He stares past his buddy, locks eyes with who else only me, and fully reveals the emotionally frigid look of someone whose body has been snatched in one of those living dead movies where an innocent well-decked girl, not awfully unlike me, crops up midway through the second act with the sole function of wondering, just like I'm doing right this instant, what can it all mean or add up to; am I being sensitized for some greater implant; and if I have a role to play in some larger scheme, will it guarantee my life, my liberty, my sanity, will it be the same as a safety net stretched taut and invisible beneath my every thought, my every move?

I'm tensing, fearing a rush by unidentified hostiles from the kitchen area, and experiencing a Technicolor flash wherein I hold hands with the Canadian movie actor, Donald Sutherland, while fleeing with him through a suburban mall in a desperate search for a sporting-goods store where we could arm ourselves, to the teeth if need be, and repel the undead hordes. A round through the forehead is all that will stop those zombie demons. Worst of all, I know we're in the wrong movie.

Of course the lightning-scarred man is familiar in some protean way. Like I've seen him on TV, possibly

America's Most Wanted, or even on a CSPAN broadcast from Capitol Hill as I flicked past some coverage of an anonymous House committee that was unable to hold my attention. My pulse plays these tricks, skipping and racing, folding back on itself. I have no intention of getting sucked in for a dunk in the void. I'm on my feet, grabbing the baby, my bag, hurrying breathless for the door, leaving Evan to pay or make his excuses, I don't care which, I just have to get away from this man whose voice, whose peremptory style, whose compelling, paranoid concerns, remind me so much of Edward, the stories my mother told about my father. Fuck them all.

We find rooms at this motel in Springdale. I pay with my Visa, go upstairs to bathe and change the baby, put him to bed. And while Evan drives off to buy gas and some snacks, I put a call through to Vegas, and when Edward picks up, I'm speaking it all in a rush without breathing, telling him I'm staying away for a while to help me get some perspective. He demands I tell him who I'm with and where I'm calling from. I listen for a moment to his tinny, disembodied voice clanging away in a remote, cartoonish way, and hang up. I wipe a finger along my upper lip, sluice away the film of perspiration that's formed there during the truncated phone call. I'd intended telling him tearfully he's the only one in the world after Serge whom I love, and know he loves me back, as much if not more so, only that's no longer enough, I now need more, much more. What more might be, I have no clear idea.

Evan shows up, carrying this cheap Styrofoam cooler

packed with bags of ice, water, soda, Snickers, Pringles, milk, bananas, gum — apparently his idea of essential nutrition. I tell him I feel like having a swim, ask him to sit here and look out for Serge. Considerately, he steps out on the balcony while I change into my bathing suit, this expensive black Lycra maillot with a rhinestone belt which Edward believes, or at least used to believe, makes me look half my age and glow like a juicy piece of God-given jail bait.

I'm circling the pool in a slow deliberate doggy-paddle, watching the sun burn out against the pink bluffs that back the town to the east. A lovely roseate colour seeps through to me, through my skin, to my blood. The one other time I've been here, this town, this motel, it was my honeymoon, and Edward had swum with me in this same pool, compared the effect of the sun on these cliffs as happier than Prozac, and I'd dunked him for his irreverence. Tonight there's no Edward to dunk and no Prozac to comfort me.

I climb from the pool just as a boisterous family of Italian tourists race one another to leap in the water. Back in the room, I shoo Evan out into the corridor, bat away his feeble attempt at kissing me goodnight. I peel out of the wet bathing suit, leave it to soak in the basin while I shower. Wrapped in a towel, I step outside and hang the bathing suit to dry over the balcony rail. I watch the last of the Italians, two slender-chested boys in their early teens, pony around in the water, splashing and crying to each other in a foreign language that, just hearing it like this from the balcony over the sound of cicadas and the faint clinking of voices and glasses from a nearby porch makes me feel elegant and sophisticated and nothing like some cracker wife running out on her vows. The smell of a barbecue reaches from the grounds of the neighbouring motel, and I wish I had something other than Snickers and baby food to eat, but I don't want to venture down the street for fear of being noticed in too many places, and making it too easy for Edward to find me.

This flapping creature wakes me, floundering by my feet. I pull the sheet to my chin, switch on the bedside light to find it's only my bathing suit. The wind must have risen while I slept and tossed it back in the room. I get out of bed, go to secure the billowing drapes and the sliding glass door that opens onto the cedar balcony. I turn back to bed and find the swimsuit's virtually dried out. I check Serge is OK, and try to sleep, hoping and trusting Edward is hot on my trail.

It doesn't take a brain doctor to figure out all these years after the events a complete picture of what happened. It isn't even a mystery how these things are done. You just realise you know someone, a town, human nature. You just exhale and find you understand how the pieces fall into place, occupy all those levels, what you once thought of as blanks, other folks' alien nature, movie-of-the-week fare.

Serge wakes me a little after six, and I pull him closer, letting him press into my curving warmth, talking to him in a low, soothing voice about me and his daddy, and how he came to be.

'It's not like I got knocked up on purpose or

anything. Maybe your daddy wanted me that way. He wouldn't use protection – and I'm not going to bore you with where I believe the burden of that particular issue belongs, on the man or the woman or the little dickybird in between – so I guess it was kind of inevitable. He wanted me, he wanted a wife and kid, that's you, so he knocked me up, or maybe I got him to knock me up, or half and half, take your pick. We got married right away, soon as I told him you were coming. No question. And don't think we didn't love each other from the start, we did. Besides, I thought I was having a life, dating Edward Pirie, screwing around with him, getting knocked up, getting married to a man with a nice house and plenty money and clean fingers, having a baby. If that wasn't real life nothing else would ever be. I always wanted everything to be real, especially love. You dance for a living in Vegas, you're always up against stuff that's not real – knockers, noses, names, faces, the town itself – so, first chance, I grabbed, I got myself a real husband, a real baby, and your daddy got a real family. He's an important man, clever too. He can be kind of hard to live with sometimes but who isn't. The thing is, I do love him, much as I ever have, and I want him to love me again the way he used to, which is what this whole detour event out here is all about, ow . . .' I go, with Serge suddenly catching the tip of my nose in a sharp two-fisted grip. 'Always standing up for your daddy, aren't you. How would you like to talk to him? Right away? OK, let's do it.' So I place the call, and when a sleepy Edward picks up, I hold the handpiece to Serge's face, and whisper, 'Say hello to Daddy, baby.'

'Lee?'

'Say hello to Daddy.'

'Lee?'

Serge looks at me with great dishy eyes, and I realise he's not about to become a slick communicator at the drop of a pin.

I take the handpiece, say, 'Hello, Edward.'

'Lee?'

'This is Lee.'

'Where the fuck are you?'

'Don't you want to ask how your son is?'

'Tell me, who are you with?'

'Don't be jealous, Edward.'

'I'm not jealous. I just asked who you're with. Why you have my son along with you on this reckless escapade I have no clear idea, but let me tell you, if you're exposing him to any kind of sorry behaviour then you will regret this fling to your trailer-trash core. Do you hear me? Lee? Lee?'

'Nice talking to you, Edward,' I say, and blow him a snappy kiss down the line before dropping the handpiece back in its cradle.

Evan shows up around eight and suggests that seeing as how we're here in Springdale we ought to go look at the gorge. I tell him I've seen it already, and Serge is too young to appreciate the splendour. I don't want to get into a debate about it so I tell him I'd like to get started, pick up breakfast along the way.

'What way?'

'Bryce.'

'Page is nice, the lake and all.'

'This is not a tour.'

'I thought . . .'

'Don't.'

'I'm only trying to be helpful.'

'I'm sorry, look, I do appreciate all you're doing for me.'

'Are we on some sort of mission?'

'Kind of.'

'There's no danger involved?'

'How about I'll save you.'

'Buy me breakfast before we start?'

'If you're that hungry.'

'I'm always that hungry.'

So we walk down the street to a diner, quite the picture of this model family strolling along in the morning sun, he carrying Serge in his arms, pointing out all the different model cars we pass, long-windedly favouring domestic models over imports, allowing their features cope best with local conditions not to mention driver characteristics, lingering on a contrast of the stature and behaviour of redneck girls, which Detroit designers understand implicitly, against those of Seoul or Kyoto missies, which Toyota and Honda designers understandably arrange their worlds by.

I order juice and coffee for myself, cereal for Serge. I'm crushing the pre-sweetened cereal with the heel of a spoon, soaking it in low-fat milk, patiently spoon-ing the mush in Serge's mouth. Evan forks down a memorably heaped plate of over-easy eggs, ham, sausage, hash browns, beans, tomatoes, pancakes, slices of white-bread toast with butter and jelly.

'You should eat,' he mumbles through a mangled

mouthful, jabbing his yolk-daubed fork in the direction of my midriff.

I smile at him, pray he'll hurry up. Serge, small and snug in the seat alongside me, plays with a spoon.

'You call your husband?' he asks.

I just glare at him.

'Only wondering,' he says.

'You like driving me?'

'You know it.'

'And you've never met my husband, have you? So you can't have formed any opinion about whether he's the type of man always needs his wife to check in when she's just a couple of miles down the road, right?'

He shakes his head, more than a little stupidly, then nods vigorously and mouths, 'Right,' spilling beans from his ketchup-stained lips. He wipes his mouth with his fingers, then surreptitiously smears them across the Formica-topped table on his way to reaching for a paper napkin. He runs the napkin across his lips and cursorily against his fingers. Finally he wipes his fingers back and forth across his Levi'd thighs.

I'm thinking I have him whipped for the moment but he comes right back, surprising me, saying, 'Only I kind of need some idea here of how long this all is going to take?'

'You got a life you want to get back to, is that it?'

'Yes, ma'am.'

My instincts tell me he needs some small treat to keep him on my side, so I glide my hand over the table to rub the back of his fingers, and from the way his face changes countenance, lighting up, I'm guessing the little touch has done the trick. 'Me too,' I say, 'me too.'

We're heading east on 9, going north at Mt Carmel Junction on 89 until we make a turning east again, a state road, 12, through Red Canyon, and two hours later we're at Ruby's Inn, the gateway to Bryce Canyon National Park. We climb out to stretch our legs, and I buy and mail a postcard to Edward. No message other than the contracted postmark.

Evan's sitting in the shade, sharing an ice-cream with Serge, and looking at me strangely while I loiter by the mailbox as if expecting an immediate reply to my card.

A pony-tailed man in his forties approaches and introduces himself as Mescalero Apache, a polytheist, and tribal separatist, visiting from voluntary exile in Quebec. I'm finding it difficult to pay attention to what he's saying – I'm focusing so on Evan, worrying, wondering how much longer he'll remain biddable, while also increasingly conscious of the hot mailbox pressing against the back of my skirt – something about the Fed atrocities at Waco and Ruby Ridge, Reno's bloody hands, and the unremitting bullshit of Government.

The Mescalero's bijou blonde wife and kids emerge from the shade of a stall selling ersatz Native American artifacts, and he grumbles a little as they usher him toward their rental, a claret-coloured Ford Taurus sedan, whose wheels and fenders are marked by streaks of baked hard, red mud – a charm it seems, a propitiatory ornament in this country with its many tribulations.

The wife sits in the driver's seat and smiles at me as she pulls out of there, a patient, sainted smile which conveys she knows well enough what it is to fight tedium all the days and nights of her marriage.

Now I'm finding the underarms of my blouse soaked with perspiration. And I can scarcely breathe. If only the Mescalero had spoken about medicine and magic, about bears and coyotes and mother blue earth, instead of apparently being compelled to select me from the dozen other tourist types in the dusty street, and weave for my sole benefit something so painfully surfeit to my present needs, another prickly layer of paranoia and frustration. As if I'm marked out, primed to attract all the unwholesome, stray looniness in the entire southwest. I'm having to pluck my skirt away from my thighs, imagining I can feel, faintly imprinted on my flesh, a portion of the US Mail decal off the mail-box, as if I'm now a piece of freight, out of my hands, and voyaging down the seething macadamed road to my appointed destination.

I cross to where Evan and Serge sit licking their fingers, and more plaintively than I realise, ask, 'Can we go?'

Evan looks at me as if he can see those frayed trans-parent seams holding me together, and asks, 'Are you OK?'

'Do I look not OK to you?' I snap, pulling Serge into my arms.

'You're the boss,' he says, and shuffles away to climb back in his truck.

The thing is, I've always trusted in and played up my waywardness, I know it's that part of my charm

which has separated me from the herd of toothy, tits-
and-ass hoofers, my so-called peers, the more statu-
esque, the more social, the more flirtatious, the more
calculating. Waywardness which has certainly appealed
to Edward. Right from the moment we met, he's
praised and indulged my quirkiness, my blithe detours
and sudden, inescapable passions. And now, this trip,
provided Edward can read the sign properly, is wayward
in a way which I've never been before. I'm hoping
and trusting he will appreciate what I've embarked
upon. Nonetheless I can't help feeling a little tenderised
and jittery about the outcome. It's possible he might
interpret this jaunt in utterly the wrong way. I'm having
to quickly reconcile myself, thinking so what if he
does go haywire over my behaviour, I've nothing to
lose, how much worse could things be than the way
they are at the moment with him not loving me
anymore. I close my eyes, trying to resurrect the silted
theories I've heard from girlfriends over the years as
to how to win back your man and make him love
you with all his being, down to his very last frazzled
cell. But right now my mind is all a cavernous blank.

I show Evan where to turn off the paved road, and
almost right away he needs to get out and lock the
hubs.
    'How much further?' he asks.
    'Not much.'
    'Hours, days, a hundred miles, what?'
    'No.'
    'No what?'
    'No idea.'

'Fuck.'

'Don't listen, Serge,' I say, placing my hands over the baby's ears.

'You know why I agreed to drive you up here, don't you?'

'Five hundred dollars.'

'Lee.'

I'm afraid he's about to reach for me. He has that moony, devoted look to his face men get when they teeter between declaring their undying love for you and swearing they're ready to end it all rather than go another moment without your loving them back.

So I speak up. 'We'll talk about it when we get to the cabin.'

'What cabin?'

'If you quit gabbing maybe we can be there before dark.'

'Sounds good to me.'

He takes us on down that almost vanished trail. The truck swaying up and down. Serge throws up once on my lap but other than that the remainder of our journey's uneventful.

When the track fades altogether, we leave the truck in the shade of a boulder, which Evan remarks is the size of a house, pick our way out over this almost sheer cusp of sheetrock that obliges us to slow almost to a crawl. It's enough for Evan to carry the baby, and for me to follow close behind. I'm picturing what I would do should I slip – grab at the back of his pants belt and pray that I wouldn't pull him over the edge.

'You sure this is the way?' he asks, for the umpteenth time, it seems.

'Save your breath.'

'You're always telling me what to do like you're my boss or something.'

'I know where we're going.'

'I can turn back anytime.'

'You'd have to get by me, and there's no room for two on this ledge.'

'You're so fucking smart and sassy, you never let up.'

'And you never stop wanting to jump my bones.'

'Like, bad, I must be nuts.'

The words, coming breathlessly, seem light and not to matter, as if they're not ours. And the climb, though short, takes it out of us, boiling the busy world away to a small matter of another step, another boot on crumbling rock, an advance of epic inches.

We reach the edge of a vast range of broken country, and collapse to the ground to catch our breath. I can feel a trickle running along my leg, and swipe away what I think is sweat only to see my hand is red with blood, see where I've scraped my knee. Evan unhooks a water bottle from his belt, offers it to me. I throw back my head to drink, then spill some over my knee, washing blood onto the parched dirt.

'I'm guessing there's water at this cabin?' he asks.

'Not enough to swim in I don't think but usually you can wade in a rock pool up to your ankles, and crawl on your belly in it, and brush your teeth, and shave, and generally relish the experience.'

'Where's it from here exactly?'

I'm looking away from the setting sun, and incline my head. When I turn back I find him staring strangely at me, full of what I take to be doubt.

'What?'

'Nothing.'

'What?'

'I guess I just like looking at you.'

'That's nuts.'

He scoots over to my side, bringing the baby with him. I remove the baby's cap, splash some water on his head and face, let him sip from my palm. I hand Evan his bottle, watch him drink and slap a handful on his neck. I plant my hands by my side, my legs stretched out before me, ankles crossed. And murmuring, 'I love this country,' I close my eyes, rest back my head, expose my throat to the last of that dying sun.

'Can't I kiss you?' he asks softly, like a voice from a dream.

I'm taking my time, opening one eye, and looking at him sideways like he's confirmed nuts and needs reminding of the fact.

'Just a little one?' he asks again, beginning to annoy me with his perpetual pleading.

Not for the first time, I remark the colour of his eyes – that wild raging blue, not tame and watery like the rest of his nature might have decreed – and his smooth young skin beneath the pale and wispy facial hair. At the rate I'm feeding out my treats I calculate I have two maybe three days before I'll need to extend any serious delight. And Edward should have come and gotten me long before then.

I'm smiling, saying, 'But not in front of the baby.'

'Promise?' he asks.

'I said it, didn't I.'

He takes off the straw Stetson, drops it over Serge's head so it covers three-quarters of his face. Serge gurgles, catches the hat two handed, starts twisting it round and round like a whirligig blindfold.

'Don't,' I warn, thinking I detect a slight move closer on his part.

'Cross your heart you will.'

'I like you, Evan, a lot. I wouldn't have gotten you to bring me up here if I didn't. But what I said goes. Not now, later, when Serge's not likely to be spooked by someone not his dad wrestling his mom on a hot rock the middle of no damn where.'

'All I asked you was a kiss.'

'You ought to quit sometime.'

'I love you.'

I'm gagging, motioning harshly, 'So run off, make a mess behind a rock, you'll get over me.'

'Never.'

'Grow up, like a pal.'

Right now he looks so downcast, I keep on talking, trying to soften the rejection, and still not hang out too much in the line of promises. 'Remember,' I'm saying, 'bringing you up here doesn't mean I'm obliged to do anything for you. The way things have been going for me in my life lately, I need time, I need to watch where I step, I am real fragile right now. Maybe something will happen between us, maybe it won't. There are no guarantees.'

'I know I love you, that's guaranteed.'

'That's just horny talking.'

'No, it's not.'

'Did I promise you anything? Did I? Evan, did I?'

'No.'

'Don't sulk,' I say, extending a hand to squeeze on his thigh, getting him to smile. 'You got to take those chances getting to know someone new, chances someone new likes you enough to kiss and make out and like that, or chances the sight of you makes them ill to the point of screaming misery. Otherwise, if you don't want to face those kind of possibilities, you can avoid them altogether, simply run off to one of those chicken ranches, pay for your fun without any complications. You get a lot of funning around for five hundred dollars, you know, at least back there in Nevada you do.'

'Like what for instance?' he asks, his interest piqued, his tongue trailing, his blond face atop his bulky shoulders reminding me of nothing more than a dewlapped bull with an urge for bulling.

'Don't look at me that way,' I say.

'Tell me, like from the menu.'

'I'm not talking dirty to you, Evan.'

He leans across me, pushing me to the ground, pinning my hands against my tummy, looking deep in my eyes. I can smell us, our road tiredness, the hot air of the pickup, the sweat, our slick skin, though my breath in his face must still be sweet. So sweet, he whispers, that it hurts him not to lick me, lick all and everywhich part of me, baby or no baby. He can scarcely breathe. Like the way it is, I'm so fired-up beautiful he just has to drop his face to mine, force a kiss on me.

'Ow,' he yelps, and sits up straight, fingering his lip and seeing the blood, 'I'm bleeding.'

'You ought to have taken me seriously, Evan,' I'm

saying, getting to my feet, straightening my skirt, jiggling my tight little special in his face. 'I may not look it,' I say, 'and I don't know what at all you think of me but I am a serious person, and you oughtn't to treat me like I wasn't.'

I walk off, with my shadow angling bent and twisted ahead of me, moving as if I'm this proud and unowned creature. I pluck at the seat of my skirt, swat some of that dust off it, showing what I aim to be the grandeur, the splendid natural pep affected by a thousand haughty celluloid debs.

He knows what he knows, and groans, 'I can't love you better than I do.'

'Bring Serge,' I'm calling, and wait to see him springing to his feet to do my bidding one more time.

There's no sign on the trail, no prints, no litter, no scat, nothing to show that anyone or anything has passed this way in months. I'm trying not to let this bother me, since, according to Edward, the trail is a thousand years old, give or take, and I have to suppose a few months of low-level use isn't going to erase it or render it less likely to lead to my destination.

I hurry, sliding down into one of those zigzagging fissures that break open the land, my boots skimming the surface of loose dirt and shale, scarcely regretting I haven't worn hiking boots today instead of these cant-heeled Spanish ones, following the bank of an arroyo straight toward where I remember a canyon, keeping a trickle of water, opens a vein of green and cool like a minor oasis in this harshness. Now that the cabin is less than a quarter-mile away, I can't wait to reach it and see for myself the place where Edward and I had been happiest.

Edward had learned about the place from this broken-down uranium prospector who used it whenever he made it through these parts, often spending weeks here, griping about the leprous society of towns and his ex-wives who lived in such distemperate places, and when the mood took him, spending days on end in recreation, hunting and skinning snakes.

Suddenly there's a cluster of pine and pinyon, and I only have to focus to find the cabin. Only now it's become a distorted, shrunken thing, hunched in scant outline against the heat. Veils of haze seem to mask it, though it's close enough to throw a ball at. I begin to appreciate the folly of coming out here. I spit between my boots, and take a step closer. The haze seems against my eyes. I blink and wipe a finger to each eye, rub, and look again, and sink to my knees.

A moment later Evan reaches me, finds me sobbing. He looks past me, sees the burned-out shell of a cabin, blackened beams lying crisscross over a rubble of collapsed stone and charred, shattered wood. The only intact structure is this effigy of a barn thrown together against the side of the canyon wall some distance from the cabin, something made of rough-hewn lumber crudely laid, gaping with cracks.

'This it?' he asks.

He needn't have spoken. He offers a hand-up which I ignore, getting to my feet under my own steam. Now it's his turn to squat on his haunches. He wipes a hand across his brow and watches as I go trudging over the hard, baked dirt.

'We can go back,' he calls, 'find a motel.'

I step over a charred, fallen beam, move inside the line of blackened stone which marks the front wall. Just burdened with disappointment, as rank and corrosive as any I've known.

'Lee,' he says, 'Lee.'

And I turn to look at him. He doesn't seem to realise all my plans are in disarray. He doesn't seem so young any more. I'm wondering what I must look like to him. Forsaken, no doubt. Full of fear and defeat. I'm hearing my own dead mother's critical voice, gnawing at me, telling me to get a grip, to look coldly and see where my erratic behaviour has brought me, a married woman, a mother – to this. What a way to behave, running around the country in company with this irresponsible kid, risking destruction, inviting disaster. Evan places an arm around my shoulder.

'We should get back,' he says.

'I'm staying here.'

'That's crazy,' he says.

'I've come all this way. You can drive back and get us some food, whatever you think we need. There's no reason why we can't stay on here a day or two.'

'Where?'

'That looks OK,' I say, and stride away toward the barn.

I haul on the sunken door, the bottom silted by wind-blown sand. He hurries to help, and together we toe and heel away the dirt, and drag open the door to find sunken sacks of feed in the half-shade, ribs and shafts of light swimming in a sea of motes, shreds of rotten harness hanging from ten-inch nails, a family of must-be woodrats scrambling in every direction, trying to escape the light, our intrusive gaze.

'How do you know this place?' he asks.

'I was here one time with my husband.'

I'm wondering what's become of the old man. Whether he's finally gone to Corpus Christi to the fat daughter he loathed, or whether he's wandered, burnt and confused after the fire, into the desert to die like several of his wives had foretold, miserably alone and screaming in agony. I feel something clinging to my leg, and look down to see Serge sitting there.

'Evan,' I'm saying softly, my hand tightening on his arm, 'I really need to stay up here tonight.' Now wetting my fingers on my tongue, and dabbing at the baby's face.

'I'll get what I can from the truck,' he says.

'We're going to need more than that.'

'For one night?'

'Maybe you'll like it up here so much you'll want to stay on a while longer.'

He nods his head, and I lean up to press against him and kiss him on the mouth. Before he realises I'm not about to bite again, I've finished and stood down. He grins and strides away to get water and a particular bag I ask for.

And then I give him a list of what we might need, and send him back down the hill to the last town we came through. Soon as he's passed from sight, I sit on the ground alongside the baby, dab my fingers in the dirt, and taste it.

Leaving Serge to sleep, I walk to where water gathers

beneath the overhang. Looking around for sign of snakes, I undress and lie down in that shallow basin of cool water. I palm water onto my hair until it's every inch wet, let it float out around me. I want to lie quietly and look at the stars but my view of the sky is partially obscured by the overhang. On the rock above I can make out faint ochre drawings, distortions of life, showing men, children, weapons, sheep, bison, bear, horses, the sun and the moon. The light falls quickly away, and I start to feel lonely, as if I'm entirely in the wrong place, somewhere far from sanctuary, and a chill steals over me with the first whispers of a rising wind. I turn on my hands and knees, and crawl out of there. I gather my clothes and boots, and saunter, dripping, across the moonlit clearing toward the barn where my son lies dreaming. Before I reach the barn, I hear Evan come noising up the canyon, carrying boxes of store goods. I'm gauging from his groaning, burdened pace there's enough in those boxes to last us a week or so if we dare to remain here. Part of me is disappointed he's returned so quickly, surprised he's been the first to reach me. All the same, I hurry into my clothes, and buttoning up, go barefoot to greet him.

'See anyone?' I ask.

'Not a jackrabbit soul for miles.'

He stands there without moving, just looking at me. My hair lying wet about my face and shoulders. My smiling face not turning from his. The night breeze moving at the corners of my dampened blouse where it hangs outside the waistband of my skirt. He sets the two boxes on the ground, and rubs at his arms and shoulders.

'Serge is sleeping,' I say quietly.

'You went for a swim?' he says, reaching a hand to touch my hair.

I'm laughing, stepping into his arms, whispering, 'Thank you, Evan,' at his throat.

'I want to kiss you,' he says, kissing me and swinging me off the ground, whirling me round and round with my tight clamped eyes picturing the pale soles of my feet rising and falling like the sun-bleached vanes of a backwoods mill.

Wishing I could be ill, I can only gurgle, pleading, 'Put me down, Evan. Evan.'

My squealing exciting him, so he lays me on the powdered dirt and moves astride me, my eyes unfocused, his hands moving, stretching my skin, thumbs at my nipples, stirring them, fixes his mouth to mine, his tongue dives past my lips, buzzing, finds my teeth, then my tongue, small and warm, fights with his jeans belt, yanks at his buttoned flies, drags off his boots and Levi's, never takes his eyes from me, lying dizzy on the ground, my breath humming softly from my nose and mouth as he pulls at the skirt, my eyes widening, holding it high to catch the light, searching for where I might draw him inside, kissing me again, my legs moving apart, and he sweeps right into me.

I'm up at the rock pool, the sun on my neck, kneeling by the skim of water, combing out my hair, when I hear the ugly snicking sound of a shell being jacked into the breech of a pumpaction. I haven't seen such a gun in Evan's possession, though it's possible he might keep one concealed in his pickup. I pocket the comb, wipe the trace of sand from my knees, start back toward the cabin. Closer, I hear voices, and my heart swoops to think Edward's finally come for me. The dirt already hot under the soles of my feet. Edward's here all right, talking to Evan. I can see something blue-black, brown, a shotgun, hanging from Edward's hand, a finger through the trigger-guard. Behind them, Serge, sitting on a jacket in the shade, plays with a soup can. Evan swings his arms, trying to illustrate something, explain his role and function in this scenario, and Edward smacks him flush in the face with the butt of the big shotgun. Evan buckles, drops to his knees, and Edward kicks him in the mouth. I'm beginning to lift my legs, hoping, meaning to run, but they're too heavy for me to accomplish any speed. I can only stumble, breathless, unbalanced, toward them. Evan cries and bleeds and clutches at his face and moves on his knees, gasping, raggedy on the ground. Edward turns to face me, catches me in his arms and pulls me close so when he speaks his spittle gusts at my face.

'This little punk claims you love him and he loves you. Is that true?'

I'm shaking my head, drops flying from my eyes.

'Is that true?' he asks again, rattling and shaking me.

'He just drove me up here,' I say, barely audible.

'Then tell me why the fuck did he say you loved him?'

'I don't know.'

He releases me, turns and swings the shotgun one-handed, smacking the barrel against the side of Evan's head. Evan crumples, lays in a heap on the dirt. I'm screaming, and Edward hooks a boot behind my ankle, shoves me backwards, sends me sprawling onto my backside in a small swirl of dust.

'I don't know who he is, or thinks he is, but you're my wife and plainly in need of a sharp little homily on the sanctity of the family, and maybe even a slap or two.'

'Let's get Serge,' I'm saying, 'and leave here, right now.'

He smiles and says, 'OK, go get him, go.'

I struggle to my feet and move slowly past him. I glance at Evan and instantly wish I hadn't. One eye is swollen shut; his nose, all disjointed and coloured livid, drips a steady flow of blood; his lips mashed against cracked and broken-off teeth; blood flowing from the side of his head down over his ear and neck, soaking his shirt. I look at Edward who smiles at me and dips his head, urging me to hurry and gather Serge. No sooner have I moved beyond them than I hear Edward laying into Evan again.

'Edward,' I cry.

I'm screaming. Edward lunges again and again, kicking and stomping. All this in lieu of a lecture on moral turpitude. And when Evan ceases to shield his head with his arms, Edward takes a breath and turns to see where I've gotten to. My face halfway buried in my son's body. He strides over, pulls the child from me.

'You come on home when you're ready,' he says, and walks away.

My face pressing into the ground, I flick my hand behind me in the dirt, blindly spraying a scoop after him. I hear his boots scrunching as he leaves, pray he'll keep on going out of here.

I hear him saying to Evan, 'I'll pray for your soul, asshole.'

I'm waiting for a blast from the shotgun but none comes. Finally, I raise my eyes, and see where Evan lies unmoving. There's no trace of Edward or Serge. No one remains, only the boy I brought out here. I scramble over to kneel beside him, his face a rupture, coarse and flayed, this froth forming in the blood at his lips, his breath so faint and shallow, guessing his ribs are all busted in.

I start pawing mindlessly at the ground, and speaking ashamedly, 'Evan, oh, my.'

Lifting his head onto my lap and dabbing at his face with a corner of spit-wet blouse. He blinks once and his lips seem to strain about the form of some word. I'm longing for him to speak but he doesn't. I lay him down again, hurry to the barn where we'd left the water. When I return, I uncork the bottle and pour a trickle over his lips. I decide that he's swallowing a little. Which has to be a good sign. I can't tell how badly beaten he's been, hoping maybe it's only a couple of broken bones. I realise I can never drag him all the way back to his truck, so I'll have to go for help by myself. I search through his pockets until I find the keys to the truck and a roll of paper money, and I'm astonished to find myself capable of estimating this will get me out of here, get me home. I think about dragging him over to the shade of the barn but decide it's better not to move him. I prop the bottle of water against his side and lean close to whisper in his ear, 'Here's some water. I'm going get help, Evan.'

I'm thinking I should kiss him. I'm thinking I should

touch him, brush his skin with my fingers, let him understand. I'm thinking this baked air. I'm thinking hell. I'm thinking give back time. I'm thinking I would nurse him, my baby, never surrender him to another's care, so we would twine ourselves together, never look up from that bond. I'm thinking it's my dying mother's face staring back at me. I'm thinking, not caring, the same illness which devoured her might also now this instant be feeding on me. Splashing water on my face, parting my blouse to run fingers here and here, thinking all the rest of it I could bear.

Edward hasn't changed the locks or the alarm code, or posted any threats for me not to venture onto the property, so I park the truck in the drive, just waltz in there, home again. There are men's voices in the den, talking dimly about some new Mexican fighter come to town. I stay out of sight a moment in the hallway, trying to place those voices. Rose comes from the kitchen and along the hall toward me, bearing a tray of snacks, look like gobbler balls on Ritz crackers. She smiles at me like nothing's up.

'Mrs Pirie,' she says.

'Dr Pirie home?'

'He's out by the pool, I'm sure.'

She sweeps on past me and into the den. I step into the doorway and recognise the two shaven-headed men who swing from their seats to snatch at the snacks as friends of Edward's from the shooting ranges around town. IPSC shooters. I smile at them, and they smile politely back at me. The small one with the busy eyes, whose name I can't remember, had been emancipated by his father at sixteen so he could enlist underage, go off to Vietnam and kill thirteen-year-old gooks; and after the rout and shameful run from Saigon, he'd stayed on in the service to become a SEAL and get tattooed all over. The other one is Andy, a sort of Latin looker, who's been a cop with the LAPD, and now tours parties of Japanese tourists round the ranges, tutors them how to shoot the vitals out of paper targets.

'You all going the range or what?' I ask.

'Just kicking,' answers the small one.

'Later maybe,' says Andy.

'IPSC competition coming up,' I say.

'A week Saturday,' says Andy.

'Well, good luck,' I say.

'See you then,' says Andy.

'See you,' says the small one.

I smile, like none of it's unreal, and step back in the hallway, and go on down toward the kitchen. For some reason I feel relieved that they've presumed I'll still be alive a week Saturday. I can't tell whether they're armed or not but I know they have permits to carry concealed weapons. Guys like them always do.

In the kitchen, Rose asks whether I'd like something to eat. I shake my head, go stand by the window, looking out at the pool where Edward is floating Serge through the water in front of him. Shimako sits on the side of the pool, her feet kicking in the water, calling encouragement and praise to Serge. She looks girlish, calm, at home, wearing her favourite ocean-motifed blue and green striped bikini, brightly sketched starfish, crabs, tropical minnows, damselfish, swimming across her buttocks, the shoulder straps hanging redundant either side under her arms, and her toenails painted luminescent green, splashing in and out of the bright water. An oldish woman, a bright crimson paper-cut for a mouth, Edward's age, thirties, in ritzy antique shades and a white one-piece bathing suit, sits under an umbrella, reading a glossy magazine. I'm searching the woman's thighs for the dimpling trace of cellulite but the thighs are tan and sleek.

'Who's that?' I ask.

'That's Miss Tulper,' answers Rose.

'I'm going to lie down,' I say. 'You get a chance, I'd appreciate you let Dr Pirie know I'm home.'

'Sure,' says Rose, deftly keeping any hint of sniffy impertinence from her voice.

Upstairs, I open the doors to all my closets, sit on the edge of the bed and look at the wall of garments hanging there, other sides of me, days and nights gone by when I must have been someone else. Choices here which I hardly know occasions for. I'm waiting for all that's happened since I came to Vegas to catch up with me, but it doesn't, and probably never will. I realise how I might be able to live with myself and all that I've wrought if it stays that way, with me skimming the surface of everything.

I lower myself sideways onto the bed, draw up my legs, curl in on myself like a child. I can hear voices, laughter from the pool area below. Edward calling to someone to get in the water with him so he might baptise them. And a woman's voice laughing and fending off the suggestion. I weigh for a moment whether I ought to feel abandoned or otherwise hard done by. Not especially. There are worse-off people right this instant standing at any gas station or street corner in America.

Sleep hurries into me, and I dream quickly I'm dancing totally naked in this bar in Missoula with slot machines pinging away out in front, and there's no one watching save a senile old horse doctor dribbling tobacco juice in his bourbon, and his gummy Blackfoot housekeeper pestering him about it being time to start home. It turns out it's some sort of audition and I guess I fail to land the job. Too bad, huh.

I'm awake, rubbing the ball of my palm hard at the tip of my nose which is itching, some elusive itch. I look at the window, see it's still light out. I shower, put on this white bias-cut dress with splatters of jet black beading, expensive reptilian glamour kind of deal, something which someone twice my age and just as desperate for other reasons might wear, in order to reclaim, for instance, a hopeless situation. I lay out some clothes to wear for the morning. Faded black pants, an old soft blue T-shirt. Not unlike the clothes I first came to town in. Standing by the window I see there's no longer anyone out by the pool. I search through a dressing table until I find some old G-strings, select one, put it aside in the pants pocket where it makes hardly a bump. If things go badly then at least I'll have that to remind me how it's all been more than a dream. Hearing Edward come in the room, I turn to face him. He doesn't look contrite or troubled in any way.

'You the baptiser now or what?' I ask.

'Huh?'

'You bring that whore to Jesus?'

'What're you talking about?'

'I saw that whore stretched by our pool.'

'I didn't baptise her, no,' he says, sneering at me.

'You don't deny she's a whore?'

'I know she has no tits to speak of.'

'So she's a client?'

'Patient.'

'She was painted up like a whore.'

'I didn't notice.'

'You going to marry her?'

'You think she goes with me?'

'I hope you're being careful.'

'You think I'd marry a whore?'

'I think she'd make a good organ donor, that's what. I think you should harvest her organs, donate them to poor people can't afford replacements.'

He laughs and moves closer. I step away. He comes after me, shuffling, his arms by his side, his teeth bared. I'm thinking it's ridiculous, this cuckold's dance.

'You're afraid I'm going to try to kill you,' I say.

'Why would you try and do that?'

'I saw the boys downstairs.'

'Andy and Del.'

'They're here to protect you, aren't they?'

'Just friends.'

'I never saw them here before.'

'I was showing them my trophies.'

He reaches out a hand to my face, and I lean away from the faint caress.

'You remember his birthday?' I ask, backing further away from him.

'Sure I did.'

'You get him a cake?'

'Balloons, a clown, the works.'

Finding myself against the wall, I can hear myself breathe, my heart tumbling inside my chest. We're looking hard and fixed at each other.

'You going to hit me?' I finally ask.

'I ought to,' he says.

'I was desperate,' I say. 'I only knew what I had to do. I thought you would read my mind. I thought you would come and get me, and we would be like we used to.'

'I believe you.'

'I never let him near me,' I say, 'I never.'

'I know,' he says, and steps close, taking me in his arms, pressing his mouth against my hair.

'That boy?' he says.

'Don't,' I say.

'How's he doing?'

'He's at the hospital.'

'The police? He talk to the police?'

'There's nothing to worry about.'

'Anything I can do?'

'I thought I was lost. I thought I wanted to die. I lay down to do just that.'

'No.'

'If you think of me at all I'm just your property. You think I'm sort of chattels, goods.'

'I love you.'

'Like you love your guns, and your trophies, and your house.'

'I married you.'

'You can't marry a house, that's for sure.'

'I sleep with you.'

'You fuck whores.'

'Now what do you want me to say?'

'Nothing,' I say, hoping he will keep on saying it.

He's tugging at the dress, pawing at my flesh. And I can't understand it but I'm impatient now, trembling, expectant. Through the night we move at each other, harsh and unremitting, like we're making up for lost time, the faults we've found in each other.

'You won't leave,' he says, 'ever again.'

'Only when you want me to.'

I'm looking at him shortly before dawn, seeing that he's sleeping, and I think about stealing downstairs, entering the den, taking down the sword which I bought him, thinking how it might feel to come back up here and strike at his head. In the morning, after he's left for work, I dress in the clothes I've laid out, carry my son to the truck, and as I prepare to drive away, I'm doubting, somewhat bleakly, whether this time he'll care enough to follow me.

unzipped

Farther . . . all this continental drift, reversely long
sluice of night flight fending against the swing of time.
These hours of ill-digested meals. Movies – like Larry
says, 'No flipping,' but can I help it if the feature sucks,
loses itself in genre mishmash, gratuitous woe, studio
imperatives, reckless resolution. Amiably forgettable in-
flight magazine. Sky-map's jagged slow trajectory.
Longueurs mimicking the blue cast of repugnant
narcotic withdrawal. A dash of slit-eyed insomniacs
cloistered round about, men, cold mortiferous beings,
feralised, yet staying in their seats, staring at me as I
glide past in the penumbral aisle, wearing comple-
mentary bee-striped in-flight socks, stretching my legs,
searching for juice, water, a drink. 'Some ice to go
with that?' 'Why not.' While seven miles below shriek
lonely ice-fields smeared with moonlight. Hushed
exchanges with attendants. The intimacy of transient
warmth and practised civility. Snowy translucent
blouses, crimson laundered skirts, bare arms, trim
stems, *soignée* stamp all over. Hinting at a career choice
I might have pursued, flitted in and out of. Machines
alone don't thrive in this high compact galley. Nubile
Shiksas, Saxons, Lorraine Bracco look-alikes, a solitary

Nubian, flourish here as well. Wanting them to hold me. Also the humming of RR turbines. Circulating air imposing its own co-option. Another infected communion. Uneasy sleepers, open-mouthed, anonymous voices, groans, amorous souls, timorous beings, torment, lost shards, mumbled suppressed exchanges from beyond. 'I can't live without you, you weren't to go first.' 'You know how to boil a lobster, don't you, Elizabeth.' 'Don't talk to me about kosher sex.' Followed by indistinct somethings about a Paiute Casino and the Bishop Chamber of Commerce. Worrying an instant it's someone from my neck of the West. Probably just another sun-seared tourist in a Bart'n'Buffy T-shirt. Counterfeiting meaning where none exists. Taming the vast expanse of unexplored night and terror. Here be cannibals. Others. Deploying frail myth and deceit to ward off those wraiths and pea-green moulting demons. We cannot abide that abandonment, that openness, that unimaginable eternal vastness, that godless lack of scheme. There's no plot here, is there, no pilot by any other name? This better not be shark-food denouement. The very enclosure of this tub tells tales of safe passage. Take heart, it's been done before. Someone whispering, 'You're my gorgeous,' as I pass. Meaning me? Who else. Also a very particular taste of mango dessert repeating sickly like a mandala from stomach to throat and back again. Remembering that time my uncle over by Livingston haemorrhaged, his oesophagus's secret disintegration. Too much beer and bourbon they said. A geyser of blood filling a pail. Earthly trials. He survived and died. That sort of reduced morphology applies equally to organisms, rocks, words, especially words, promises made, never to leave, always to return. Frights we take and grow to expect. Rivets popping free. Sequential deconstruction. Sheets of metal cladding shearing off into monstrous space, leaving behind the frail heart soughing its last feeble expiration, the silent scream, *Put me down, you shedding leprous ghoul,* as we tumble once more into gravity's bottomless maw, bringing me up in a deafening, dizzying rush of arrival.

As soon as I disembark I think I get it where Araki is concerned. Araki is all about impotence. Male impotence. Impotence in the face of a life teeming with opportunity, temptation. Now I wish I'd brought an Araki for Billy. Help him to know himself better.

My feet feel swollen from the flight but I resist the urge to remove my shoes and walk barefoot through customs, immigration, appreciating how that would be too flamboyant, even for me. My face looks puffy, and my eyes are red behind oversized shades. And this is what I'm wearing: black virgin wool sweater and white pants a little too tight across my hips. Getting a touch beamy, I appreciate, all too painfully. Maybe why life has lost its edge, maybe vice versa, whatever. I realise it's coming time to step back, appraise options, strike off anew. I doubt whether anyone will recognise me looking like this, as much as I doubt whether I could fake a smile if I needed to. Long, sleek hair, tailed and looped in a silk scarf. Feeling bloated, awkward, stiff, like a collagened, suffused movie star, or a touch overdone country singer with rowdy dramatics on a hair-trigger. As for the cause of my present unease . . . Too much salt in the airline food? Deep Vein Thrombosis? Pregnant?

Hardly.

Nothing more than all of it so far, every morsel of my life, mingling carelessly to assail me. This morning I estimate I look years older than my true age, closer to forty than thirty, closer to either than I care to be. Over the hill and still underachieving. I can picture Billy telling me as much. Such a cruel breach in my easy faith.

People begin to notice me. Women, men, giving me second glances, as if they recognise me as someone they should know but can't quite nail. Something I've learned to live with. I suspect if I'm ever going to feel it, now is the time to start thinking it's great to be back.

Someone calls, 'Lee,' someone coming toward me says the name again like they're not so sure it's me.

It's contagious. Even I seem unsure, as if there's suddenly some grave doubt over who I am. Hesitating, slowing, not quite stopping, tilting my hip, my shoulder, my jaw, brandishing the lot, snowy sparklers, icecap molars, welcoming the flash, the momentary warmth it offers. Peripherally, from inside the dark lenses, I sense someone else staring at me, notice a girl, someone vaguely familiar, apparently someone off the flight.

The photographer thanks me as we walk along, side by side. I imagine it must be gratifying to recognise, almost as much as it is, sometimes, to be recognised, even to find oneself mistaken for someone else, someone more glamorous, more famous, more celebrated, someone without my irregular history. The photographer appears old, frayed, tired, burdened. His close-shaven face starting jowly. His eyes smoky, suggesting setbacks stacked up at life's choke point, stasis freezing over him. His grey suit wrinkled and sad. His necktie awry. A shirt thread squirming free of his partially undone collar button. His shoes squeaky, rubber soled. All of it, the reality, the unmediated humanity, reverberating with some forgotten frailty, making my heart shudder as nothing has in days, and thinking, on top of everything else that's happened, that somewhere out there is the man my father is, looking a lot like this one.

The girl from the flight keeps following, glaring, no doubt wondering who this woman can be, what it is about her makes her a target for an airport paparazzo. Not very bright that girl. What else only horror, shock, spectacle, irreversible decline, constitute my notoriety, my professional stock-in-trade. Maybe I'm mistaken about the girl being someone off the flight, maybe she's just another damaged soul frequents the airport, on the look-out for a mother figure, someone celebrated, beautiful, haughty, someone forever breezing past, never granting her the time of day, just what she's accustomed to at home, what experience informs her that mother-hood entails. Silly girl should stay there, home, stare at the wall, develop inner resources, await the Lord's tender mercies, rather than look to me or my kind for any hint of how to cope with the relentless bullshit.

The photographer extends his hand, and the shock of his flesh, soft, warm, and tremulous, against mine, strangely renders the passing gesture of civility into something grander, life-enhancing, that overused and almost invariably misunderstood term. It's astonishing that strangers are still capable of such contact. In a moment I know I'll start blubbing. I mouth the words, *Thank you*, silently wishing him well, wondering an instant why I've never noticed him before among the pack that hounds me on and off, and hurry away, not daring to look back lest I disappoint, or disappear, or be transformed into something base and useless, more hollow and disordered than I already am.

And here's my driver, Harris, approaching, circling like an amiable old dog, blue-rinsed, moustached, apologetic, puttied hands reaching for my case, same old metallic twinkle in his mouth.

The first thing I do on reaching home is pour half a bottle of butter-coloured Neutro Roberts bubblebath in the tub, and soak in it for thirty minutes straight, trying not to fall asleep and drown, trying to figure out what I'm doing here, trying to remember where things might have gone wrong.

No better place to start with than Dr Schnabel, the shrink with whom I've had more than a passing acquaintance since the move to London on the back of Anaconda's breakout second album, *Kangaroo Girl*, whose sessions are always more accessory, faddish comparative conversational fodder than any crushing want of absolution for any shortcoming, sin, psychic, otherwise, and who used to call me, depending on his humour, either his Marilyn or his Maria de' Medici. I honestly don't mind what Schnabel calls me, or how he views me, so long as I don't have to listen to his crypto-Freudian pap about the incidence of confused paternity among hysterics. Denied maternity is an altogether separate kettle of fish. Besides, all of that surely concerns my mother more than it does me, and I never understood where it impacted on my day-to-day life, the psychological frailties, the lack of focus, or killer instinct, which deny me the glory many commentators deem my talent, albeit late-blooming, deserves. Of course the Marilyn and Maria de' Medici allusions intrigue me but I'm not about to flatter Schnabel by enquiring further. The walls of his Albert Street rooms are decorated in this hazy cathouse style, apparently an unprovable version of either Rome or Paris during the Second Empire, I forget which. It seems everyone is given to decking their lives with the conceited trash which intrepid shrinks claim offer a window to their souls. Honestly, I believe all this shrink stuff's nothing more than a pile of chickenshit voodoo. Which obviously doesn't begin to explain Schnabel.

Nonetheless, soaking, propping myself gleaming against the rim, I call him on my cellphone and confirm a long-standing appointment for later in the morning, feeling clever for having remembered to consult my diary, lay down appointments like my life wants structure, spokes fanning out to cover yawning lacunae either nightmarish or . . .

Slipping now, wishing hands, others, seizing me, my quivering . . .

So round I scoot to Schnabel's only to find nothing has changed in my week away. Abusive relations, Schnabel, as usual, wants to know about, wants me to elaborate.

'Let me tell you about abusive relations. For one my father shtupped my mother, begot me. I never asked for it, for this, for any of it. And two . . .'

I can't go on. This is customary. As far as I'm concerned. I regret using language, the word *fuck* for instance. Especially in relation to my parents, mother deceased, father fugitive and untraceable, last heard of in Northern California, sighted in Bolinas, playing Bay Area clubs wreathed in cloak and mystery, no big deal, believe me. Hence, shtupped. I regret everything, every word, every revelation, regret going so far, tentative and all as it is. And Schnabel understands. We've been here before, this benighted neck of the woods. Schnabel and I.

Languid and patient, he watches as I light up a cigarette. He doesn't seem to mind that I smoke. He puts up with a lot where I'm concerned. I know that he likes looking, is perfectly content to just sit here and run his eyes over me. Never mind that I'm paying, he's the one, it's evident, gains the most from these sessions, as if these encounters are arranged and honoured primarily for his pleasure, his benefit, his profit. Of course it never goes beyond the eyeballing, the significant surveying of me in whatever my current state of dress, or strait of demeanour I happen to show up in. And if I challenge him, stare back at him, his gaze will simply lock, just rest on me, one part of me, my hair maybe, my nose, my hands, my chin, an elbow, some non-erogenous part of me, some part of me he deems to be non-erogenous. He probably thinks it's OK to do that, safe. But it's not.

I tilt back my head, let my hair hang free behind me, blow smoke at the ceiling, then check my watch, see there's still twenty-five minutes' worth of session remaining, sigh somewhat expansively, cross over my knees the other way, this time placing the right one on top, his favourite, straighten my skirt, brush at it, the fresh cream linen, regret again every pound over a hundred I haul around, bring the cigarette back to my lips, draw deeply. And laugh. A great loud smoky effusion of a laugh. And the sad old bastard doesn't know why I'm laughing. And that's what I like. I wipe a tear from my eye, say, 'Sorry,' and before I know it I'm laughing again, spluttering, laughing so hard my face feels flushed, my eyes stream, and I'm aware I'm no longer a picture, possibly so unattractive, and as I fumble for a tissue and clear my nose I feel good, light and purged. But still not happy.

'Why can't I be happy?' I ask him finally.

'Happiness,' says Schnabel, 'is . . .'

And whatever he says goes right by me. The same as ever. The story of my life. Deaf to someone who possibly holds the key, a fragment of the key, the guide-book, the repair manual, the rules to this outing, this so-called gift, this life, this juggling of, on the one hand, angst, and on the other, well, what else only despair, this joke to which everyone knows full well the punch-line, the hideous, vile, perfectly unfair, inescapable fifth-rate certainty. Deaf to one whose arcane learning and keen wisdom might lead me from this pit, this unwanted, unasked-for pit of deep dark doubt, swarming hang-ups, ravenous guilt, snarling remorse, anticyclones of repression and cowering from the world. Ah, the world. And the cowering.

So this is how I come to regard myself, a case of greetings

from the abyss, hi, and all of that, and the thing is, the one thing I know best about myself, my current straits, I know my life is full of spectators, spectrous bother- some beings, and it looks like I am closely connected to each and every one of these sad creatures. Strangers stop me on the street and tell me things about my life that I don't know myself. How they saw me triumph in Eugene, or lose my way in Shreveport, Louisiana, how we used to be involved, how we routed each other and rutted together. All sorts of claimants. And I just look at them, glassy-eyed, nod like I remember, like every word is truth, like none of it bothers me. Sad specimens I prefer to believe I'd never go within a schoolyard of, or the width of a towncar. And some of them have the tattoos to prove it, their version of events, my name alongside some SS Lazio or Chelsea FC emblem, or a swarm of track marks like it's a marriage licence or a deposition or an affidavit, never hearsay or fantasy or hysterical urban legend, which to my mind is all it ever is or can be.

But that's not all. There's magazines, there's TV and radio shows, book blurbs, police reports, press releases, album sleeves, inflated low-grade memoirists, wholly devoted websites, bug-eyed stalkers, anonymous lech- ers and letters, lubricious late-night phone calls, bill- boards, obituaries, blind dates, advertising hoardings, taxi-sidings, lurid claims daubed with ultra-lucent paint on the shutters of my favourite shops on the Via Condotti, other streets all over the so-called civilised world, all contributing their little titbits of biographi- cal trivia to the bilious fricassee that is now and has always been my life.

How much is apocryphal?

The shame, the sweat, the desperation, the pills, my aversion to wanky do-gooders and the out-of-doors, my limited intellect, my heedless libido, my profligacy, my leaping out of windows, my bulimia, my rosy pink secret, my certain sometime soon death much foretold, my flame-tattooed labia, those Bulgari piercings, my outright amorality?

Snap, snap, and snap again.

Certainly this item of graffiti I happened bizarrely upon in a dead baking interlude while striving to make my stomach lurch and sicken in the otherwise pristine terrain of the backstage washroom of Dublin's Vicar Street venue, no more than a year ago, cannot be regarded as anything other than mischievous burlesque. The Byzantine felt-tipped script had been cunningly inscribed beneath the rim, and consequently was visible only to the most diligent of cleaners, or anyone on their knees – toilet paper laid craftily, cushioning, hygienic, on the floor – embracing the vitreous bowl, straining bug-eyed to emit a light repast of seafood chowder, three thumbnail-size croutons, and a glass of so-so spumante. The gist of the message was that I, Lee Annis, am a monster, hell-spawned, a porn slut, and a firehole witch. Hurtful in its bare-bones pithiness but no more cruel and inaccurate comment than what I am long accustomed to being the subject of.

And if it's truth they're seeking, these night-crawler commentators might better busy themselves chasing details of my time with the Montana Ballet Company, paying tuition working double shifts at the Safeway on Bozeman's Main Street before moving on for a time to Pony Espresso and then the plum Montana Ale Works where I learned to weave between tables, high-stepping, almost tittupping, as well as parry the inevitable hands and come-ons of diners, local blowhards, out-of-state anglers, skiers, movie stars, politicians, all of them hot and eager to have me realise how easily I might transmute a fat gratuity into a modest down payment against a little more of my time, slipping me their room numbers at the Lewis & Clark Motel, pencilled on the backs of fifty-dollar bills.

Fifty minutes after leaving Schnabel, home again, coked up it must be said, in my cool basement, to find Libby Elapida's on afternoon television being interviewed about her debut movie as a director, at fifty-five, a domestic drama featuring a runaway Brahmin wife, pursuit, adventure, travail, romance, death in the very last frame, gunned down by sinister associates of her husband. A sort of indie *Chinatown* it's being hyped as. In other words nothing to do with the women-in-jeopardy-made-for-TV-blaagh '90s genre but a dark and adult cinematic reprise of the kind of movies Libby made her name in during the '70s, the last fair bloom of American cinema . . .

All of which sends me rushing nauseous toward the bathroom, disturbed for obvious reasons . . . suddenly distracted by a shadow racing on the sill, the darkened unwashed glass bubbled opaque to begin with, hasn't had a refit since the late '60s, what I like about this place, the peeling wood frames, the ill-hung doors aslant, the skirtings shot, but it's only the outline of a Belsize Park squirrel halted there beyond the jagged skyline range of shampoos and unguents, its grey tail cocked upright, hands or paws, whatever you call them, moving sure, forensic, busy, feeding, turning something minute on a lathe. I reach up to tap the glass but not before the creature abruptly speeds away again, frantic in a search for what? Its practically alien intrusion wrongfoots me, leaving me with no idea how to accommodate it here in the coiled sequence of what else only calamity and triumph.

A little short of four in the afternoon, refreshed by a shower, some couple of Vicodin washed down by a perfectly pitched gimlet, I call Lucy Rhea, sometime stylist and record-label alumna, tell her over the hum of the ill-advised hairdryer – it's my time to be reckless – where I've been and why, tell her lies, tell her not so much and no more, tell her how badly Billy mistreated Alessia, mistreated me when I admonished him for same, tell her how he availed of the opportunity to restate his reasons why Anaconda must die and cast itself onto the . . . 'scrapheap of modern dirge and honky-tonk heartache . . .' where it belongs, tell her he'd cited my slowing him down, along with my inhibiting his growth, tell her how he'd cast his light on my patented shortcomings – musical, personal, manifold – my failure to match his combustible ambition, attend his scorching vision with all due devotion. These amongst other points thrown in my face, menaces, rudimentary jibes – short on clarity, substance, fixedness – as if we were no more, nor less, than a heartsick can of worms. Even as I speak I feel myself lurching out of step with myself, incline toward excusing him, making allowances for his unease, accommodating his making so light of me. Though Lucy is not so benign. She immediately offers to butcher him, tells me she knows some Portuguese boys Kilburn way, Shoot Up Hill to be precise, Bruno is one, would happily do her a favour. I thank her, say no more favours, please. Lucy asks if she should skip work to spend a little time with me. No, I say, I'm fine, suggest maybe later in the week we can meet for a drink, squeeze in some shopping. So now we confine ourselves to phone talk, the sheer inconsequence of . . .

'Therapy,' I say, 'is supposed to help but it seems like all they're interested in is my sex life, who I'm doing, where and how, how well, how often. And I don't feel any unresolved issues I may have revolve around sex. Sex is fine. It's what comes after sex is where I appear to run into trouble.'

'And what comes after sex?'

'Gonorrhoea, chlamydia, I don't know.'

'Mature relations perhaps?'

'I'm too young,' I say, in my most appalled put-upon tone, 'to be interested in mature relations.'

'I went to see a psychic the other day. She assured me I'd die fulfilled, an old and blissfully married woman.'

'And that's your dream?'

'What's wrong with it?'

'You believed her, this charlatan?'

'Olivia's no charlatan.'

'They're all charlatans, honey. Trust me.'

Before we can pursue this Olivia any further, I receive another call . . . it's Pearl, phoning from LA, explaining how she's been to a spa in the desert out at Two Bunch Palms, and consequently has lost touch in a day with developments, LA happenings.

'How was it?' I say.

'What?'

'The spa.'

'That's not really why I'm calling.'

'You hated it?'

'To tell you the truth they had these mud baths whose main constituent seems to have been, I can't begin to explain, gardening by-products, milled peat, horrid shredder stuff, that sort of vegetative detritus. I'm still plucking twigs out of my butt, believe me.'

'That's not why you're calling?'

'No.'

'You contracted some other sort of lifestyle affliction?'

'It's about your friend, Scott Weaver.'

'He's dead?'

'Not quite.'

'You're seeing him?' which strikes me as being just about the next worst thing to his being dead.

'Only on the TV news,' says Pearl.

'So, what'd he do?'

'You know that night you met him, you went to his house?'

'And yes?'

'Well, someone made a phone call from there, called 911, complaining about the noise coming from this party up the street? So the cops come, and because it's fancy dress no one knows the real cops from the guests? And one guy thinks it's a gag when the cops come round the back of the house, just suddenly materialise out of the dark without any warning, you know, wearing cop costumes, masquerading, trying to grill him about the noise, get everyone to quieten it down a little. And this one guy raises his hand, points his hand at them, makes like it's a gun? And the cops, one cop . . . shoots him.'

'Shoots him?'

'Shoots him dead.'

'No?'

'Just, yeah, for real, shoots him. And now every-one's saying how Scott Weaver's responsible, you know, because he dialled 911, called the cops there in the first place, complained about the noise. The cop who shot the guy, that's bad enough but everyone knows who Scott Weaver is. They're saying he never should have called the cops, had no reason to, apart from which – I mean even if he had reason – the fact is he should have known better, been cooler, you know. Everyone's, like, asking how can he live with himself, how can people ever think well of him again. He's saying nothing. No one knows where he is. Now he's disappeared. But it's no use what he does or says because they have tapes. They have the tapes, the recording the cops make when you call 911. They're playing it all the time on TV, and, like, it's his voice all right. No doubt about it. The guy is finished, you know, in this town. And Jesus, you were there. You must have been there, right when he's making the call. I think it has to be, according to what I guess the timing is. I mean what time did you get back here that night, do you remember? It was late. You probably hadn't even left there before he made the call. Do you remember him making the call? Jesus, Lee, think about it. It's, like, so weird. And you were there.'

It's not so clear to me why Pearl's so excited. Someone died in LA. People die there all the time, and more often than not in stranger circumstances. It's not as if either of us knew the dead person or even the policeman. And as for Scott Weaver, certainly I slept with him, or at least with someone who looked like Scott Weaver, and lived in Scott Weaver's house, but who never once admitted, all the hours I was with him, from when he picked me up to when he dropped me off, that was who he was. And OK, I've slept with a few people in my time, but if I need to worry about, or feel in any way burdened or responsible for what they get up to when I'm not around, then I'm sure I'd have a lot to think about. And another thing is how Pearl sounds so animated, so unlike her usual aloof and imperturbable self, just being a hyper little cunt for whatever reason, trying to whiz on my parade, and I never, for an instant, imagined I even had a parade . . . so fuck her.

The photographs come in the morning post. Along with a note signed, Regards, Poole. Photos of me coming through Heathrow, looking pallid, beset, retentive, less than my vivacious best. Deducing he's the photographer from the airport, I phone around, asking who this Poole is, who he works for or sells to. No one's heard of him. For five or so minutes I'm content to dismiss him as just some loner, some fan, some wannabe snapper, until I realise that somehow he's gotten hold of my address. Which is worrying as I'm not in the phone book, live quietly on a quiet street in a quiet neighbourhood whose residents, being quintessentially English, refuse to acknowledge my presence, never mind going so far as to induct me into their impenetrable sense of community.

Feeling caged, I pace around the apartment, trying to soothe the yo-yoing motion of my stomach, suppress my panic, my racing pulse, fight the urge to make some grand gesture to prove to myself how worthwhile my existence is. I resort to television, find myself exercised by too much significance. An analysis of recent events in Genoa where the police shot a protestor dead. Which is what happens when you put guns in the hands of children. Somehow the police seemed to think the array of confiscated pocket knives justified their brutality, their risible inept efforts at propaganda. I wondered at the time, and again now, why the police didn't just raid the meeting of G8 leaders, the Bush, Blair, Berlusconi gang, see what grade of weaponry they might have found to confiscate there. Instead the police raided a school and people were brought out on stretchers. Rocks against guns. That's the kind of fatalistic struggle I crave. I read about the President's son. Everyone knows who killed him. Yet his wife's family receive a fifteen-million-dollar settlement. Soon I'm back in Wonderland Avenue, in Scott Weaver's house, wondering what's he about to tell me. That he has an STD? That he loves me? Can't live without me? Has to see me again? That he knows Billy? That he's coming to London? That he has two weeks to live? That he's not Scott Weaver? That he's a phoney? A trans-gender imposter? Neither man nor woman? Selling a strain of steamy delirious weirdness?

Harris collects me for the short drive to the Salon Mystique where I'm to rendezvous with Lucy Rhea for a noontime bout of beautification. Harris, this occasional driver, one of the few remaining perks to Anaconda membership; and I'm set foursquare on milking it, getting the most from his nervy diligence. Propped in the corner of the back seat, my eyes heavy, my head tipping, battling lack of sleep and what else, residual jet-lag. Thinking of my photograph which appeared in last month's Italian *Vogue*, part of an article entitled, *sesso e potere*, which I ripped out, put with the other tear sheets, other references to me and Billy . . . including a newspaper headline which a thoughtful anonymous someone recently clipped and sent me, *Lee e Billy, fine della love story*. Just the caption, no story. Those Italians really have a thing for me and Billy, *fuck him*, seem to confuse being in a band with some sort of romantic affair, unless they know something which no one else does? I wonder what they'd think if they only knew half the truth about my life, the mundanity of one day following another. Suspecting, day after day, that I may have dozed off somewhere along the way.

The motion of the car feeds to a feeling of panic lurching in my stomach, rising into my throat, forcing me to flick through the years since we came to Europe with the sole purpose of what? Attaining fame, sex, power, riches? I don't know any more what we ever hoped to achieve.

Looking to blame my nausea on someone else, anyone, anything, Harris's driving, city fumes, tap water, snotty fucking locals. Desperately trying to discern achievement, substance, assuagement, realising that all my life amounts to is a series of men, none of whom have names, so that they all appear the same, interchangeable, and so the chronology is fluid, disorienting, with events occurring either in the past or present, faces recurring, confirming nothing, validating less. Everything else, the music, the money, the modest fame, that vacant splendour, do nothing other than illuminate their own transient, bogus nature . . . like anyone should be surprised by that, right, or need a yogi or a maharishi or the Panchen Lama to point it out. Unless the source of my nausea is more immediate, less mystical, such as Harris trying to get my attention.

'Hey, Lee,' he says.

'Yeah?' I say.

'Did you see that?'

'See what?

'Just there, that skinny transvestite, ballsy fucker, in the buff.'

'Transvestite?'

'All made up, lipstick, mascara, tits, hips, hair, the fucking lot.'

'No.'

'Pity.'

Soon enough, caged again, a whimpering comes across the salon, sidles and laps from one to the other. Lucy, plangent, plumpish, getting her brows sculpted, a Revlon pro-model tweezers flashing, flying in the hands of a tight-bloused ogress, another pin-eyed enthusiast, sadistically plucking short strawberry hair in this relentless mowing sweep, trailing a geometric crescent thread, precisely what's desired, the discomfort – who would ever classify it as pain? – reaching a pitch, staying up there, beyond gravity's reach, never lulling, never falling back, and Lucy's hardly conscious that she's whimpering, hasping my senses, burning my ear, making me fidget, irritating me to the point where, stretched supine nearby on another paper-sheeted bench, I question, not for the first time in my oh-so-brief life in this noxious town, whether or not I have anything in common with these people, with Harris, with ballsy invisible transvestites, with Lucy, how could I, how could anyone ever think the two of us share anything, split chromosomes, instinct, background, neighbourhood, education, genetic definition, mascara wand and bottle? Just consider my lovely youngish skin, effulgent, pure, what am I doing here at all, having gunk – zingy lemon and dairy ripe, not even proprietary gunk but something bunged up by some junior, some twit, some bright-lights glamour-dazzled west-country yokel – slathered on my face at fifty quid and rising per hour? I certainly don't need much clarifying on that account. Then of course there's the mostly ectomorphic build – slender, angular, fragile – super-appealing, they keep telling me, as an urchin's, or an angel's numinous dimensions, setting me apart along with my contumacious peepers, big beautiful promising, never mind those innocently understated bazooms, deeply adorable, upsetting to men, confusing and derailing those aspirant clowns to the point where they lurch at me, believing the overall package signifies an easy virtue, mutual attraction, mumbling their crass inept come-ons, chafing in their pants, delirious with visions of my mossy untouched quim, my moistly, uh . . . and I have to live with this. No wonder I bridle.

Once more, fumbling my way into daylight – feeling disoriented the way you do on emerging from an indulgent early-afternoon trip to the movies – hoping to rescue something of my latest self the best way I know, visiting one after the other, boutiques, emporia, overpriced purveyors of shrouds for the quick, attempting to supersede the revelations of yesterday, Pearl's voice flaking me out on the phone, retrieve some forward momentum, trying on Alberta Ferretti, how *she* manages to make black translucent, trying not to think about Billy, about Pearl, or Scott Weaver, about anyone, just stepped in to kill an hour, turning it into a slaughter.

Suddenly aware of this man in a grey suit, blue and white striped cotton shirt, an elegantly knotted salmon necktie, staring at me. Know him from somewhere. And then it comes to me. Introduced to him once. On Ibiza at a diving contest. Boys, men, holding their breath under water. Homeric twinkies. Has some tenuous link with women's tennis. A sort of creepy groupie on the Sanex Tour. He'd been sweet enough, hosted huge parties, confided in me, said I reminded him of Ally McBeal with fifteen extra kilos on. Scoping him here, an alien in these parts, like myself. Oh, now he's coming over. Toss him one of my venereal half-smiles, too late to worry about how I got here, the whole back-story of my day so far, preceding weeks, months, years, that whole tumult of arms and legs like a massacre of hope, fallible instinct shunting all of that messy distraction into some dark and gaping annexe of my mind.

'Hello there,' he says.

'Hello yourself.'

'Shopping?'

'Browsing.'

'See anything you like?'

'Oh, this and that.'

'Well, why don't you tell me more about this and that, and I'll tell you whether or not I can afford it.'

'Oh, no,' I say, 'I couldn't.'

'Oh, but yes, I insist.'

Insanely, I allow him take my arm, and as we move along, I strain to remember his name, and soon it all becomes a glimmering swoon, his voice soothing and the store so gay and his scent a little much, and I start to think this is how life is supposed to be, and you never imagine bad things can happen to you or to those whom you know.

Two hours later, laden with shopping, I'm accompanying him up in the lift to his flat and expecting we're going to indulge in certain activities, and he reaches out a hand to touch my hair, tells me he's so happy he ran into me, that all day he's been vaguely aware of some need clamouring for his attention, and now he realises what it was he wanted, to spend a little time with someone like me, and my turning up unexpectedly is just ideal, and also he's sick of paying over the odds for domestic models, foreign imports, plastic enhancements, uncultured nitwits, braying ninnies, who would sooner betray or rob you than keep their side of the bargain.

He looks at me like he thinks I ought to be feeling flattered, as if he's only repeated what he's said before when I remember him as a gentleman, seductive, that I'm some sort of exquisite desert rose, pale, exotic by his lights, full-haired, somewhere between the fat girl you can see struggling to prevail in Nicole Kidman's face and an overweight Calista Flockhart, lugubrious flower, fragrant, shimmering, languorous, shadowy, soft and willing, sweet as Turkish delight, something pure which he's free to foul in the course of the be-all bargain. Of course I unveil my dumbest, least complicated smile, and estimate how much I'm going to deceive him for treating me like such a prostitute.

Inflating his sense of male bravado, I insist that size matters, and a measuring tape is flourished to confirm it's a three-foot line, the longest line of white either of us admit to having seen, and I leer as he falters and retires around the twenty-eight-inch mark, leaving me to lean over, one hand holding back my fall of hair, and tidy off the remainder.

My legs pinned up against me, chest crushed, face turning from side to side to escape his kisses. Remembering his name, his wife's name, his father's name, his sister's name. Wet dripping from his lips agape. The shine of crowns in his mouth. His hands tightening in my hair, jerking hard to get my head still as he drives inside of me. Aching, with tears running off my face onto the pillow. Forcing himself in and out, in and out, in and out. Kissing me, whoever

I am, I hardly know any longer, his hot hurrying breath suffocating me. Picturing myself as a list – laundry, shopping, resolutions – rubbed, remade, scratched, scuffed illegible, lost and found and lost again. The new black and jade-green detailed basque tugged this way and that, the unfamiliar straps biting into flesh, the pale reaches, the pearly radiance, the burn of folly. Piles of hair soaked in sweat, his and mine, his spit and mine. As he spills, his neck twists away and he sighs, mutters something smothering, what I guess is some sort of imprecation, names, none familiar, none mine. Watching as he pulls out to show his furry brown chest and damp abdomen, his slack anterior, the dark penis glistening and shrivelling in the laden bright pink rubber.

As I'm walking down the street, trying to conjure up a taxi, all these shopping bags preventing me from raising an arm, I'm trying to figure where that fuck feeling came from, skin slick beneath my dress, thinking I should have showered before I got out of there, still can't work out what it was about him made me want to, the man who's just fucked me – he has more shirts than suits, more suits than shoes, more shoes than books – though lurking somewhere is a hazy thread, just another unsubstantiated red-top rumour linking him with someone else, someone English, someone blonde, patrician, someone tragic, only the facts refuse to surface, remaining beyond definition, but persecutory, like a hammer beating dissonant inside my head.

Waking in misery. This cock-to-mouth existence is

doing me in. I may be prone to regular reserve after all. Conclude what I need is a five-year plan. Perhaps a five-day plan to begin with. Money and space. And focus. Some augmented focus. They're really my priorities at the moment. I have $187,849. Give or take. Accumulated capital. Plus expectations. Not least some Anaconda royalties. The secret being to act as if you have $187,849,000. Wonder how people, friends and strangers, if they knew, would relate to the true state of my finances. People are beginning to frown when they spot me. Even in this so-called liberated age there is so much ground to be won, and I am going about it as best I can, doing my bit valiantly, and no doubt other women regard me as a liability to their cause, as if I'm putting the struggle back decades, whereas I regard myself as the new way. A little lightweight perhaps but heck I'm out there. And sometimes when I see the pictures on TV or in the papers, my conscience is tugged as much as anyone's, and I want to give over all my worldly goods and treasures to relieve world hunger, and smite tyrants and arseholes, and all of that, devote myself, apply my talents to the cause of justice, equity, bread for children the world over. And I genuinely think that. I feel it so intensely that I perspire, relinquish blood pressure, fall limp, while simultaneously appreciating how stuck-up *soignée* twittering witches in their Galliano outerwear and Eres knickers scowl at me, the very idea of me, rubbish me behind my back, to my face even, heap scorn upon me, speculate I'm a whore or something in that milieu, misogynistic fodder, the neighbours do. I'm nothing so available. I have a heart that beats and flesh which yields. I'm a human being, a woman. Remember, none of which I asked for in the first place. And always, I keep trying my best.

My latest dealer, King, is an imposter. King is neither queer nor impotent yet never shows the slightest interest in me. That at least cuts off one slippery slope avenue of procuring and paying for life-sustaining blow. He is proper and boyishly a gent, always trusts I will pay, always happy to extend unsecured credit. He has no friends to push on me as a means of balancing the books. He is self-contained. A dream. But underneath the dream, the smiles, the accommodation – no one's fooling anyone – lies the steel that subtly informs there's a limit to his munificence, that he's not to be taken for granted, that this relationship is one that will not be salved by means of anything so insubstantial as a token headsuck, or anything so nightmarish as a bestowing of such oral outrage on some unwashed smegma-fouled bonehead enforcer-slash-slasher-slash-associate of his, that very steel inveigles us into a taut wrapped relationship as sturdy and superficial as that which ties Posh and Becks, Phil the Greek and Liz the Second, Igor and Stravinsky, lemon and curd, Roald and Dahl.

I make the call, say, 'King, hello.'

And right off, King says, purring, 'Ms Lee, baby.'

'I have a situation.'

'What do you need?'

'Apart from direction and a life, money would be nice, acclaim, adulation, recognition in my native land.'

'A couple of grams OK?'

'Thank you.'

'You come round or you want me bike it to you?'

'I'm in this pub off Seven Dials, you know the one?'

'Stay put,' he says, hanging up.

Twenty minutes later this girl in beaded blonde hair, black sucked-on Lycra cycle shorts, loose grey sleeveless Nike tennis top, struts in the bar, her face all sheeny from exertion and health, smiling when she spots me, though I don't know her, have never seen her before, handing over a three-pack of Durex, turning away, leaving. I tip back my gin, stare down the Japanese tourists peering at me over their maps and offal-pies, strike for the toilets, wondering about the Durex, whether it's a sign of things to come. Course there's no johnnies in the box, just blow. Laying out a third on the front cover of this month's *Total Film*, thinking how evolved a consumer society we live in, lean over, provides for the likes of me, my irregular wayward abrupt requirements, line up my improvised biro device and suck white off Angelina Jolie's air-brushed cheek.

Out again, seeking to regain the same seat, only this moron, floc-jawed, peanuts swimming in his pint, steps into my path, huffs in my face, squawking, 'Ey, skinny, don't I know you?'

'Hardly.'

'I do, you're . . .'

'Push off, will you, and don't call me skinny.'

'I never, what?'

'Ey, skinny, don't I know you?'

'Excuse me.'

'And keep your hands off me or I'll rip your fucking head off and scream rape, you hairy fuck.'

Excuse him? Ey, skinny? Oh, my. Sometimes I suspect my hearing's impaired from too many nights gadding, nodding like a simpleton and screaming to make myself heard, or else worrying that I'm mentally ill and prone to discerning affront and insult, a conspiracy of hate, in the blandest of come-ons. Telling myself, Don't go there, honey.

Let's appraise.

Cons: No man, no family, no home, so-called career in deep-ditch cold-storage.

Pros: My looks.

Straits: Stray tits, blossoming gravity-loving arse.

Outrage: People think they understand love or fucking because they do it, they don't. To them they reduce it so that it's all about feelings like in a weepy TV movie or *Madame Bovary* or *Anna Karenin*, when there's really nothing to it. It's a primal fact without provenance or consequence. Do it or not, no one gives a damn, I don't. Excuse me, said the geek, sounding like – yes, vacancies – he knew he shouldn't have called me skinny.

Sure enough I come face to face with Alessia. An inevitability given the limitations of our shared society. Less inevitably, both of us anxiously fingering virtually the same décolletage, part of the daring dishabille which composes the distinguishing element of the same designer's strictured vision. Immediately concerned we appear too much like sisters, twins even, not quite identical, to the uninformed passing observer, whoever he or she might be. Mirroring the same distracted intensity for almost a minute as if we fail to see or recognise each other – nothing to do with her nicely healed, barely altered nose – and then having little other choice but invoke, nearly synchronically, the same poise-saving estimation of Billy's sheer inconsequence to our lives, as best illustrated by our phlegmatic presence here at the launch of nothing more crucial than a refurbished shop, one of Guido Maffei's visions for *Allegria*, an expansionist Milanese fashion collective, cool and cavernous, before realising our patent similarity, what Billy must have seen, both his type. An unsparing, cold recognition. And only now able to breathe again, move, stiffly clutching each other's chiffoned arms and shoulders to graze cheeks and swap particles of Clinique and L'Oreal face powder with equivalent transparency levels.

Hardly pausing for prudence, I leap right in, asking, 'The nose, you're happy?'

'Absolutely, it's what I've always dreamed.'

'What about you and Billy?'

'He's a mountebank.'

'A what?'

'A boastful, unscrupulous wanker.'

'Don't you love him?'

'He made his bed.'

'Did he?'

'Don't let on not to know, Lee, don't take me for the born-yesterday type.'

With which Alessia swings away, brandishing renewed gaiety toward strangers. Of course I'm relieved neither of us confessed anything intimate, broached for instance the question, impossible or otherwise, of simultaneous impregnation, whether Billy was sufficiently potent, his grubby pingtongs diabolically capable of nosing their way into primed ova and establishing beachheads there within hours of one another. Or perhaps that Gloucester Avenue bed, the three of us pawns to its hoodoo, what else, two at a time, traversing its surface, Alessia and Billy in the hours before she went in the hospital to have her nose fixed, me and Billy in the hours following, that guilty bed ordering our future in the space of prurient minutes.

Retiring to a corner, flute in one hand, Ericsson in the other, feeling the atmosphere turn close, oppressive, sweat beading through the powder of lip and brow, scrolling frantically, searching for someone to call, settling on Fisk, do just that, letting him know that I'm back, followed by silence as if I've woken or dragged him from some Duchamp pointed-finger or cluttered-box reverie, or even a commoner dose of Hirst-envy, as if he'd never missed me, as if he might not have caught my name just now, recognised my voice, as if he's failed to allot me significance on any level. I mention Billy and that seems to do the trick. Immediately he tells me the portrait's finished, and I accept his invitation to view.

Hurrying from the chattering, choked shop, I step into the street, wave down the first cab I encounter, cry Fisk's address, change my mind, redirect the driver to take me home where I switch to the scooter, ride on to his studio where he makes no comment on my harried state, hair awry, lips parted, breathing audibly through my mouth, blurred pencil as though bruised recently ravaged lips signalling another man's, or why not woman's, kisses.

He admires my what he calls my frock, mentions Balthus, this year's Spoleto Festival poster, the last before the artist's death, assuring me mutely our age difference is surmountable, he's early forties, pressing softly against my arm, as if the Balthus allusion escapes me, the warm glow of light and strangely adolescent-seeming flesh, torso swept flat, latent and unbound, a shock of loose ashen ripe hair, a high-plains vision, twitching, turning sideways, closer to him, so he gets to breathe deeply the scent adhering to me, shower gel, perspiration, traffic, the reception I've so restively abandoned. Now leading me to where he unveils the painting which was Billy's idea, introducing me to Fisk, recommending we commission a portrait just as his work, reflecting, it was widely reported, an obsessive love affair with contemporary enigmas, among whom, Billy flattered himself to think, he at least, of us two Anaconda, must be counted, was attracting ever and exponentially greater éclat – something which we'd both acquired an immoderate appetite for during our time in Europe. So, significant money changed hands and we sat for the artist in a puritanically archaic fashion, as if the camera or video recorder had never been invented, as if the subject had to suffer endless discomfort in order for there to be any chance of achieving a successful rendition. While I'd been attracted to and excited by the vaguely masochistic and time-consuming process, Billy had promptly declared the experience tiresome, not to mention detractive and debilitating to his own artistic imperative, and had scuttled off to Rome, abandoning both me and Alessia, while claiming he needed to find space in which to work on his, no longer *ours*, overdue third album. So, the commission had shrunk to a portrait of me by myself. And all through the weeks which it took, I'd failed to discern any ulterior motive in Billy's unflagging avowal of the exercise. He was always accessible at the other end of the phone, ready to cheerlead, shore up my resolve, urging me to see the matter through for his sake as much as mine, reminding me how Fisk's work would surely prove a prudent investment, flattering evidence of our prescience in selecting him, as well as a confirming illustration of our eternal bond, and finally confiding that there was record-company approval for the completed portrait to feature on the forthcoming album cover. Now, all these months later, that possibility seems as improbable as Billy ever discarding his latest amoureuse, Sylvia-sucking-Glade, in favour of my bruised and set-aside self. The entire exercise exposed as a scheme to occupy my time while Billy was freed to abuse my love with the help of the same plush and thoroughgoing Sylvia.

So, it's with some detachment that I discover Fisk has painted my tits so they look like plums, small yellowy green plums, a little way from ripe. Not so far from the truth, size-wise. He asks if I'd be interested in doing some further modelling for him, wouldn't be able to pay very much, though his smile seems to suggest there would be certain other rewards to be gained from the experience: satisfactions, illuminations. I tell him I don't feel it would be such a good idea, and ask when to expect delivery of the painting. Not for a couple of months he tells me because he wants to place it in a forthcoming exhibition.

I say, 'You mean other people are going to see this?'

'Does that bother you?'

'I have green tits.'

'If you let me paint you again you can have whatever kind of tits you like.'

'Avocado?'

'Of course.'

'And kind of more, telescopic, conical, not so much big as out there, you know, jutting.'

'That's doable.'

Looking again at the portrait, I decide that despite its unhappy associations it's not so gruesome. There are axillary – he calls it, referring to my armpits – clusters of unfamiliar flowers, leaves in my mouth, ivy binding my waist, a laurel choker, legs spread, hips swathed in a puffed ballerina skirt, eyes downcast, hair pushed back off my face which is half veiled by this wing, a gossamer wafer of white tulle, an aigrette of bright red berries sprayed on my crown, thistledown lashes, photographs of old women on the wall behind me, wrinkled and bowed – depicting my future? – more photographs of Mediterranean villas and boys in short pants standing alongside large dusty motor cars with running boards and curvy pre-war lines.

I wonder how he managed to do that, achieve an effect like photographs of photographs. Projecting slides onto canvas and painting over? Could it be that simple?

Outside again, the humidity cloaks me, and I hate having to wear the black helmet, but once I'm moving, skimming along, the wind catches my dress, runs cool over my skin.

We fly separately to Tokyo. Billy departs on a Tuesday.

I follow on the Thursday. No sign of a fiancée. Someone tells me the Glade in question remains at home – Billy's place – in Gloucester Avenue, busy redecorating, attempting to install some natural light in that gloomy house, a task which involves no less than luring the sun out of its way if it's ever to strike that north-facing curve which the street takes just before turning over the railway bridge. All within her powers according to the consensus hereabouts.

This is to be the last of Anaconda, our final show together, dispatched by mutual consent, ha. No matter how much it pains some of us there's no escaping the obligation to fulfil this final, long-standing commitment. Too many grim grown-ups – executive types – have graphically outlined the grievous legal and financial penalties following any failure to show.

A gaggle of Japanese reporters, tiny girls in tiny skirts and collegiate sweaters, interview Billy. Watching him wallow in the attention makes me think if only I'd been his wife I might be coming out of all this further ahead than I am, due at least a settlement, worth a pound of flesh, or a nut or two. I feel feverish, ringed in, squeezed, hardly able to breathe, unable to enjoy the milling experience that's Tokyo.

Hours before we're due on stage I'm shuffling around, trying to muster ideas, some means of derailing Billy's fixation on his apparently scintillating bride-to-be. What I seek is a scheme to expose the interloper as a ninny, shatter whatever spell she's cast upon him. Unsure of how to attract his attention I consider mutilating myself, wading into the ocean, walking into free-way traffic at rush hour, making him regret all the hurt he's causing me. But rush hour comes and goes, and I remain neglected, a peripheral figure, bowed translucent face, fingers pushed into my sleeves like a nun – OK there's a boy-child digital-diarist lurking, aiming his three-chip Sony at my lips, my eyes, attempting to harvest my soul or more, but he's too young, mid-teens, and sad for the world, to signify.

Even as we go through the motions of the final sound check, assorted delusional scenarios present themselves, all involving the same conclusion, the same elements of contrition, forgiveness, restoration, blind faith in our future happiness together. Maybe it's time I revealed to the world what it's like to be me. Maybe the years when he wasn't around. Share what that all entailed. The smell of myself in solitude and fear. The roaring desolation. For years I've held myself to the discipline of never looking back. Now I ache for him to approach me, to rub up against me in the presence of all, the knowing view of many. It breaks over me, the need to reveal myself once and completely to him, so I strike off across the hollow stage, snag him by the waist of his two-sizes-too-small T-shirt and drag him away from where he's discussing acoustics, playlists, formulaic melodies, syncopation, slant-eye pussy. Over-riding his protests, I remind him he has other obligations, in particular, to me, his only, his first and ever-lasting conquest. And, ensuring that the weltschmerzy local boy's recording all of this, I go pressing Billy against the dusty folds of an ancient stage drop, admitting him into the mayhem of another truth.

'Either we're dead,' I say, 'or I'm a part of you nothing can deny.'

'So what's it like being dead?' he says.

'That's not what I . . .'

'What?' he says. 'That's not what you what?'

Unsure how to articulate all that's weighing upon me, I fling arms around his neck, and rising to my toes, heave myself at him, pressing hard lips at his, his cheek, his eyes, whispering my breath into his ear.

'Fuck it, Lee,' he says, pushing me away.

Waiting out the ensuing interlude on my lonesome, backstage, watching the bowl of noodles I requested congeal. Sitting here, my face in flames, telling myself our timing sucks, has always sucked, prey to hit and run logistics, chance, lousy fate. A few exceptions to the contrary, it's almost always the case that whenever he looks to me, I'm unavailable; and when I look to him, he's disinterested. And not that I'm turning into an inchoate moralist but right now I feel humiliated. As if this has been another episode to brush aside, to shunt away, hopefully well beyond the reach of memory. Though experience informs me, there's no escaping regret, panic, sentiment, hysteria. One thing always seems to lead to another, and before you know it you're right back where you started.

And suddenly it's time for the million-yen spectacle — hardly worth my while, is it — taking a final breath, detaching myself from fear and the shelter of the sunken dressing room, stepping from the private gateway out onto the runway into a roar of sound, a flood of heat, shaking off the breath of pain, assured at least no hem nor thread nor button nor cuff nor collar, no hair no ruff no colour out of place, no heel scuffed, no nail jagged, no scent uncultured, no line visible, nothing to impugn the local *soignée* daftness I've so enfolded about myself in armour against the inevitable ravenous eyes in search of frailty, flaw, or crevice to worry into utter rank ragged destruction, and warming up, swerve and swivel, use the hips, deploy the innate sulking eye, peering, quivering close to tears, elated, down the line, crossing over from left side to right to gain the greater light like evening sun postpones a chill, surfing the bright clamour, another rank of snappers, beyond which, rafts of floating faces jostle, green like parachutes filling the night sky or swarms of jellyfish swimming overhead, knowing when to veer off to avoid the intense gust of unearned adulation, hellish air off the pressing scrimmage, targeting the scope they have of my pudendal crest, mispronouncing my name, crying en masse, *LeapLeapLeap*, like blind runty piglets, little baby birds in a nest clamouring to be fed and all I have to offer are portions of my self, avoid that brazening of spirit to engage with their marshy viscera. Billy's guitar already noising, raw and broken, rumbling, growling, homemade, true. Removing my shirt, caught behind by the collar, and pulling it that way over my head and tossing it, soul gyrating, kneading the crowd into a howl of approval. Some practised stagehand plucks the shirt out of the air before it reaches them, the gesture having been repeated endlessly, show after show. Crying out, 'You want me?' And they roar their souls away. And I tell them everything they want to hear, cry out, 'I'm coming.' Doubtful how much they understand. Followed by most of *Zombie*, all of *Kangaroo Girl*, some bloodlust covers, 'One More Cup of Coffee', 'Gloria',

'Rock'n'Roll Nigger', only for it all to end abruptly
with my take on 'I Bid You Good Night' –

> Lay down my dear brother
> lay down & take your rest
> I want you lay your head now
> upon your Saviour's breast
> I love you oh
> but Jesus love you the best
> oh I bid you good night Lord
> good night Lord oh . . .

. . . Billy having to drag me off stage to yowls of
protest, disappointment. Chilled and sobered by the
lack of tenderness in his face. No other choice but to
adjust instantly to the gloom. And request a coffee like
a sane woman. And stand here waiting. A sweaty hand
towel round my neck, the ends covering my chest, the
white vest with *SINTERTAINER* sequinned onto it.
My hair tangled, snaky. Running my gaze over the
ovoid faces here, without purchase. Crinkling my eyes
in delayed acknowledgement of their cooling applause.

I've had four years of this, three hundred dates to
prepare for ending it all in a swirling black-hole town
like Tokyo. By the time the others have left, waved
away to party, I've finished crying. Back out on the
glazed street in tights, black boots, speckled grey and
black skirt, black mohair sweater, scarf, searching vainly
for the cab they said was waiting. Aching all over, the
ice-pack on my knee proved ineffectual, I can barely
walk, probably needs strapping. How could I work and
wear strapping? Wheel me out on stage, rock'n'roll

quadriplegic? Brought along my book, my water, my phone. Remember him laughing, telling me, 'You don't have to try and seduce me, Lee.' Hair clings wet, shampoo scented, about my collar. Forcing myself to walk toward the end of the street in hope of another cab. Rerunning my eighty minutes on stage – desiring I was in the sun that much each morning, not ramp lights, real sun, that pervasive heat. Finding a bin to toss away the book, the water. Looking around for a chance of that cab. Turning away and striking off along another street. Neon and black night. A street of vending machines: Kirin, Cokes, and Luckies. Staying on the sidewalk, limping, swinging my arms, singing low to myself –

> Lord I goin walkin in the valley
> in the shad'r of love

. . . imagining the sun, growing accustomed to it, forbidding myself to falter. The money I borrowed for the cab fare scratching, ¥20,000 up my sleeve. Thinking, doubting that Billy will have gotten rid of the liggers by the time I get back to the hotel where we're supposed to be anonymous, registered under Mishima. Questioning whether I ever believed we would be together until we were just another pair of shrivelled old fish, stinking in some Sierra Vista, Fort Huachuca, Tombstone, nursing home, barely hanging on to our voting rights.

Wearing my favourite delicate rosy Kristina Ti's, wishing the red tsunami would hit. Resisting the urge to look, confirm it one way or the other. Imagining what if they're ruined, 155,000 lire down the drain. The luxury of being able to claim, *It's not like I planned it on purpose or anything. It just happened, you know, as it does. So Billy's in the clear.*

The same for Alessia?

I wonder.

Feeling relieved?

Of course, who wouldn't be.

Anyway L.155,000 was the full price, and the girls at the Via Mario de Fiori branch know me, had let me have them for L.108,000, the sale price, even though the sales were still weeks away when I saw them. The matching *reggiseno* discounted from L.110,000 to L.77,000. Don't need an excuse to go back there. Regret the black under green dress I left behind. L.550,000 for the black *abito*, L.150,000 for the jade *sottoveste*. The time that guy drinking water from the street pump squirted my skirt, his finger stopping the spout, redirecting the flow, shooting out through the second aperture, right at me. I squealed and shied away. So improbably fucking girlish of me. Should have made him apologise, only some sense told me he recognised something about me. Besides, it dried before I got to the end of the street. Forever seeking relief from the heat. Spending entire afternoons indoors. Running into that tall girl, efficient Pariolina type, a guide, associate curator, in the coolness of the modern art gallery wearing the identical denim skirt, the identical green twin set, the cardigan wrapped around her hips, everything the same except for the shoes, the hair, the complexion, the height, the cardigan draped over my shoulders. And the same night, across the street to see Patti Smith in concert, as she urged the crowd to help her out, abandon the steps they were seated on, and swoop down to press the stage. Closer to midnight I came across a pod of the most beautiful slender boys, like cast-out angels, perched cross-legged effete on stone pedestals immediately inside the gates to what seemed like the zoo, waiting for business. The Viale delle Belle Arti.

Paula Lennox lives in this big house I keep thinking must have gargoyles poking their snouts from somewhere round the cast-iron gutters but I've never seen any. Tonight there are cars parked higgledy-piggledy in the drive and all across the lawns. Leaving Lucy to find a space, I go inside, where Paula greets me, finds me something to drink, champagne, pink, and tells me Johnny Depp, who's in town, promised he'd drop by. I let on to be thrilled by this piece of pathetic nonsense. Paula's nineteen, floating high on the age-old craze for blue-blood mannequins. She moves away to greet and devour, leaving me to scan the crowd, the usual assortment of actors, models, musicians, upper-class layabouts, louts, druggies. I hate myself for being here, thinking if this is life, if this is rock'n'roll, if this is how it's all dressed up, dusted down . . . I wish I wasn't wearing this dress, this minidress, this piece of salvage knitwear. I wish I was somewhere else, anywhere raw, basic, dirty and be damned, how it used to be, me sucking on a microphone, Billy, sweaty, troubled, fucked up, on guitar, vocals, punk R&B, garage rockers. I know this is supposed to last me to the end, these few years, but it isn't enough, it isn't fair.

Matthew Davis leans into a woman who must be forty-five or fifty, an entertainment lawyer's wife I think and Rebecca's mother. She wears this lowcut black top with spaghetti straps. Her boobs are great, signally evident, look like they're never going to founder, not in this life anyway. She keeps her back to the wall, and Matthew leans close, so his bare arm touches her hair, her face. She turns her lips against his wrist as her gaze meets mine, and I smile at her and turn away, wondering whether he'll still love her when she's vanquished, bring her fuck and flowers when she's opiated, dying, lying mired in her own shit and treacle-heavy piss. I don't see Rebecca here.

I trail after this endearingly freckled girl, follow her outside, thinking she's someone I should get to know, but she's not, she turns and stares at me, cold, possibly a little frightened, and I feel my face puffy and eyes piggy, and I should pursue that theme of fear and walk up to her, eyeball her, go, *What?*

There's a guy in the pool doing distance. He's got on these white mini-briefs, and his legs beat the water with barely a ripple, without splashing.

The freckled girl moves alongside me, flexes her lips, and points her empty glass at the swimmer, says, 'What do you think?'

'Who is he?'

'JD.'

'Don't tell me, he thinks he's a fish?'

'That's funny,' says the freckled girl through clenched teeth.

'No tan line,' I say.

'No.'

123

'When's he going to stop?'

'I don't think he's ever coming out.'

'Neat,' I say, unable to help myself.

The freckled girl looks hard at me, finally affronted by my tone, the accent, the dress, all of it, says, 'What did you say?'

I shake my head, tilt the glass at my lips so it slowly empties. The swimmer swims on. The girl scowls.

I say, 'Maybe he does interiors?'

'Tell me, who're you?'

'Lilly Gruber.'

'Don't be such a bitch.'

'I'm not, I swear. Lilly Gruber, like on Italian TV. Lilly Gruber, you know her, that's me.'

The freckled girl calls, 'JD,' calls to the swimmer but he doesn't look up, he doesn't slow, he doesn't stop, and she calls and calls, 'JD, JD.' Still he doesn't acknowledge her. She hurries down beside the pool, and clutching her elbows, waits for him to return to her. I wave but the freckled girl doesn't see me, and I go back inside and run into Lucy and indicate the girl, the strangest girl, outside by the pool, and Lucy explains that the girl is JD's sister, and that they're really close, like especially. I should have guessed it was something like that.

Someone fires a flashgun in my vicinity, and I swivel to face it, baring my teeth in enthusiastic reflex, scrunching my eyes in party-snap-happy mode. A boy, T-shirted, tall, undernourished, German, languid ungroomed campness, a camera in each hand, strapped to each wrist, Contax, little shiny point-and-shooters, attempts to frame me, capture my congealing enigma,

124

leans in to buss my powdered cheek.

And I say, 'Dieter.'

And he says, 'Honey-pot.'

'Don't you ever stop?'

'Never, never,' he exclaims. And touching my hip, his fingers stroking the material, seeking more than retro-design details, the flesh moving beneath the creamy beige cashmere, his brows arching as he asks warmly, apropos the dress, 'Now, tell me, who is this?'

'Lucy's mother's,' I say.

'Never, never,' he says.

'Really,' I say.

'It's . . .' he says.

'I know,' I say, as his fingers go tracing deftly the gentle swag of gilded chain at my waist, finding it decorates the front alone, ends at either hip. His eyes busy, shamelessly flitting from outlined nipples to kohl-rimmed eyes and back again. Our faces inclining toward each other, lips parted, eyes wide, until at the very last instant only cheeks brushing, pressing an instant, a dance of teeter-tottering attraction exposed as gamine habit. He passes on, the grace of a feral starved cat high on a perilous hip roof, the flashes, cried greetings, indicating his passage through the crowd.

I go drifting toward the kitchen, trying to recall how many cameras that Poole had . . . out at Heathrow. More than one? I can't remember. There's a tall skinny boy in here with his hand up Paula's skirt. It seems Paula's not wearing underwear anymore since there's a puff of faint black gossamer on the floor by her feet.

'Hey, gorgeous,' says Paula, 'say hi to Lee.'

Gorgeous says, 'Hiya, Lee,' and takes his hand from underneath her skirt, and holds it out to me.

I'm guessing he expects me to shake it, and thinking, weird, I take his hand, slickish from Paula, and he pumps me four or five times, making me thirst for escape, hard labour, *Top of the Pops*, flu, guesting on The sly Priory, a night with an obese throwback Brylcreemed Tory politician of my choice, anything but this.

Paula says, 'Lee, this is Tim.'

'Tim.'

He releases my hand only when I say his name, and it's a struggle to keep from bringing fingers up and sniffing.

Paula says, 'Tim's in a band, bass, lead vocals.'

They're waiting for me to react. I'm sure I must look out of it, like it's so unusual to meet someone who's in a band. Like am I supposed to know every fucking band pops up in London. Absolute morons. Morons mate with more morons and beget bigger morons. Generation after generation. Paula was born without a brain but her parents had all this money so no one ever noticed. As for Tim, who knows. At least he looks like he could be in a band, he's crucially mop-haired, gaunt, cadaverous, decked and dyed in black, and he appears to have two tennis balls and a tuberous anatomical prominence, carrot or parsnip, stuffed in his vacuum-packed crotch. Paula gets Tim to share the name of his band – Popeye.

And Paula adds, 'You've heard of them, they're like really . . .'

I wait for it.

'. . . shredding,' says Paula.

Crikes. I nod my head, agreeably, mustering a fake little flutter of awe. Paula tells me to go upstairs to her room and put on Popeye's CD, *Animal Pleasures*. Any excuse. Any escape.

So I'm stretched out on Paula's bed, listening to Popeye thrash their way through five or six or seven songs, and I get a little lost in there, the songs are all essentially the same Ramones rip-off, and someone comes and sits on the side of the bed, it's Tim, dropping his clammy hand on my leg, squeezing my calf, and I roll over on my back and search his face for some flicker indicating he knows better than he's behaving, and I try not to shudder or tear at my arms, and he takes my hand, and turns it over, and studies the palm which is white, dead, terribly petite and ladylike.

'Looking for something?' I ask in a small weary voice.

Tim says, 'When I was seven, my old man topped my mum with a Bacardi bottle, then went out and drowned himself.'

Whether or not in Bacardi is unclear and probably on balance not crucial. I don't know what to say so I say, 'Groovy,' say it very quietly. It seems to do the trick. At least it doesn't agitate him. Where the hell is Paula? I attempt to sit up some more on the bed but it's difficult with him clutching my hand so tightly.

'My old man,' he's saying, 'was a terror. I have his nose.'

'Where?' I say, and he turns to show his profile.

'And his dick,' he claims.

And preemptively I go, 'I believe you.'

'You're different,' he says.

Tragic, I think. 'Not really,' I say.

There's flecks of something frosty on his lashes – not sleep – and more at his nostrils. And his eyes are shot with something flagrant and ugly that should be far away but is really close up. There are four black swastikas penned in smeared ink on the knuckles of his right hand, KUFC on his dyslexic left.

At least his voice is quiet, 'I hear you, babe, I hear you.'

'Where's Paula?'

'I threw her in the pool.'

'No?' I squeak, unavoidably picturing the Lennoxs' other pool, an ironically tacky, contra-Council strictures, ornamental puddle out front with rockery facing, and featuring a threesome of concrete, brightly Duluxed flamingos. Give it another couple of hours it'll be soured over with party detritus, cans, butt ends, upchuck, spongy vol-au-vents, socks, matches, patches of burnt foil, broken-off stiletto heel, a plastic barrette, primary-coloured condoms, at least one oversized condoom, that Dutch Cees is downstairs, the stale wind picking up, stragglers searching, hearts hurting, contusive, crying out the names of lost dates, sisters, drivers, loves, Lucy? Freckles? Harris? Mary?

Tim says, 'I think she must have drowned.'

'Oh.'

He takes my hand and slowly, very deliberately, bundles my fingers, inserts the lot like fasces in his mouth. I doubt whether he'd be less enthusiastic over a warm package of my faeces. He takes his time, sucking and running his tongue over each finger individually, suggestive of some Eastern, Far Eastern, courtship routine, Persian, Chinese, Turkestani, somewhere on the open Silk Road, where the suitor expends prodigious amounts of spittle until his beloved radiates homologous moistness. He stops, parched at last, and finally I manage to extract my hand, clear my throat, say, 'Tim, sugar, I have this . . .' gulp '. . . condition, menacing condition actually, called trichomoniasis.'

Nothing. Like he's in the dark here as well. So I press ahead, 'Tim,' slower, 'I have mono, more this cocktail of mono, gonorrhoea, one or more strains of what-do-you . . . hepatitis! . . . some really nasty ugly grungy warts, more ulcers than warts in appearance, real weepers, but warts are indisputably what they are, perhaps, even, who knows, they're leprous.'

Something lifts fractionally from his eyes, and like a lazy lethal 'gator into water he slides into some campus character we've seen in a hundred movies, and says, 'Pity.' And then, 'Oh, you lovely.'

He retrieves my hand, runs my sleeve up over my elbow, kisses the inside of my arm, finally biting and sucking the crook so hard he hurts me, blood sliding beneath the skin, capillaries flooding, discolouring, haematomatic.

The door opens, Paula's here, wet through, hair a tangled mess, bearing this empurpled aggrieved aura I don't like the look of. Tim drops my arm, and I go scampering off the bed, keeping it between us, flicking my hand to sluice off his wet. Paula crosses her arms, tugs off her top, unsnaps and drops her skirt, steps away, grabs a towel. Tim stares at her. I stare at her. Paula has a blurred bluish circular birthmark, or maybe it's a tattoo, like a cattle brand, the lazy C, high on the inside of her thigh; an almost invisible teased blonde bush over the tiny pink lesion of her sex; sharp jutting high-set hip bones Tim's probably right now fantasising about exfoliating himself with. Her skin gleaming, she stares at him, bypassing little old me.

'I'll call,' I say, driftingly, going out the door, doubting whether Paula hears me, thinking nothing bad can ever happen to me.

And another week goes by, and someone calls, waking me at 8.20 in the morning, and I'm flailing at the sheet, tangled disorder, pillows all over the place, trying to establish my bearings, finding my rings have rubbed off in the night, lying scattered on the sheet beneath me, and it's Pearl calling to tell me Scott Weaver's OD'd.

'But he's going to be OK, right?'

'He's dead, Lee, dead, he OD'd.'

'God,' I say.

'No,' she says, emphatically, 'OD'd.'

No one I know goes to funerals. Besides, Scott Weaver is going to be cremated and his ashes scattered in the sea somewhere off Baja California. Everyone I know dies. I try to estimate how many dead people I've slept with. Of course none were dead when I delved with them. Maybe I'm some sort of a jinx where certain people are concerned. Sleep with me and die. Fuck Lee Annis and embrace eternity.

Scott Weaver seems such a long time ago. So long ago in fact, I doubt whether I was the same person I am today. So long ago, I probably don't even need to be worried about having picked up any nasties. So long ago, I probably don't need to take a test. So long ago in fact, if he had anything to pass on I'd be dead already. Fifteen, twenty days. A lifetime ago. Forget it.

Wake again, knowing I'm in trouble, having dreamt about sex, my pimp having fled, one of those dreams, I'm all-out anxious about who's going to feed business my way, weed out the loons, keep everything discreet, when I get a call to a hotel, and however the message was passed on it's a deaf guy in town for the deaf games, *19th Giochi Mondiali Silenziosi, Roma 2001*, and I've never done deaf before. In the morning it's like I dreamed everything, a dodgy wooden encounter, a high odour of something harsh, a chemical abrasive, chlorine? in the room. The deaf man is anxious that I leave as soon as possible. I stare blankly at his empty mouth, his pointing to his watch, the door, his taking my elbow, trying to tug me, urge me up out of bed. There are other deaf people in the hotel, and he doesn't want to be seen with me, with someone so obviously a pro, but I delay, wanting to make him pay a little more, suffer, feel a little shame, embarrassment, indicating I need time to dress, ready myself, put on my face, so I proceed to ignore him, sit on the edge of the bed, turn on the TV while he goes away to shower, and finally find a channel showing the police crawling all over Scott Weaver's house, my own body lying at the bottom of the pool, a phone cord wrapped biting tight around my neck, my hair floating up over my blue-white face, my staring eyes, a phone beside me as if it anchors me, illustrates my crime, and even though I'm dead, I can see, up through chlorine murk, sun haze, and six feet

131

of unfiltered water, to where Scott Weaver raises his hands in surrender just as the cops open fire.

Harris says it's contagious, menace runs to fear, he's certain he's being followed, shows me the knife he carries beside him on the front passenger seat, concealed beneath a stale copy of the *Evening Standard*, soon he's going to get himself a gun, a proper gun, offers to get one for me too, if I'm of a mind, if I've got a prudent wisp in my body, I'll do it too.

Walking late at night as far as Swiss Cottage, standing outside a Japanese steak restaurant, inhaling the warm draught from the kitchens. When we first came to London, occasionally during the winter I'd come out here after too many hours with Billy, too many hours watching him worry over a song he was writing about some other woman, just to walk past and savour the fumes off the street mingling with the scent of broiling marbled beef.

No one recognises me, approaches me. I think about what I might do after Anaconda, think about getting myself another band, messy Kentish Town girls with customised guitars, short dresses, Nadines and Justines, tangled heaps of hair, endless shaved legs, Nutrasweet lyrics, dickhead junkies, Westminster old boys, backstage every night, intrigue, fights, jealousy, fingernails, pussy.

'*You want to do him?*'

'*No.*'

'*You do.*'

'*Not.*'

'*Don't lie.*'

'*Fuck you.*'
'*Bitch.*'
'*Bitch.*'

Of course I'd walk out on them long before anyone could lay a hand on either me or my Gibson.

Now tonight I find I've strayed off Finchley Road, a foul taste in my mouth, follow the sound of boys calling until I find them playing football in a series of floodlit walled courts, turn back to encounter couples emerging from the theatre, and further along crowds flooding toward a late show at the Odeon. The air oppressive. I wipe the back of my hand to my mouth, run my tongue around my teeth, decide I need liquids, a place to lie low, ride out the evening.

Inside forty minutes I'm checked into the Anubis Hotel. No luggage. Just brain and a gold AmEx. £300 worth of suite. £20 to the bellboy. Send down for Tom Collins's, a Revlon Orange Fire lipstick, and a selection of fashion glossies. £20 to the girl. Remember to smile. How to win pals and influence their outlook. The staff appear predominantly Eastern European, Estonians, Ukrainians, tall, blonde, Viking Nazi types, and expect such munificence. They take one look at me, read me for dumb American, believe they know the type, remittance girls, either possessing a private fortune, marriage settlement, or else some sort of glamour trophy date for an endless line of rich men.

James Spader and Vincent D'Onofrio are on TV, different movies, different channels. I turn the sound down and stare at the picture, sucking up every second of screen-time Spader's got. The Tom Collins runs out. Spader runs out. Credits roll. Apply the lipstick with a shaky hand, and call down for more cocktails. It's the same girl. Make sure to smile at her while clinging desperately to the wall. The girl picks up the first tray and the £20 I've left on it for her. The girl thanks me profusely, so much so that I realise the second £20 is a mistake, and snatch it back. The girl doesn't seem to mind or question my sanity which is something I know quite a bit about. Neither do I let go of the wall until the girl has left. I pour myself another drink. Wonder how much the girl makes in tips, wonder whether it's a line of work it might be worth my while to explore. Sit on the floor with my back against the bed. Knock over the glass, spilling my drink. No need to worry. There's more than enough. Close my eyes.

When I wake again, Vincent D'Onofrio is staring at me. Manage to get to my feet. Ankles all rubbery. Neck hurting. Head hurting. Stomach hurting. All of me, even my hair, hurting. Throw back the covers and crawl into bed. Turn my back on the TV and D'Onofrio and those lethal rays that just insinuate themselves into your bones.

I dream how D'Onofrio fucks me with tears in his eyes, then drives me far into Mexico where he operates on me in this unlicensed clinic for fourteen hours to remove a tumour which is colonising me. It's a risky unapproved last-ditch operation, and when he digs out the tumour it's the size of an avocado pear. He holds it up in his two hands to show me, and I force a smile, proud and relieved to be delivered of the bloody little bundle. But I die almost immediately, and ever afterwards he keeps the tumour in a jar of tequila set on his desk so he'll never forget me.

Lee Annis,
Undead,
Anubis Hotel,
London W1.

Wearing shades to conceal these pink rubbed eyes, and a pink and green suit, short-skirted, and Kristina Ti beneath, and new pink Miu Miu shoes. And that's it. Grotesque, I know. Accepting coffee, perched on the edge of a chair in Lucy's mother's living room. Lucy looking like her mother must have looked thirty years ago. A cup and saucer held poised over my knee. My smooth bare knees clenched in place. Touching a finger to the roar in my head, trying to tell me something significant, something critical to my well-being. Their voices rumbling on. Lucy explaining what I do, how I used to be part of a band called Anaconda.

'Called what?' she asks.

Both of them focusing on me, like I can't begin to fathom what they want, why Lucy can't tell her mother what she wants to hear.

Finally, 'Called Anaconda,' I say, stammering.

I consider turning my head to look out the window, but I know it's going to require more effort than I can manage, so I raise the coffee cup to my lips, my hand trembling, but don't sip, only inhale, just a brief moment, long enough to make me nauseous, lean forward, stretch out to place the cup and saucer rattling on the table, finding it difficult to gauge where the table starts and saucer ends, and as for space itself, well, my face just appears, smudged in the silver swell of the coffee pot as I very carefully place the cup and saucer on the table, avoid disaster, and careful not to topple from my seat, lean further forward to nudge the coffee pot toward the centre of the serving tray, feeling like my body's too large for this room, its elegant décor, too bulky even for my own skin, always having to tidy it away, hair spilling, move my legs, my feet, watch my elbows, careful of that vase, it's no way Ikea Dynasty, or is it?

Lucy appears to be outlining what she believes I need, now that Anaconda is history, and I'm not so ingénue anymore, or getting any younger, which amounts to the same crux, and my appeal is wearing thin, the vulnerability shtick, the verge or aftermath of tears looking dated, tired – holding nothing back, sometimes she's too English for words – suggests something like television work, weather, news, *TOTP*, how difficult could that be, something like cultural commenting perhaps, or PR, or something behind the scenes, given my intermittent bouts of stammering, though that tortured glue-trap effect has its own devotees. Which is the moment when Lucy's mother offers her pennyworth, suggesting what I need is a day job, regular employment, suitable to a nice girl, a daughter of good family. And this is intended to be helpful, this kind of saturated loopy advice.

'That's not exactly Lee,' explains Lucy.

'No, it's not,' I whisper hoarsely, sitting back, relieved to be rid of the cup and saucer, of having to attend gingerly to Lucy and her mother's streaming waffle.

'How do you know,' says Lucy's mother, 'until you try?'

'She's tried, and besides, what would it do for her?'

'Money, introduce her to new people, experiences, challenges, even travel, why not.'

'What type of day job do you envisage offers all this, these fabulous rewards and amenities . . . ?'

'What is she interested in?'

'Lee?'

'I'm sorry?'

'Mother was just saying . . .'

'I was merely wondering . . .'

'One thing, before we go any further, you know Lee's really not what anyone would term a morning person.'

'That would rather restrict her options all right.'

'And if something came up, if say she had to be somewhere, an opening, or a premiere, or a very important benefit perhaps, then she should have to leave the what-do-they-call-it, the office, early, dash home, change, all of that, very probably arrive all flustered and dissatisfied with how she looks, and how one presents oneself is always, you know, super critical.'

'I never considered . . .'

'You see, it's not so straightforward as one might expect.'

'Still, I'm sure employers are very accommodating these days.'

'Sometimes I think I would like a job.'

'Really, what would you do?'

'I don't know.'

'Exactly, that's exactly the point I'm endeavouring to . . .'

'Don't listen to her, dear, just give it some thought.'

'I can do that.'

'Good.'

'You're not serious?'

'Why not.'

'Just give it some thought, that's all I'm saying.'

'Well, I shall.'

'Good Lord.' Turning to her mother, 'How's Oscar?'

'You know Oscar. Frenetic. Bloody frenetic.'

Laughing, they both attend to a police siren growing ever louder as it approaches, both probably with sufficient reason to believe it's coming right here, for one or other of them, is going to pull up outside the front door directly, but it doesn't, and they both look up at the same instant, catch each other's eye, and smile these thin-lipped minor smiles, both of them relieved, though also partly disappointed, deprived of an injection of drama, and I begin to wonder why Lucy's mother chose to use the term day job for what I initially took to mean a regular seven-hour office placement but which now strikes me as having implied anything, anything at all, that doesn't involve labouring on the flat of your back.

Not thinking about Scott Weaver. Not thinking about Billy. Thinking what about an epidural. An epidural for life. Already passed on one. Someone, somewhere, owes me an epidural. Thinking about repairing relations with Billy. Thinking about calling him. Until I remember we've crossed over, he's gone back to Rome, taken the English girl with him.

Coffee with Poole. He looks indisposed, admits to vague peptic upset. I feel I ought to be taking notes. The way his fingers, trembling, neatly manicured, tear open the sachet, spilling sugar across the table top – is it me, do I make him nervous? The way in which he reminds me of Francis, the Sky weatherman. The way he gently remarks my accent, the soft hybrid of America and Europe. The way his hair curls at his collar. The way his eyebrows meet when I light my cigarette.

We talk about the spate of murders where fathers, unhappy over the level of access to their kids, take those little lives, then kill themselves, as if the world must then empathise with their pain, their mad inverted reasoning. I ask him whether he has any kids. He shakes his head. So, either he's not my father or he's denying me. I ask him how he got my address. He says contacts, as if that explains everything. Nor does he admit it's strange my coming out here to find him, inviting him to have coffee with me.

One after another, my life's turning out to be this litany of wrong men. But do I consider for one moment trying something different, such as celibacy, or amnesia, or devoting myself to my so-called career, or good causes, or even to shopping, or travelling, or art for goodness sake. I know there are never enough dilettantes flitting around the world at any one moment, parlaying significance, sham poignancy, the visceral vulnerability of the human condition, like so many smoke-shrouded heathen shamans casting spells over their stooped, knuckle-dragging constituency.

Poole suggests I may need to calm down a touch. I want to tell him who I really am. I want him to save me, restore me. I want him to understand me, pardon me.

I tell him all about the dead princess who had this

really unhappy private life, wanted a new one, made a deal, they faked her death, promised her money, access to her kids, a chance to attend her own funeral, wear something specially run-up by her favourite designer, Gianni, but events moved too swiftly, they spirited her away, sent her halfway across the world on a military transport, not at all how she was accustomed to travelling, plus Belize, she had imagined, would be some sort of undiscovered beach paradise, a Club Med where she could upgrade her tan while waiting for her new face, her new life to start, but it proved to be none of that, it was an unmitigated jungle, crowded with spiders, tics and serpents, steaming shadows, demonic eyes watching every breath she took, every thought she ventured, a horrendously humid atmosphere, neither an ocean aspect nor a suggestion of an offshore breeze, not to mention a sort of fungal infection she seemed to pick up on arrival, a kind of curried rot between her toes, the same repellent scum plastered on her crotch made her pee burn caustic, forcing her to seek alleviation, experiment with messy posturing, bitter setbacks, squally and obscene, demanded to see a dermatologist or at least get some antibiotics, a cortisone cream, Mupirocin, but all they did was bung her some Vaseline, entomb her on an army compound, her quarters scarcely tolerable, a bed, a bucket, having to squirt for mosquitoes, bugs, imagine, every evening, check under the bed for those darting chameleons which appalled her and managed to get into everything, her guard never once met her gaze, as if he feared death was contagious, of course she ached to grab him, shake him, tell him touch, feel, see how much vibrancy remained, how much flesh and blood she retained, no spectre yet, not dead at all, nothing to be frightened of, also the food was turgid, though the guard claimed there was a chance they'd be able to source some Guatemalan beer, no way as punchy as Mexican, but what could one expect being exiled rather than dead as everyone believed, appreciating how Napoleon must have felt on Saint Helena before they poisoned him, this was not the first glimmer suggesting they might be planning to similarly hasten her demise, all they'd need to do was let that fungal malady ripen, go untreated, deny her access to a medic, a genito-urinary specialist, then dispose of her remains in the jungle for ants and bats to gorge upon, all the bugs and carrion birds to scatter her in microscopic ways over miles of green fetid hell, better than quicklime, on top of everything they claimed to have mislaid her luggage, not simply a question of having something decent to wear, a change of underthings would have been nice, it being so humid and the loo paper chalky to touch, but also her make-up and wash articles, life-sustaining scrubs, brushes, unguents, men can't begin to realise the importance of, family mementoes, photographs, her Discman, her mobile phone, all of it, not even a hairbrush, never mind a nail file or a tweezers or a Tampax, all she got were excuses, the face surgeon had been detained in California, her luggage misdirected to Diego Garcia, all the usual paranoia, starting to appreciate how cleverly and completely they'd duped her, she'd presented herself on a platter to her enemies, thanks to her they were in position to erase her with impunity, and every moment she itched to contact her children, friends, family, let them know she wasn't dead but alive, that soon she would have a new name, face, identity, that soon she would be back where she belonged, fêted at glamorous high-society parties in her honour, seeking pleasure and fulfilment hunting designer thrills on Rodeo Drive, Fifth Avenue, the Via Montenapoleone, even Bond Street, shopping until the plastic warped, and the treasury lay spent and plundered, the new her, anyway, fuck, it ended badly, terribly, nothing new in that . . .

Stubbed-out cigarettes and ash overflowing my saucer. Whatever happened to my mother's injunction not to smoke? Poole's eyes defused, no longer fixed on mine but strayed onto the steady stream of flushed and sweaty travellers, searching for a mark, unguarded celebrity. An air of almost post-coital lassitude stealing over me, thinking of Rome, Billy walking dazed among the morning shoppers and African traders on the shaded side of the Viale dei Parioli.

Lucy's mother buys a sunbed, tells Lucy I'm welcome to use it whenever I like, then changes her mind, sends it back. We smoke cigarettes on Lucy's mother's balcony, tip ash toward unwitting strollers, dog-walkers, fifty feet below. We walk Oscar, Lucy's mother's cairn. Lucy's mother instructs us on the innate vulgarity of over-sized diamonds, lectures us on the necessity of acquiring as many large diamonds as possible, setting them aside in one's prime against the guaranteed depredations of later life.

Withdrawing my fingers, my hand, my raw knuckles,

even as lunch – a basket from Tofu Heaven – gushes past into the lined bin, a Waterstone's carrier bag quarter-full of wasteful rankness. Sweat beading my face and chest, pinpricks on my extremities, feeling like someone's hijacking my soul, a manual jacking, without benefit of anaesthetic, a fist and arm shoved all the way down my throat, speculatively probing.

Panic attacks triggered by the thought of rain on shoes; sight of rhinestone-collared Dachshund manufacturing poo that emerges looking like a baby mini-Dachshund; spider in the bath; dead Ericsson; leaves in the garden.

Gaunt with love. Thinking about getting a T-shirt made, with *Are you Billy Annis?* on the front, *Am I Billy Annis?* on the back.

Moleskine notebooks to write songs in, Pilot G-1 pens in blue, red, black ink to write songs with, wanting to write a song about love, about banished love, about the impossibility of love, about fucking your way to uncertainty, about exile, about loss, about bastards, about spending days, nights, entire weeks by yourself, aching for the relief of wrapping your arms, your legs, about some flesh and bone, some other life, becoming whole again.

To Manchester, of all places, for the evening and Fisk's *Pretender* exhibition, featuring my portrait, fruity bumps and all, along with a sequence of golden-era Godard actresses, Marina Vlady, Jean Seberg, Anna Karina,

Chantal Goya, Anne Wiazemsky. What is that all about? Wondering why he wants me here? Wearing: virgin wool, cropped, off the shoulder, pale pink, pure, adhesive; Duarte tulip-cuffed jeans with a lace-front fly and parrot appliqué; black suede front-zippered Sigerson Morrison boots. Limpid eyes. Displaying teeth in a fixed grimace. Keeping my head empty. Takes no more effort than holding your breath under water. Essential. Swatting away the amateurish efforts of the men who approach, wanting to touch, breathe on me, the women who want to compete, to compare me with the canvas version, themselves, probe why no one's painted them, explore that purgatory, why I'm not so special, they already know I can't sing, keep a man longer than a month. They turn away, grimacing, straining to displace me in their minds, demean me. They remind me of cadavers. Hoary, bristled, and chalky daubed faces, eyeless.

Feels like I'm coming down with something, some kind of fever. No one to take my temperature. No one to press a big cool hand on my forehead. No enormous motherly soakpit eyes gazing steadily, unconditionally, into mine. No gentle voice to shush, call me Girly. When I go pee, it's stinking rich, dense and clouded. Also this desire to bolt assails me. There's no one to stop me, to steer me toward bed, to nurse me with hot drinks and warm towels. Feeling tentative about everything except this urge to escape. No one to offer to accompany me. Finding the prospect of being alone alarming. No one to look worried and ask where I'm planning on going. No one here whose unselfish concern for me wrings my heart.

'How do you feel now?' he asks.

'So much better,' I lie, without looking at him.

I was sick before we left the party, sick again in the street. Too much gin someone had mouthed. I believe the fish, grouper, which I'd eaten earlier is responsible for my queasy stomach. Or perhaps someone slipped me something ugly without provenance, for a giggle. One benefit is I've gotten to ride up front, the better to settle my upset tum. I rise from a slouch, check see in the back seat where two girls from one of those East London vacant-spaces modern galleries sleep entwined in each other's arms, hoping they might provide some clue, some bearing. The car cruising, humming along at a soothing eighty-eight. Gliding through the night.

Looking at me, he says, 'You want to get out and walk a while?'

Shaking my head. Fisk is a funny fish. Vaguely cultured, thoroughly hip, or the other way, I'm not sure how the blend works, yet always in a suit with the collar done up, and his silk ties knotted tight and close instead of wide and loose as seems to be the fashion especially with the footballers, those beacons of style, I see on television. A surfeit of critical and commercial success seems to have warped every sense of style he might once have owned. Shaking my foot free of an unzipped boot, planting it solidly against the dash. The nails all carefully painted red. The faded tan, I'm ruing, is merely the sunbed variety, and not charred enough to strike in the gloom of the speeding car.

'I miss the smell,' I say.

He says, 'You do?'

'Is that strange?'

'I shouldn't imagine so.'

'Really,' I say, 'I think it's pretty fucking weird.'

Looking again at him, realising he can't know what I'm talking about, is happy to concur with anything I might say or suggest. He tosses me a small sideways smile. I wish he would undo his tie and loosen his collar. All that flesh and vein squeezed at his throat can't be good for him. And if he suffers an aneurism while driving, I don't know what I could or should or would do to gain control of the car and save us all from crashing off the motorway when one spark, I know, because of all the cognac I've drunk, on top of a bucket of gin, would be all it would take to flambé my tender hide.

'You smile,' he says, 'I mean, you smell nice,' sounding like he's been thinking about it for quite a while and it's finally this huge relief to express.

'Cigarette smoke,' I say, 'and someone spilled Dos Equis on my sweater, I think it's ruined, and don't forget I did puke, twice, both occasions involuntarily, I hasten to add, before you jump to any cheap conclusions about my sylphid figure.'

The memory steals over me, depositing once more some essence of indecorous helplessness. Swiping at the leg of my jeans, saying, 'And here,' as I turn to puff a small warm exhalation toward his face, 'my disco-breath, and somewhere underneath all that is some AG.'

'What's underneath?' he asks, seeming a little plaintive, choked, caught short for air.

'Annick Goutal.'

'Sorry?'

'Scent.'

'Yes?'

'Eau du Sud,' I say, extending a bare forearm in front of his nose for a tantalising moment, there is no doubt of this, and saying, 'like it?'

'What's that?' he says, plainly relieved I've withdrawn my arm, and no longer obscure his view of the road ahead.

'Annick Goutal.'

'I don't know it.'

'It's French,' I say, and, 'here,' I say, taking the bottle from my purse and splashing some on my fingers, flicking them in the air between his face and the windshield.

'That's,' he starts to say, and gasps, a little playfully.

'It's not like Jesse's certainly, Jesse's was the most wonderful smell in the world, I'll never forget it, an amalgam of sweat and hay and mud,' I smile, 'and *moi* of course.'

'Jesse was who exactly?'

'My pony, didn't I say, when I was a little girl, I was fearless, would pilot him at breakneck speed, heels down, elbows tucked in, from one glorious weekend to another, picked up oodles of prizes,' catching him stifling a yawn which makes me squirm close to grandiose indignation. Saying, 'Tell me, am I talking too much?'

'Please,' he says, 'I like listening to you.'

'Hooh,' I say, 'that isn't so very gallant,' throwing him a sulky look, my lower lip curled way over, draping one arm across my chest, my hand slowly gathering and clutching faintly damp sweater material under my arm. Scraping out of my other boot, bringing that foot up to the cool leather dashboard, setting it alongside the first, slouching a little lower in the seat so my sweater rides up, and now I'm lying on my spine with my neck cramped against the back of the seat, with my right hand dropped between my thighs, settling fingers modestly across the bevelled swollen outline.

'You'll get roadsick,' he says, dragging his eyes from me.

'You mean carsick,' I say.

'Are you sulking for any reason?'

'You going to Billy's wedding?'

'Possibly.'

'You know he hasn't asked me yet, I'm awfully upset.'

He laughs at me, no doubt my manner of speaking amuses him, my posh Madonna-like posing. I touch the button to roll down the window, incline my head so all that hair is sucked and snapped into darkness, gulp after air, gather myself inside the car again, the walnutty interior, shiver as the window glass glides up again. The girls in the back seat stir, move closer to each another with scarcely a murmur.

I go, softly, 'I hope it rains, don't you?'

'Frankly, no.'

'Frankly, no,' whispering his words back at him, doubting, in my present state of mind, whether he can ever be more than a blip. Now it's my turn to laugh at him, surprising myself by asking, 'Fisk, are you married?' when I've already met the incumbent, Beattie, also American, several occasions, worn Beattie's dress, whatever that was about, wearing his wife's dress, posing, in the cause of art I suppose, bluey black silk skirt with a beaded bodice, thousands of gilded bubbles, trim at the waist, widening toward the neckline and shoulders, not shiny, just gilded, matt, and round like bearings, marbles, Maltesers, Christmas-tree decorations, typical Beattie, of course it's a size or so too large and lies off the shoulder on one side, my hair heaped unevenly, close and tight around my face, wisps at my ears, straggly duck-tails at my neck, while he directs me to stand in a window, not touching me, telling me exactly where and how he wants me, hands me this book, asks me to read aloud a certain passage, something by Hegel – I mean *really* – regarding *Property*, *Taking Possession*, and *Use of a Thing*, reading for what seems like hours, finding a voice and a rhythm, soon appreciating how he understands less about what I'm reading than I do, soon forgetting about him, the dress, the book-lined walls behind him, begrimed skylights overhead, stretched canvas stacked against another wall, the smell of oil, paint, thinners, the open window at my back, and sounds from the garden below, where Beattie turns raucous on her phone, and the city beyond the high walls, wondering how much the place is worth, the vast garden, someone once told me that Fisk, Beattie's money, has very nearly the largest private garden in North London, reading until my throat becomes sore, feeling as if some of the meaning rubs off on me, relishing the sound of my voice, feels like it vibrates and echoes through my head, resonates through my bare feet to the bare boards beneath, my heart beating through my skin, marvelling at Beattie's perpetually surging intellect, her marshalling of lucid opinion on a myriad issues, her penchant for Pierrot-designed orange sweaters, woollies with handguns, paired revolvers, like grasping hands, emblazoned on her chest, evidence of a boldly ironic post-PC cast.

'Why,' says Fisk, 'would you marry me?'

'Ask me when I'm older,' I say, yawning, turning away to sleep.

Soon we're in the city and he's dropping off the two girls, and next he takes me to my place where I put on some Nino Rota film music, some coffee, spill McVitie's Digestives onto a saucer, all in all a whore's breakfast, and as if I've been encouraging him, he reaches over, taking my foot in his hand, presenting his face for me to move my bosoms against, telling me I smell of lemons, my ankles, my knees, my elbows, something a schoolboy might say the first time he got near a girl, wide-eyed, open-mouthed, gasping like a fish, greedy to explore everywhere, touch on everything, I don't know, expecting me to respond like I'm thrilled, but I tell myself he might as well have stayed in the car the way he's uselessly sniffing every bit of me, the novelty of a woman practically volunteering herself, all the sense in her dimmed like she's something he's happened on by the side of the road, some creature suffering, not too much difference to a kick on the head, what it means to her, to me, to Lee, stifled, lying here, scuffed at, with him labouring obscurely, thrusting and thrashing, if this is just the beginning, Lord preserve me, surging past the . . .

'Watch out, will you watch it.'

Too late to save the lamp from falling.

He says, 'I'm sorry.'

And I say, 'It doesn't matter.'

He says, 'I'll buy you a new one.'

'I said it doesn't matter.'

'I'll replace it.'

'There's really no need.'

'I want to buy you a new one.'

'I never liked it to begin with.'

'Please, allow me.'

'Fine, fine, if that's what you want, buy me a new one.'

'Lee.'

'What now?'

'It doesn't matter.'

'. . .'

'I was thinking, maybe.'

'No.'

'But you don't even know what I was going to say.'

'I know.'

'I never even said.'

'Fisk, I know, honestly, and the answer's no.'

'Once.'

'We already once.'

'Once more.'

'No.'

'Please.'

'Don't whine.'

'Please.'

'No.'

So he goes, half ecstatic with what he's achieved, half despondent with what he's failed to attain. Later, in the afternoon, waking to the realisation that, not for the first time and unlikely to be the last, I've slept

151

with the wrong man, his smell all over my sheets, along with a pennyworth of stain.

It's reasonable, thirty pounds for thirty minutes, offering insight, guidance, cosmic channelling, guaranteed uplift, comic diversion. Madame Olivia's Dolphin Square salon-cum-boudoir is stuffy, darkly carpeted, cluttered with dust-collectors, knickknacks, dark-ages, 1970s, '80s, mementoes of what appears to have been a frustrated theatrical career. She takes the thirty pounds, folds it, pockets it in her ankle-length cream corduroy skirt, says, 'So you're a friend of Lucy's?'

I can't help but be impressed, saying, 'How did you know that?'

'You told me on the phone, remember?'

No, but I ascribe the lapse to Fisk fallout, on top of a gobbled Valium, and then the unsettling encounter with the new woman at the dry cleaners, a witch with a faceful of warts and without a word of English, she'd shrieked repeatedly, ignoring the receipt which I'd proffered so naively. Strange how some days just take a turn for the worse at the most unlikely juncture. Perhaps that was the moment when I ought to have neutered the rest of the day, turned for home, retaken that nap. Instead, here I am, lying to a most dubious clairvoyant, saying, 'Oh, right.'

'When you're ready,' she says, indicating I should occupy the small brocaded cushion on the floor.

I can't help wondering what I've gotten myself into. Perhaps the witch from the dry cleaners and this Madame Olivia are in league. I drop to the cushion, start unbuckling my shoes.

'Just the one will do, my darling,' says the woman, holding up a cheap-ringed hand.

'Which one, right or left?'

'It's entirely up to you, whichever you prefer, whichever will always be the correct choice.'

'They're not identical, you know, I've got these calluses on the heel of one from these designer crappy boots I bought in Schiphol Duty Free, I should never have bought in the first place, never mind worn, I mean what kind of disturbed dysfunctional personality buys shoes in an airport, you're not going to be able to return them easily next day, are you, not if you're two or three hundred miles away, and no real excuse for going back there, and on that particular day my feet were swollen from walking and flying and . . .' I finally notice the woman's ever expanding impatience, realise she probably has woes of her own to tend, and I say, 'I should zip it, shouldn't I?'

She smiles agreeably, and I begin to wonder whether she really has powers, and if she has, whether she's picked up on the frisson relating to another occasion in Schiphol. Discovering Billy's in love with Alessia, bless, a stolen half-hour turning into an entire afternoon, running on and on through early evening, their heedless carry-on in that airport hotel, the antique diamond ring he'd bought for me but which he preferred to give her to put in her wetness for luck, and bear to the show in that fashion. That was a crock anyhow. So much for charms. Ignominious repercussions in the Dutch media, suggestions of our appearing jaded, indifferent, and that way disrespectful. Less than besotted by the subsequent circus, Billy and Alessia skipped town, leaving me to offer excuses. Answering the question on TV of what Alessia was like, I said, 'She's sixteen, long hair, very beautiful, very stupid, he's in love.' Alessia adored the fact I lied about her age.

Madame Olivia strikes up, cuts across, 'I can see clearly,' she says, 'you are a mass of tiny misgivings.'

'That's brilliant,' I say.

Somehow she finds reason to be affronted, going, 'I'm not obliging you to do this.'

And never one to inflict gratuitous offence, though a touch disconcerted by her hair colouring, thirty shades of red, massed thick and wavy about a jaundiced complexion, I rush to assure her, 'No, no, I mean it, that's brilliant, because that's what I am, a mess, a mass of misgivings, about everything, not just me or you or this whole thing, it's normal for me to be this uneasy, sceptical, even queasy.'

We seem to come to an accommodation. She takes my foot into her lap and proceeds to read it, interpreting bumps and veins, lines, other cutaneous imprints, before solemnly saying, 'You want to know whether you'll ever marry?'

'No, no, that's not why I'm here, I'm not like that, I'm not.'

She looks at me like maybe I'd like to take a moment to reconsider. And I have to confess, I am partly, sneakily curious, eager at least to know whether my toe cleavage holds any special significance, so I waver and bend, say, 'Will I?'

'I see many, I see legions who will want to marry you.'

'Legions, that's interesting.'

'But true love is elusive.'

'That doesn't mean I won't find it, does it?'

'I see you have a lot of clouded issues in your life.'

Surely she means my feet. 'Such as?'

'You want a man to love, and who will love you fairly, yet you fear being tied to a layabout, loser, mutant freak in the terminal grip of a thirty-year-long mother fixation, clings to you,' she gasps, 'frustrating your chance of happiness, smothering you.'

'What?'

Now there's no doubting the woman's dredging from bitter personal experience here.

'Or some hairy-arsed son of a bitch sleeps with your sister, squanders your savings, tries on your clothes as soon as your back's turned, ruins your shoes for ever with his stinking gouty feet, makes off with your microwave, your CD player, your best friend.'

'Look,' I say, 'I'm terribly sorry to hear about your bad luck.'

She sobs, and while I appreciate I'm paying for this, this is my time, but really, the woman's in distress.

Nothing for it but a sisterly sharing of tissues, saying, 'Listen, Madame . . .'

'Olivia.'

'Yes, what if I pay you for, let's say three sessions, and you just tell me what I want to hear?'

She sniffles, deigns not to have heard the last suggestion, and continues, a tad enviously, saying, 'I see four children, a large house and garden, a place by the sea, cars, holidays.'

'And a husband?'

'I'm sure,' she says, uneasily, 'it goes without saying. I see . . .' sounding and looking ever so evasive on what suddenly for the first time in my life seems the critical question, 'ten, eleven, twelve, fifteen grandchildren, healthy and strong, wise and beautiful.'

'Forget the babies for one second, will you, what about true love?'

'Define true love,' she says, looking fiercely in my direction, as though it's time I shared in some of the harsh lessons in line for all womankind.

And clueless as to why I should be so rattled, I say, 'You're the one brought it up. I walk in here and first thing you do is go true love this and true love that. You tell me what it means.'

'I'm sorry,' she says.

'What if I make you out a cheque?'

'It's no good,' she says, shaking her head, 'your aura's fogged.'

'You mean my feet smell?' I say, raising my foot, hooking it toward my chest, straining, attempting to sniff it.

And she says, 'A word of advice, you're still young and attractive.'

'Thank you,' I say, slipping on my shoe.

'Crush the bastards,' she says, 'while you still can, crush them before they destroy you and ruin your life.'

What else can I do only smile in the face of such fervour.

Seeing as I'm so far south, I pass on over Vauxhall Bridge, and knowing where to go from when I used to live this side of the river, I ride by the park to

156

where in the shelter of trees, I can purchase recourse from the Cameroonian, whose cohort of coal-faced boys, lined five, six, seven, in a line like crows with bright white teeth, some in jeans, some wearing djellabas, perched on the wall, stare at me, impervious to me, as if my rude flesh offers only malediction.

All it takes is thirty minutes there and back.

Another fifteen to take the elevator, forget myself, cauterised, in a swoon, forget where I started and where I'm looking to end. Barely able to contain myself, I slam the door, gather a magazine off the floor, a knife from the breakfast tray, step up to the bed, fumble with the folded paper, and with trembling fingers, spill out the white onto the back of *Vanity Fair*, using the knife to slice and divide the pile into first one line, plump and high, more of a hump-back ridge, then two longer narrower lines, then into four lines, then back to one line, a sharp-edged arête, starting over again, trying to gauge how much to do right away, how to pace myself, bringing it all back together again into a little pile, rubbing my palms on my thighs, temporising, gathering, refining, stroking it into three lines this time, two lines, who knows what's best, two big fat lines, parallel, a thumb length apart, press a finger to one nostril, drape my face over the bed, the magazine, the cocaine, and gather half inside, then the other nostril, clean it out.

Hating to look back, think of all the jokers I fellated, the money I funnelled up my nose, causes a din in my head, how I feel after a show, the big shows, the intense fleeting camaraderie, the friends you make that you never see again, you learn to live without them.

157

Thinking, people hate me because I'm vacuous, hate me because I'm American. Others love me for the same reasons. I never know, from day to day, to which camp I belong.

Forty frantic minutes searching for the foot reader's business card, find it midway down a stack of CDs, whether there's any significance to its nestling between Captain Beefheart's *Trout Mask Replica* and the eponymous *I Am Shelby Lynne* slips by me.

　　She picks up before the second ring, 'Lee,' she says.
　　'How'd you know it was me?'
　　'Caller ID,' she explains, 'how may I help?'
　　'Don't you know?'
　　'I suppose I could give it a shot.'
　　'Be my guest.'
　　'You feel pregnant.'
　　'Yes, but . . .'
　　'With what?'
　　'That's . . . you're good.'
　　'It's only a feeling.'
　　'I'm sure that's all.'
　　'On the other hand.'
　　'Oh, fuck.'
　　'Now, I doubt your mother raised you to speak like that.'
　　'What do you know about what my mother did or didn't do for me?'
　　'Let's take a step back here, a moment, and reflect.'
　　'Where's all this going?'
　　'Another life.'
　　'That's impossible.'

'Then you're in the clear.'
'Oh, Christ.'

Sometimes, it really strikes me how I'm not a serious person, not serious enough, not so serious as certain events in my life – some recent, some not so recent – might require me to be. And I think it's true that everyone would prefer to be regarded as a serious person. Life is a serious matter with certain inevitable grim consequences. It behoves us all in the meantime to take it seriously, to be serious in turn. But me, I seem to be operating with a not insignificant deficit where seriousness is concerned.

Take the other day, Jennifer, one of the publicists at the record company, called me, and I just know I'm a disappointment to her. She'd gone to some trouble to set up an interview for me with an extremely serious journalist, one of those clever columnists who live in million-pound houses and whose husbands write voluble novels offering insight on issues of culture and civilisation, as well as contemporary psychosis, drug abuse, self-realisation. Whatever I said, something irreverent, facetious, off the cuff, something hurtful to Jennifer, dismissive of her efforts on my behalf, something which I sincerely regret since not only did it leave both the columnist and Jennifer with an impression of my dearth of professionalism, as well as a gaping hole in their schedules, but it made me loathe myself, want to swear off ever uttering another word to anyone anywhere on any subject or occasion whatsoever.

I resolve to be mute and serious, sober and dull, and to go through life without alienating one more person. With that in mind I call up Jennifer and invite her to come shopping with me. I buy myself a silk-satin floral minidress. She buys herself a hairclip. I attempt to restore myself in her regard. Over coffee I confide how much I regret the absence of a father while growing up, a father figure, someone to warn me off tattoos, drugs, boys, someone to lay down the law. It wasn't so much that Billy and I lacked a sense of there being some things you don't do, but rather that we appreciated how much we were by ourselves, had only ourselves to turn to and steer by. Jennifer doesn't seem to go for what I'm telling her. I start to get a sense that of the two of us it is she who is the golden girl, she who would be perfect for Billy.

No one calls, no one writes. My money leaks away. I take dance classes, traipse around showrooms looking at new cars, thinking if things get really tight I can always find a job as a receptionist in one of these shiny inviting places. I get my hair done, nails done, brows done. I sort through my wardrobe, binbag innumerable sweaters. Sweaters I decide are done to death. And right away I realise it's late August, twenty-seven degrees, not the time to be appraising sweaters, no, sweaters are beyond done to death, put them all back in the closet. My mind goes blank. Apparently this lasts for days. Nothing happens in fifty different ways. Days go round and round like so much soap scum in a basin, circling the drain. That weekend with the dead Australian, sticking close to him as he circled the buffet, remarking how he never knew which way round he should move, clockwise, anticlockwise, being

Australian, some connection he supposed with the different way water circles, up this side, to where he came from.

Billy leaves a message. He's back from Italy, and wants to see me. I can't begin to think why. It all seems an age ago. I find it difficult to remember who he's supposed to be. When we'd been together nothing had gone right. And then the ending had been bad. When I return his call, he tells me he just wants his credit card back. Something else which has slipped my mind.

After Dr Schoen, in a sullen mood, removes the stitches, I don't feel like doing anything except sleep. I wake after an hour or so, my hand still throbbing, the sun still exploding outside, and I can hear someone, a gardener, working with some motorised machine, strimming or blowing, and I hate having slept for ninety minutes in the early afternoon in my underwear, now uncomfortably awry, and run up tight on me, catching and pinching, damn near garotting me, it seems like, in some role as this short-term amputee, some Tokyo amateur bondage deal, this dreamy afterimage of a funny-looking, little, round-bellied, toothy, ferret-like man, balding, bespectacled, suspenders *and* belt, trousers half-masted up around his shins, bright pastel socks *and* sandals, pointing something incongruously large at me – a Pentax, medium-format, 6x7, 200mm lens, which is what it says when I look down the barrel at it – when there's so much else I ought to be doing, and I want to blame somebody but there's no one really to blame, not even me, so I blame everybody, and my face is sore and wrinkled, and my mouth is stale, and my hands are shaky, and that left one aching like the devil where I put it through the window and Schoen stitched it up again almost like new, the idiot, looking at me like he could read my soul, like I was thirteen, not twenty-eight, and I feel anxious that different people right now are thinking about me, making moves to contact me, involve me, unload on me, *also* my stomach hurts, so I consider going to throw up, instead I roll over onto my side, try to keep my eyes shut, try to sleep, but these thoughts keep crowding, questioning the strength of these too few painkillers the miserly wank offered me, of course I took them, as if he'd put two and five together and instead of ten fingers came up with self-abuse, immo-lation, blood on his hands whatever happens, and I'm nostalgic for 1971, 1972, the years before I was born, the years before I was conceived, pressing my hands between my knees, weeping silently, my tears soaking the pillow, leafy branches flicking against the windows, someone's shut the blinds, I could swear, someone's been in my room, someone's seen me like this, no one else has the keys except, he's seen me like this, or did I shut the blinds myself, soon enough it's going to come down to being no more than this wrinkly, haemorrhoidal, arthritic, anginal creature, and suddenly I find I have all this surplus vigour, imagination, youth, so I choose to run it off, first brushing my teeth, then dressing the part, black tennis shorts and shirt, grey ankle socks, white Lycra knickers and sports support, blue Nikes, headphones, Discgirl clipped at my waist, clutching Ericsson cellphone the size of an After Eight, hair tucked into a green and black baseball cap from Babbitt's in Flagstaff, and the first thing I do when I leave the house is rush through a précis of my usual stretching routine and worry why nobody's called me in five hours, or why I don't feel like calling anyone, so I head out the gate and run and run and run through leafy shadowed streets, keeping an eye out for rooty eruptions, lippy paving stones, meandering past mothers pushing buggies, pernickety pensioners towing shopping trolleys, layabouts with extended legs, toppled refuse bins left out to impede the likes of me, run on and on without stopping or stepping even once in dog poo until I reach the park, in through the gate opposite Oppidans Road, my ribs flexing, sides quaking, legs leaden, breath rasping, and on to the summit for the view and a recuperative smoke, I knew I'd forget something, nothing in these pants pocket but a, what seems to be a rabbit's foot, a bit in the dark here regarding this charm's origins, snowy white, soft, furry, must have been an arctic snow bunny's once, the size of my thumb, half a thumb, knuckle to nail, rub it, press it to shiny cheeks and brow, half mopping, half hoping devotion will refresh me, turn up some smokes, nope, what else can you expect from a wadded scrunch of forgotten Kleenex, look around for someone to touch but it's hopeless, I'm abandoned, adrift, alone, harried by invisible forces, surrounded by this vast hiving city, the air here sluggish as myself, yawning expansively, awash with pollen, and sneezing, clogging up, I turn around and walk home, back up the hill, takes me forty minutes, every part of me aching, every so often licking my palm where the sutures were, and even though it's only early afternoon I'm surprised how short and featureless my days are, and at this rate it's all going to be over before I ever do anything.

I've this early-morning flight to Rome, where, curiously, a magazine wants me to adorn their October cover, and I've decided I need to nurture Italian celebrity in case certain other prospects fail to materialise, certain debts fall due. I'm sure there's an opening going, somewhere on Italian TV, dancing, singing, juggling, conjuring.

The shoot coordinator's booked me into the Aldrovandi Palace Hotel. It's midday, mid-thirties when I arrive. Immediately I change into my bathing suit, take some baby-factor lotion, go lie by the pool. There's no one here but a young Asian woman with two kids, German accents, little S-shaped bodies. A man walks by but I'm not interested. He goes to sit by the Asian woman. Later when they're gathering up their belongings, the woman scowls at me. As if she's affronted by my not showing any interest in her husband, never mind not managing the minimal courtesy of letting on to be either intrigued or charmed by her broiling brats. And my phone goes. Everything's starting to unravel. I don't move. I let the phone continue ringing until finally it stops. I remove my sunglasses, study my toes, nothing the matter with them, no hint of my mother's hexadactyly, which anyway always seemed less freakish than distinguishing, how she used to claim Picasso had made her, sculpted and shaped her, painted her, brought her to life with a snap of his fingers, the magic words, *testa di donna, hexadactyly*, the fun she had teaching us how to spell that word beginning with h e x. The wind rises. Leaves rain from the trees around the pool. Bright, white and pink, petals float on the surface of the water. Bugs engage in a vain struggle. No escape. Casualties not victims. I think about getting in the water, swimming. I don't move. I really don't like that word – unravel – don't like it at all.

I go to dinner over the river in Prati with people from the magazine, the photographer, his assistants. Some new people, some people I already know. Maurizio, Daisy, Marta, Marilena, Rachele Radaelli, Alessandra, Piero Taccani, Chiara Sparaciari, Olimpia, Camilla, Lodovica, Marilena II.

I tell them my story about this cosmetic surgeon I used to know who once had a consultation with a family, non-nuclear, of Saudi women whose patronage promised to be extremely lucrative, and by way of illustrating their wealth and idiocy, they'd shown up in his office, flourishing not the usual pages torn from *Vogue* and other magazines of that high-fashion ilk, but rather reproductions of favourite works by Picasso, Giacometti, Modigliani, which they wished to have portions of their temporal selves modelled upon, more Giacometti in the flank, more Picasso in the bosom, more Modigliani in the face.

Alessandra comments how un-American I seem. Marta remarks how there are thirteen of us at table. After a moment's hesitation we laugh off the risk posed by that inauspicious number. A stranger comes to say hello, leans over Lodovica, kisses her, his eyes on her tits showing small and manifest inside a loose bodice. 'Like eggs,' he whispers in her ear, 'soft white boiled eggs,' urging her to laugh with him as if he's said something particularly intimate and flattering, even amusing, though everyone knows how much Lodo abhors eggs, has often stated her immovable aversion to any man who ate eggs for breakfast, could never countenance his lips, his tongue, against hers.

Rome is relatively uncomplicated. I wouldn't mind living here again. I think about calling Billy in London, letting him know where I've washed up for the night, seeing what kind of reaction that might trigger.

Back in my room I undress, take an orange in the bathroom, peel and eat it while standing by the basin, the juice running sticky on my skin. Sitting on the rim of the tub, I scan the newspaper I brought from the plane. I'm hardly surprised to discover that Pearl Mundy got it wrong, someone somewhere got it wrong, at least according to the agency report I find on the obituary page.

DIED. Scott Weaver, 19, movie actor; of an apparently self-inflicted gunshot wound; in Big Bear Lake, California. A badly decomposed body, identified at week's end as Weaver's, was found in his home by friends who had become worried about not hearing from him for several weeks.

Early in the morning I'm collected by minivan, and we drive the short distance to the Villa Giulia where they dress me, take the photos before the sun turns severe, set me loose with an afternoon to spare.

Running into this Cockney actor by the fountain outside the Hotel Locarno, who tells me what he's doing in town. 'I'm playing the fucking pope,' he says, clapping hands to his belly, trying to get me to laugh.

I make an early evening flight, a car collects me at

the airport, drops me home by what I think is eleven
until I remember to reset my watch.

'My little bunny,' he says, and more, mumbling what I
can't make out. My teeth showing. Helping me to my
feet. Staggering in the gloom, away from the light, away
from the booming music, all the way down into the
farthest depths of the garden where the grass turns to
daisies, dandelions, weeds, and this whatever, must be
acid, he's given me, makes everything seem wreathed
in crystal strands, spun kaleidoscopic candy. His arm
around my waist, seeking, his fingers pressing on my
hip, his tongue on my neck, worrying. The thing I
remember best about being a child, galloping round
the limit of that naked paddock, grazed and trampled
arid. On my knees now, throwing up, rushes of empty
nothing, followed by aftershocks of the same dry retching. I just want to be the best. My hair matted with
rain, sweat, smoke, twigs, shards of grass, leaves, petals.
Touching the mud. When did it rain? My forehead on
the ground. My tongue feeling among the black tundric
muck, finding the plastic nozzle of the garden hose
hard against my teeth. Realising this is Surrey. Thinking,
hoping, no one expects me to fill in the blanks. For
an instant, I think I've been following the clues or
rather making an effort to do so, even if, as seems likely,
it all leads nowhere. But there were no clues. There
are no clues. At least none that I can see. My mouth
full, cheeks fat with mud. Slowly, tediously, masticat-
ing. He cries at me to get up. 'I'm up,' I sigh. Thinking
for an instant, it's my father calling, but it's not. He
starts away. I want to follow. I have to follow. There is

no end to anything, this hell. My head down. My chin on my fugitive whoops. Funny how at least one always somehow manages to slip free, away. Numbly trotting, now blindly, into the dark. Now wheeling like a bat. Someone calling my name. Finding I've lost a shoe. And up the stone steps to the wall of glass and the guests, monkeys, turning to look and stare. Whispers and muffled laughter. Wet grass stains on my dress, streaks of dirt. My step lopsided, muddy shoe, muddy foot, moving with a hip-fractured tilt, trailing muddy tracks. Turning hostile. 'Gimme a pal, like a drink,' I gasp, snatching the glass from the woman with dangling hoop earrings, resisting the urge to exclaim, Jesus Christ, don't you realise they went out in '84, don't you know who I am, I am the bitch of Salem, the whore of Arabia, know them by their shaved crotch and pits. Someone grabs me by the arms, shakes me, my head lolling, smiling, my teeth rotting in my mouth by the second. Those sons of bitches, camel-rich. My skin gone coarse, broken out on my arms. This is gone too far. Vomit staining my dress. Grass, semen, beer, cigarette burns. And my nails are awful, fucking awful. I must do something about these nails. A girl in my position simply can't afford to go around with nails in such wretched condition. Lying to myself how there's never been anything tentative about me in my entire life, and I'm not about to start now. Being led to a car and driven away. My teeth grinding. Waking caked in vomit, blood, spit, semen. Waking sheathed in sweat and beer. The sheets tangled on the floor. Nothing on the mattress only a cooled coil of stool, a not un-attractive light beige colour, blessed with a mucal sheen.

Relieved this is not my room but some hotel, some suite, generic, like something at the Ritz-Carlton in Pasadena where Adolfo Luna, or was it Corinne Day, took our photograph, posed together like lovers on a rumpled bed, less like the Quisisana on Capri, it's simply too hard to tell, where duff regulars bow to strangers. A distant picture of someone pressing me as to who Billy is, what relation he has to me. 'Why,' I said, 'he's my . . .' and whatever I said, always trying to make it sound like a lie, remembering the other lies we'd floated, the various guises playfully assumed. One day, honeymooners. The next, bereaved parents mourning a lost child. Another time, a divorced couple seeking reconciliation, and ever propelling ourselves further apart. Purposely clouding the picture so that people would crave to know more about us. And sometimes in a muddle ourselves, wondering whether everything was the other way round, in reverse order, that first we'd met, married, divorced, and only later, as if it were a great story, a fresh aspect, had we thought to present ourselves as brother and sister. And always appreciating that if people found us hard to like, it didn't mean they didn't want to fuck us, or be us. Now when I try to move I find I've stiffened. It takes ages, seems like hours, to loosen enough to crawl in the bathroom, feel my way into the shower, sit there cross-legged in the steam until my hair straightens and I lose the smell of beer someone must have poured over me, mottling, breasts flushed and sore, sharp hair starting beneath my arms, all along my thighs, wiry murk of pubic hair someone not so long ago compared to the stale colour of Guinness spilt on a cloth, linen. Partying at fifteen, fucking a path through all the ages, experimental, glee-ful, running flushed, chasing a basketball, rust-coloured T-shirt, ass-hugging Levi's, white briefs, clothes make the girl. Every boy, hovering victims of ravenous wild homicidal continuum, more stupefied than apes, one step from dangling out of bushes, swooping for me, what a prize, stroking my innocence with their long leaky cocks. Enthusiastic individuals nailing me in the grass, to the peeling eucalyptus bark, the tomcat smell rolling over us. Tilting my face to meet the falling water. Another day in the life. Another beautiful day. Finding myself retching when I reemerge to face the stool lying so neat, composed, and placed there by some invisible set decorator, unlikely feng shui, in the centre of the bed. Wondering whether I'm responsible, whether I may have to deal with it, remove and flush it, or is it OK to leave it for the maid. Before I can decide anything there's someone at the door. Checking to see whether I'm decent, the answer's not, still wet from the shower, going back in the bathroom, wrap-ping a towel about myself, shuffling out again to the door, opening it a crack, shielding my eyes and going, 'Yes,' my voice low and deep. And this man, this man standing in the corridor, whom I don't recognise, English, long dirty blond hair, lank to his jaw, a deeply lined face, looks like Iggy Pop and maybe the same age, that old, but it's not, his name is Woody, he tells me, he's the manager of this band, Rudimental, and he's looking for somebody. I mumble regrets, I'm unable to help him, and close the door without going into details or long convoluted denials which I know only get you into ever more involved explanations, excuses, deeper water. And when I turn round I see the drummer's there, lying partially under the bed, only his upper half visible. The stool must be his. I could never have done, managed, such a thing. Going over and prodding him, my foot on his shoulder, my toes at his jaw. 'Excuse me, hello, but I think you've done a terrible thing.' And he moans. And I think, what is the matter with me that I keep attracting these kind of people, drummers and goalkeepers. Saying to him, 'Fuck me, won't you fuck me again?' And he does, in a kind of disinterested way, deliquescent, desultory, so that afterwards I wonder whether he was ever properly inside of me, that's the kind of fuck he was. Maybe he was distracted by the small fire I manage to set in the bathroom basin, singeing dark-stained underwear, must have been his, opening the window to help dispel the smoke. I guess I hoped his coming would do something, scattering, send a bolt of truth through my deep, a burst of electricity, knock me from my drift but it didn't, there was nothing there at all to write home about. Starting to weigh the other Rudimentalists, the guitarist-vocalist, the bassist. All tattooed, pasty-headed, pierced and stapled, hard bodied, early thirties, less than average height. Why not the manager? One of whom might have the means to jolt me from this rut. This hint of sulphur in the air. Splendour expended. Starting to tidy myself up. See what I can do with this dress. Wool black top and flannel grey skirt. So stained it's hateful. How have I become so old-world elegant? Limping around the room on one shoe. The drummer smoothing his hardly prepossessing cock, petting it lightly as one might a dozy snake, mumbling inanities, baby-talk, 'There, there, poor snakey,' whose venom I remember makes me bleed from every pore, every orifice. Repudiating no option, he claimed my backside's the perfect size of a shirt button, the colour of dulled amber. Watching me, all the while making comments, appraising the fucking Prada dress, this body, the nest a tangle of old-straw-coloured bush, the deathly hint of cellulite dawning. Some joke to him. He thinks he can provoke me but he's no picture, only gaunt and deathly pale, with deep-pocked skin and freckles on his shoulders, splotches the size of quarters, summer raindrops on a paving slab. In the end there's nothing to do only put on the dress, pray no one notices how rough a state it's in, and, once hooked and fastened, venture barefoot out of there, my hair half dried into a wheaten darker jumble which downstairs shields my face from the crazy marauding photographers packed into the lobby.

Listlessly spooning grapefruit into my mouth, worrying about the true circumstances of Scott Weaver's death, where and how he died, whether he died at all. Remembering something he told me about Di, the princess, about the confusion surrounding her death, the possibility she hadn't died but rather slipped away to start a better life somewhere else, resurrect herself in another guise, another territory, assume another identity. Remembering his speculation about what type of person Di would choose to return as, finally narrowing it down to someone like me, as if I ought to have felt flattered by the notion, by his claiming to find it credible. Remembering perfectly the wired cast to his features, the glint in his eye as if he credited his own speculation, as if he believed for an instant he really was sitting with Di, as if he really believed he had just fucked a princess.

It's the kind of sell-your-soul straight-to-hell fairy-tale wedding little girls dream of but has always left me cold. Caterers in white coats, guests in dazzle wear, casual and formal. Mrs – something sounds like Obnoxia – Glade, the bride's mother, everywhere, fluttering, trailing hauteur, crème de cacao breath, touching up what's already as near to perfect as it's ever likely to get. A marquee set up on one of the higher terraced lawns. People drifting in and out of the hotel, moving from buffet tables to the barbecue area to the band playing swing beside the pool.

And I'm wandering, lost, unrecognised, and unassailed, wondering how difficult it would be at this late stage to acquire some gravitas, transform myself into something sturdy along the lines of a tennis pro on the Sanex WTA Tour, or a war reporter, venturing blonde and full-figured into the Congo, Uganda, exposing tyrants, injustice, sanction-busting multinationals, speaking out on behalf of the exploited, the downtrodden, the persecuted, the displaced, wondering what I'm doing here, uninvited, at Billy's wedding, hardly less perilous a venue than Ebola-visited equatorial Africa.

Alessia's staying away, as etiquette prescribes, having been his girlfriend for so long and until so recently. On my own behalf, despite the lack of either a welcome or a formal invitation, I believe my absence from the celebrations would only generate invidious speculation and comment regarding my oblique relations with Billy and his new wife. Of course, where I'm concerned, my presence here has varied implications, at once suggesting an affable wish to congratulate him, convey gracious and affectionate regards, as well as a by now ingrained deviation from sound thinking and moral rectitude. Having to remind myself regularly of his offences, his shedding me so completely is insignificant – and certainly I don't care to have him back, I can have anyone, have had more than sufficient, am sure this is not a factor – though not so insignificant is his triggering both Scott Weaver's and the Wonderland Avenue 911 death, and especially not, oh yes, especially not his apparently having so recently managed to knock me up. Out of however many men I've had during this recent phase of non-exclusivity, somehow I'm sure he's the one with the necessaries.

And so my eyes are obliged to track him all day, right through the ceremony, the photographs, the reception, the toasting, dancing, speeches, sideshows, almost panting to discern the best moment in which to make my move, extract my righteous vengeance. If he hadn't slept with me, then crushed me with his betrayal, then I never would have gone to LA, never would have encountered Scott Weaver, and then who knows how that night in Wonderland Avenue would have turned out. No 911 call, no cops, no shooting, no shame, no suicide in Big Bear. Fair enough, it's addling, but I'm convinced he deserves summary punishment.

Next instant I'm wishing I were in the Congo,

Uganda, Rwanda, trying to remember what someone told me about the Belgian role in that genocide, the Belgian cowardice, how their soldiers ran away, left Tutsis unprotected in those refugee camps with the Hutu killers converging, screaming their murderous intentions. They simply got in their trucks and drove away. Those fucking Belgians. Remember Lumumba? I worry about empathising too facilely with the vengeful impulse, visiting unto others as they have unto you. This is what you get when you mess with . . . wait, here's Fisk, tracking me, wheedling arcana regarding canopic vases, vainly striving to paper over the ever expanding lacunae, the gaps which he perceives in my knowledge, when all I want is to forget, and enjoy a leisurely homicidal stroll through the gardens, not hear about canopic vases carved from alabaster, limestone, typical Egyptian tomb furnishing, containers of organs – brains, lung, stomach, liver – extracted and mummified separately, protected by the sons of Horus, the baboon Hapy, the man Hamset, the dog Duamutef, and the hawk Qebemsennuf, whose heads are carved on the vessel lids, the baboon Hapy not to be confused with Hapy, god of the flooding Nile in fountain shape.

There's also this unwelcome sense that Fisk is outlining some of the options he envisages regarding my destiny. Bits of me potted in vases, stored about his studio, or on display in the British Museum, or perhaps most alluringly, jostling for position on Charles Saatchi's mantelpiece. Though his immediate preference probably has me faced up against a tree with him attempting to horse me, wrecking my dress, mussing my hair and face, upending my poise. No mention then, I bet, of the baboon Hapy or the dog Duamutef, as I struggle, dry, batting away his abrasive visitation, gasping, deprived, unbalanced by his awkward pounding. What if he knew he was assailing a pregnable position, would he hesitate, even desist, or would he press to annihilate me? He probably thinks there are rules of engagement in play here but it's closer to terror. Billy invaded me, I assailed Fisk, nothing's left to be won only deny victory to others.

Looking up, I think I see flags, banners, streamers everywhere. Now, reeling, dizzy, imagining I smell the ocean, the sea at Ostia, the Cape, Bayonne, Will Rogers State Beach, with dunes and pines close by, imagining I could start over, another new life, go to the beach every free moment, destroy my skin, meet a man who goes to the beach every free moment, destroying his skin, marry the man, mourn the loss of youth, make babies, go to the beach together every free moment, destroying all our skins in turn, deriving identity and bearings from such futility. The sky swivels. I reach out to steady myself, find nothing only an episode from our month in Rome when Billy had been busy with Alessia, leaving me time on my hands to languish, beset by – and I quote the suave Via Gregoriana practitioner who treated me with several unfamiliar brands of barbiturate – 'a chlorotic disorder of spirit'.

Those colours overhead, AS Roma banners, the year they won the scudetto, this year, only this year? the year Billy decided he could make it without me. An oppressive July when I shopped at Kristina Ti, and cheered Patti Smith, and the Texan pilot and his wife tried to save my soul, took me up to the Opus Dei headquarters on Bruno Buozzi to see where Blessed Josemaria Escriva is interred. Although all the initiates I encountered there were perfectly hospitable and charming, wearing tweeds and seersucker, and owning these shiny barbered necks, once the door was barred behind me, and they led me down into the crypt, I became claustrophobic, began to panic, to fear I would never again emerge into daylight, freedom, never return to my life, remembering the stories of how dark and extreme OD was reputed to be, as paranoid and vengeful as it was secretive and influential, how a Spanish journalist who'd been investigating them had disappeared. I couldn't fathom how I'd accepted the Texans' invitation to visit with them. They never took their marbled eyes from me, probably weighed me a suitable case for treatment if not actual recruitment. I hastily made a cash donation, took their pamphlets, promised to read, reflect, return, none of which of course I ever did.

And any time afterwards that I found myself going past the anonymous building with CCTV covering every facet – and it was only ever a couple of occasions that I permitted myself to take that route – I could sense the menace – real or imagined is irrelevant – I knew they could discern my doubt, and doubt equated in their minds to animosity – I dropped my head, hunched my shoulders, touched the accelerator, gunned the Piaggio, needled the late-night taxi driver to speed up, whatever means of transport I was using, whatever hour I journeyed, I sped through that stretch of Bruno Buozzi as fast as I could, fearing they would sense I was outside on the street in need of salvation and damnation in equal measure, and dispatch para-religious forces to grab me, incarcerate me deep inside their Masonic-seeming monolith, an ideal candidate for vanishment because no one tracked my move-ments, my whereabouts, no one cared about or loved me enough to worry about me, to wonder where I'd gone, what rabbit-hole I'd been suckered into.

'What do you want now?' I ask.

And Fisk says, 'I thought you might like some company.'

'Well, I don't.'

'You're never wrong, are you.'

Looking down at my toes, all tinged in pink, I say, 'I wish . . .'

'What?'

'I wish you'd creep off and die, fuck, or if you'd rather, just fuck off and die, creep.'

He hesitates, seems to have difficulty gauging my meaning, whether there is any, whether I really intend for him to feel the force of my abruptness, whether anything I say or do can be regarded as affecting.

'Lee,' he pleads.

'You're not listening.'

'And you're always either . . .'

'You don't know me. Everyone keeps trying to invent me.'

He stands there, quizzically, looking, searching. I'm clenching, unclenching my hands, frustrated that things are not going so well, not that I have a plan or even expectations as to this occasion, being here, today, tonight, down to wondering what am I doing in another fucking dress, standing with this dilettante in a beech grove, listening to discordant voices straying imbecile from someone else's wedding party, somehow unable to move away.

Strangely, the next moment I'm mulling over whether or not to dredge from the recesses of my memory and divulge information as to my formative period. Itinerant the length of the Rockies. Up and down. Seems like we spent too many of those years ceaselessly traversing the Continental Divide. Over and back. Worming our way through Utah, Colorado, Wyoming, Montana. The jobs our mother took.

TRADING
BEADWORKS CRAFTS ANTIQUES

Yards full of cannibalised wrecks, desiccated firewood. The twinkling lights of Lander, Wyoming. Pregnant ranch-girls withering in town over winter. Baled hay stacked as a windbreak north of the house. The basketball hoop on a rickety pine pole. Months-old tyre ruts and footprints, froze solid into the mud like rippled rock, you could break your leg, crack your hip in. Everyone said it was inhumane to keep women and livestock in that country. Frosted, lonesome ponies. Brutal-haired ladies. Neglected houses dwarfed by satellite dishes. The hollow booming sound my boots made on the Dubois, Wyoming, boardwalk. The travelling man, his name was ... Dancyger, Rob Dancyger, standing in his socks there, leaning back against his life-laden car in the winter sun, hitting on my mother who'd so recently been instructing me in notions of sophistication involving Marcello Mastroianni, life in Europe, France or Italy, nothing like this grizzled homeless soul in his faded jeans and soft plaid whom she seemed to all of a sudden find so compelling. The waitress urging Billy and me to speak up – she hated mumblers. Iced water in a wine-coloured, hazed, plastic beaker. The furnace roaring in the haberdashery basement. The entire town a cradle of backwater civilisation, an invitation to disappear.

GIFTS GUNS SOUVENIRS
REALTY
TAXIDERMY
JESUS
BILL'S PARTS – SALVAGE USED
HUNTERS WELCOME

Coming north into Colorado, suddenly the waitresses were younger, whiter, prettier, because there happened to be a prison outside of town.

ALL YOU CAN EAT
ALL THE TIME

Ski apparel, sex appeal. Billy's first guitar. Billy wheedling me to take a shot at drumming. Billy making out we were just a regular pair of aliens, misfits, out of sight on those Stanford-Binets, those Wechslers. Fort Garland, Colorado. Hayden, Colorado. Steamboat Springs, Colorado. The Lazy Sportsman Shooting Range, a series of dirt-bank berms, the middle of nowhere, our mother contemplated leasing, everyone soon realised had been this horrible close call. Jackleg fencing zigzagging through my dreams. My best friend in seventh grade, Karin Schmauss, whose stepdad's junkyard promised,

WE HAVE ANYTHING YOU WANT
IF YOU CAN FIND IT

. . . showing me how to fellate an ice-pop. The Gallatin Valley. Paradise Valley. Pendleton blankets. Buying winter outerwear, underwear, at Gibson's. Fog in the valley, mountain tops clear, the first snow. All that open big sky country. Parked out at Axtell Bridge precociously reviving, then receiving an MSU Bobcats linebacker. Other fishermen still in the river, chunks of ice crashing against their chests. Driving out to visit where they shot my great-great-grandfather in 1884. Wandering off during a field trip to the pishkin south of Logan. The rest of the class, Mrs Tessuto, climbing all over the cliff face, searching the base of the buffalo jump for bones, artefacts. Encountering ghosts, malnourished girls my own age, realising that I was privileged, making it past fifteen was always a bonus in these parts. And when I finally show up, thirty minutes late, Mrs T taking a dim view, telling me I'd jeopardised everyone's safety, never mind the punctiliously prepared schedule, telling me I'm irresponsible, a victim of the pleasure principle, destined to live only a Donkey's Tail of a life, patternless, pathological, shallow. Not having the faintest idea what she's talking about. Busting my knee playing volleyball against Great Falls High. Choir. Roping, learning to rope, the allure of roping – not for show but the hard knocks prelude to dehorning, branding, castrating, vaccinating. Who was it, which of our mother's beaux, used to practise his roping on Billy, aged seven or eight, having him run around, trying to evade the snaking, flying loop? Moving again, turning south, never far enough. Montpelier, Idaho. Butch Cassidy's Restaurant & Bar. Grimy, good-humoured hunters with quads, llamas. Never pet a llama. Smelly mean devils. Surly, bite you any chance they get. Back in Bozeman again. The fall our mother and God were dying. Days when morphine persuaded her she was about to marry Marcello Mastroianni, when doctors failed her, when in a moment of clarity she suggested Tim Allen, TV handyman, might be the one to figure what ailed her, help her recover. The meat-cutter who walked me home five nights in a row, wading ankle-deep through dead leaves, south off Main, up 7th, over Olive to 5th, south again, lights in every window, house after house, regular families, cozy interiors. *Winterize your home*, the fly sheets advised. 'Winterize your life,' he forewarned me. So I traded him for a paleontology major, who cried out the names in his sleep, not of dinosaurs, but of sophomore gymnasts, rubber-heeled, elastic-jointed, cheerful sorts.

Finding myself in the car with Fisk, his hands moving on me as if he aches to become me, nudging my breasts up out of my dress, pressing my nipples – never beady or hard in arousal but elongated, brighter, like they've pupated, emerged from some forgotten dark interior – at the moistly socketed corners of his eyes. It's not even dark out. Itching to do something, drugs, shake myself, fuck someone new. These are restricted options. Kill someone, anyone.

Trying to get him to understand, saying, 'I want you to know.'

'What?'

'This isn't me,' I say, shyly restoring my breasts, palming them down in there as he turns embarrassed, then swiftly, offended, angry. And my hand searching the door, finding the handle, pushing against it, extending one leg into the evening. Somehow managing to move in two directions simultaneously. Waiting for what? as he grows more and more agitated. Unsure of what I expect or would accept from him. Unsure whether I've been manipulating him even while he's been scheming to get me. The confusion ending in another second as I propel myself out of there, flounce away into the glowering light.

But it's only this bedlam in my head as I'm walking, stumbling. Faces blurring, voices merging, occasional teasing glimmers of the way you ache for the morning to come, offer a fresh start, erasing the impact of some interview I gave months before, or will grant months from now, responding to the rumours regarding the true nature of my relations with Billy, my forthrightness twisting into cheap effects, now haunting me, punishing me. Running where to throw up by a pergola. Lock-jawed rictus spilling couscous, shellfish, polyps, bean sprouts, ginger. And it works like a spell, conjuring up who else but Billy, surely coming to reprise the same old, same old, break my spirit, hoe my bones, press my jaundiced flesh.

'Hello,' I say.

'Hello?'

'I thought you were avoiding me.'

'Why would I do that.'

'Different reasons.'

'Jesus, Lee, what're you doing out here?'

'Not avoiding you?'

'That's clever, that's really clever.'

'Fisk brought me, but if any of you think that means something, it doesn't.' And, 'she's . . .' I say, flourishing a hand, managing to suggest his new wife, somewhere close, illuminating the occasion, her special day.

He says, 'Forget about her.'

And I say, 'Oh, OK.'

'You're so,' he says, moving closer. 'You know you're nothing like the others.'

'Huh, what others?'

'Other women.'

'What's that supposed to mean, I'm not like other women? I mean, damn it, you're not exactly Hannibal Lecter yourself, are you?'

'Where are you going now?'

'Dance,' I say, moving off, wishing, half expecting him to follow, maybe even dance with me, keep up appearances, and for once I find myself craving more of those grown-up pointless conversations he seems to always wish upon us. As if that would launder our entire life, neuter and obliterate these capricious urges, this tenderhearted lunacy.

He's not giving up so easily though, keeping pace, saying, 'Lee, try to understand.'

I turn to face him. His hand's on my arm, pressing gently, looking like he only has my welfare at heart.

'Was it so terrible?' I say. Then harshly, 'Don't tell me.'

'As if you care, one way or the other.'

'Fine, I'm so hard it's not even a matter of having a lousy memory.'

Now pushing at me, breathing on my bib, staring at my bust, as if I'm about to adjust to becoming his eager inamorata on the spot. Not likely. Never again. And this seems to be some sort of clarification to the fury storming in my head.

'Lee.'

'What is it now?'

'I just wanted to say.'

'Say what?'

'I just wanted to say that I think . . .' suddenly distracted, '. . . that bruise, there. Right there on your . . . ulna.'

I'm thinking, weird, these bastards, men, with their hang-ups and formal depravities. And scrunch up my face, stricken. It sounds so serious. Curious as to where he acquired the term. No doubt the English cake, the Sylvia person's responsible for his expanded vocabulary. Obliged to ask him, 'My ulna?'

'Your radius,' he says, really freaking me now, reaching a hand as if to touch me. 'There. There.'

'Don't touch me.'

'Your . . .'

'My arm?'

'Your arm, yes.'

I'm so relieved. Wondering why didn't he just say my arm instead of all that totally bogus ulna and radius crap which sounds so, you know, earnest and genital at the same time.

'Well, don't,' I tell him and walk away.

The nerve of some people, married people, absolute freaks, making personal remarks, upsetting folks without call. I'm thinking, later I'll get more drugs from

185

Fisk, maybe fuck him in order to make Billy jealous? Crazy note, scarcely relevant. Plant drugs in Billy's pocket, call the cops? Why ever not? Who's my dealer now? Where's King? Where's Alessia? Why doesn't someone know? Why doesn't someone care? Why isn't Alessia here? Why isn't Alessia answering her phone? Keep expecting Alessia to turn up, reclaim Billy, make some waves, announce she's been knocked up, the only one's been knocked up out of all the imaginable candidates. The usual drama, the frail nature of events, human relations. Who gets to keep anyone? Who gets to keep Billy? Who cares? Alessia? Sylvia? Me?

A swift sortie through the trees and on over treacherous, declivitous ground throws up no sign of Billy, Fisk, Mrs Billy, no trace of Alessia, mortal combat, commercial enterprise, artistic innovation. Mindful of my hair and dress as the weighed-down boughs and eruption of roots threaten to entangle me, trip me, entwine me in ivy vine for ever. Flailing at branches, fighting to escape the thicket, evade the spider-limbed prickly threat of a monkey-puzzle pine.

Almost right away I spot Mrs Billy in her frou-frou gown, circling methodically, mopping up guest after guest, cluster after cluster, thanking everyone for coming, sharing her wish to be known henceforth as Mrs Glade Annis, and that's when it hits me, not so much *that he married her, not me*, but *why am I even surprised*.

And instead of hanging around with a fixed smile on my face, waiting to wish them both a happy married life, or praying disaster befall bride and groom as they take turns riding a specially hired mechanical rodeo bull, or excusing my failure to bring a gift, or feigning interest in their honeymoon, almost certainly a trip to Namibia, Botswana, culminating with a week on the beach at Zanzibar, I head for reception, ask them to call me a taxi, and instantly withdraw the request, saying, 'Never mind, I know someone.'

Twenty minutes later, Harris drives up. He has Anaconda's two albums with him, wants me to autograph them, particularly requesting that I avoid defacing my image on the cover of *Zombie*. I'm looking at him, trying to figure him, his sudden familiarity, his boldness. Of course the *Zombie* cover features nipples, mine, the same as a stranger's, glimpsed on hoardings, off glossy promotions, detumescent, more brown than pink, incontrovertible proof, some say, whispering, that I'd once had a child.

Minutes after midnight, Lucy calls, despairing, says she's considering getting a flat, with CCTV, a website, a maid, changing her name to Plum, all on the off-chance of running into someone halfway decent. Disabuse her on that account, unless what she's seeking is some trucker with haemorrhoids, nicotine-stained teeth, and a clammy pecker the size of a lipstick you'd have to get all worked up over.

Let her know my life also is this hole. My life is wake, eat, drink, shower, brush, paint, dress, coffee, drugs, shop, run, wallow, drink, sleep, dream, wake, walk, chat, wash, dress, phone, scream, sex, eat, weep, bleed, sweat, drink, pluck, paint, slop, swallow, weigh, shop, exercise, wax, drink, use, fall, crawl, rise, expire, wake, eat, drink, shampoo, pee, poop, pray. How am I doing? Definitely got this entire hole thing going.

Soon as she's yawned and bid goodnight, asking myself why I no longer see him in other children, no longer picture the way he must be, growing tall, going to school, playing with friends, confiding to whoever his father employs for that purpose, the little triumphs and setbacks of his day, the dread and longing of his nights, bonding with his father in the rushed moments that can be spared, wondering occasionally who his mother is, where she is, why she doesn't live with him, visit him, call him, love him.

That Fisk, so damned tenacious, coming back at me in the early hours, like he knows something about me, as if we haven't had enough already, exhausted all the possibilities, calling me up, sideswiping me with the suggestion a there-and-back trip to Berlin might prove to be welcome diversion for both of us at this uneasy juncture, wants me to adorn his arm at some awards ceremony, absolutely no more than that, no pressure whatsoever, like it's a dream I've been waiting all my life for, the chance to act decoratively vacuous in Berlin, his trophy for a night.

Four hundred guests, followed by dinner for four dozen at a restaurant called Barcelona, then to a club in the east of the city, all of it hosted by Claude, a rich, old, fifties, moderately well-preserved, pouch-eyed, diamond-studded fairy, boasts a serried black hair transplant with the bonus features of both a minitail and a topknot, operates several labels, music, movies, under the Charlie Varrick, he explains, crop-dusting, bank-robbing badge, *Last of the Independents*, collects aggressively, which is where my pig-eyed Fisk comes in, has a helicopter piloted by a strikingly glamorous woman he introduces as the Baroness von Hehl, his companion for the evening – who would believe any of this? Calling over the roar of a sudden downpour as he ushers us, sweetly protective of my hair, my oh so flimsy dress, toward the club's canopied entrance, he shares his old codger criterion for music – if the singer dances it's crud.

Everyone at Club Schwerkraft seems intensely cultured, speaks precisely formal English, the competition fierce, the crowd according to Claude, notoriously predacious: brimming with displaced person model-types; a pair of leggy, possibly frigid, ex-pat American painters in blood-curdling matching hot-pants; Russian avant-garde installationists; concept peddlers; Ukrainian hookers ever poised with the chloral hydrate; painfully rational Swiss divorcees; horny Moroccan dentists; strawberry-blonde Belgian reporters; Serbian diplomats; Saatchi scouts; minor Polish-Swedish nobility; rehabilitated, satellite-hawking communists; one ex-mayor of West Berlin; a severe troika of young Dutch politicians; queers; junkies; highrollers; heiresses; hairdressers; dilettantes; dealers; Mexican photographers; Irish ceramists; English glass-blowers; Greek dancers; Italian actresses; hobbyists; financiers; law students; footballers; TV executives; bourgeois middle daughters; beautiful, uncomplicated, un-chic, low-key, local girls, still alluringly rough around the never depilated edges; a kelp-haired Métis movie producer in pearls, talking vicious above her weight; a Korean lesbian bitch with a talent for the violin; a Warhol impersonator; George Clooney's alleged aural guide, visiting from Northridge, California, along with his boyfriend, Warren Beatty's alleged former psychic sidekick from the 1970s.

I'm half expecting, half dreading one of these jokers is going to tell me he's fresh off the steppes, claim to be named Serge. Wondering not for the first time how and why I never managed to confirm who I slept with that night in LA. Scott Weaver? Or someone called Serge? Or someone else altogether? Now that Scott Weaver is dead, who's left to enquire of? Eddie Pope? Libby Elapida? Pearl Mundy?

And out of nowhere comes the notion, what if Pearl had set it up? It wasn't like her not to have managed to set up something. Something out of the ordinary. Some guy or other to impress, to prove the depth of her friendship. But what if this time, Pearl had set up something more elaborate than the usual dates she arranged? What if Pearl had pitched Scott Weaver, or whoever he was, with the chance to meet Lee Annis? More than meet. Much more. Enjoy and exploit. Virtually a sure thing. Say, $2,000 worth of guarantee. Who knows how much. What price a dairy-queen princess, a rock'n'roll comet tailing toward obscurity, cellulite-alerts and gin-sodden middle-age? What if Pearl knew about Scott's predilection for women who resembled his mother? What if Pearl told him about my having a son whose name is Serge, affording him the almost irresistible chance at playing my son, even as, in his own head, in the squalid movie he was running there, I played at being his mother? I realise I could *what if* for all eternity and advance my sense of certainty not one jot. Besides, hardly anyone knows about Serge, about my being a mother, certainly not Pearl . . . so far as I know. But what if Pearl had set me up, what if Scott Weaver had paid for the pleasure, what if Pearl had profited from my craving for . . . what? Intimacy? Sex? Loss? Distraction? Debasement?

Finding myself drawn toward Polissena, no second name, not Vitti, unless it's Duse. Why do I think that? A Roman actress, late twenties, milky décolletage, cantilevered black leather dress, obsidian necklace, elbow-length dark brown hair, sombre black eyes, a throaty voice rushing to divulge how she's reached this stage in her life – as if I care, as if it signifies, as if she's holding up a mirror for me to view the truth about myself – confiding how she restlessly seeks the moment, the nugget, which will define her. Always living this empty life. The emptier the better. Accustomed, until a month ago, to calling up Fabio, her agent, the best agent in Rome, asking him why hasn't he got her a movie, all she does is wait around, dreaming Fellini will somehow step from the grave and ask for her. Then she'd race to Fellini's office, the dark dusty cluttered room, his sarcophagus even, and show her mouth, reveal everything, do anything. She would even read for Fellini, dead or alive Fellini is all the same, and she never reads. No matter who the big-shot casting agent or director is, Polissena does not deign to read, believing they get what they see. Which attitude may explain why her career's so fixed in the doldrums, some forty-nine hours of television, '. . . late after midnight call games. Soft entertainment quizzing shows. Beach aerobics. Many interviews with vacationing dogs and their masters with ladies. All for the big climax in my first showing as true actress, *La Bionda Sciocca*. You know it, no? Of course, no. Which is very comedy how one day in my aunt's funeral house I confuse the information to three funerals of dead persons and succeed to find true love. Maybe you know *La Bionda Sciocca* does not receive one cinematric release. Not even to Festival of Cannes. Only it go very fast to Cecchi Gori Home Video. Now I know is where all the stupid blondes ending up. Dump blondes. Fabio telling me the dump blonde is kaput. Telling me many times Berlin is the future for all new Europe cinema. So here I am. And I tell you, Lee, my heart is puzzled with every man, the fools, very much wanting to sex with me . . .'

Somehow, countering the life-stalling spell, dreading that I'm even a little like her – kaput, like what she calls the *dump blonde* – I extract myself, and gain the relative sanctuary of a gloomy, plush-feeling booth. Having to shake myself in an effort to unsnarl the strands of Polissena's tragic saga. There's a bowl of gloxinias on the table before me, which I'm compelled to finger. Even their slipper-shaped flowers seem glutinous.

Someone, evidently American, evidently wasted, Claude's age, a taller than average old hippy sort with a shut-in's pallor and a mouthful of uneven dentition, materialises before me, painfully shy, glowering, unhappy to be here, exposed, resisting the force which compelled him from cover, glows for a moment, flares, checking me out as if he knows me from somewhere, and just vanishes, like a fatally ominous cartoon emissary, portending such as sorrow, death. . .

'Who was that?' I ask my neighbour.

'Slick,' says this girl, Bianca Schwarz, a model – she says – Bavarian, bobbing her mossy cropped head and shrugging her bare shoulders, bow-shaped salient clavicles, flashes of emerald at her ears. 'He makes movies. Epic movies for the Hong Kong market. All this philosophy, karate, satanic psycho-stuff. Curious flashes of mischief, exquisite meaning, faultless humour. Not to mention paranoia, or so he tells me. Don't worry, I'm the one he's after.'

'Sick who?' I say.

'*Slick*,' says Bianca. '*Slick*, that's all I know. It's Slick, his name is Slick,' even as she's sliding edgeways from the carmine-cushioned booth, scanning the crowd until she spots what she's looking for, and fixing a deliciously degenerate smile, strikes off toward a corner, or is it a doorway? veiled by palm fronds, wafted blue haze, draped whorls of yellowish stained muslin, more like distressed antique parachute silk, guarded by an obese figure, carved or live, I can't tell from this distance, seems to own a vaguely Kazakh face. Can't be troubled going after them to check what their story might actually be, what unexpected vistas might be revealed.

Someone else, a man, chats about the latest in drug-synthesisation, about *style.com*, about the local construction boom, about bird-watching in Patagonia, Arizona, about the 80,000 vacant apartments in Berlin. Another woman challenges me about American hegemony. I let on not to know what that means, ask whether it has something to do with ignominy, wonder to what extent I'm being held responsible.

Fisk's been watching me, enquires good-humouredly

whether I'm being unfaithful to him, which, I recognise much too late, is precisely his kick tonight, bringing me here, neglecting me so thoroughly, abandoning me to this ragbag sick crew. Also, he informs me, he's only now heard how Billy's in the hospital following an accident at last night's wedding reception which involved being thrown by that mechanical rodeo bull, sitting up too soon and getting smacked good on the side of his head by the revolving machine. I can't fathom what reaction Fisk's expecting, can offer nothing apart from a smile, trusting that Billy's in pain. Noticing Polissena, I disengage from Fisk, swivel away, happy to quiz her about that dress, working its meat-hooks into women as much as men.

Fisk disappears, doesn't answer his phone, and I can't remember the name of our hotel, so I strike off, find a taxi, a driver speaks English, describe the hotel decor, done deal. Fisk, of course, tracks me down, shows up at my door an hour after I make it back to the Hotel Bagnasco, brushes past me, insists on calling room service, ordering up nibbles, helping himself to minibar vodka, promising he'll take care of the bill, which was my understanding all along, his treat, that and separate rooms, asking me, 'Um, do you think maybe I might use your bathroom?'

OK, so he wants to freshen up a little, why's he feel he has to ask me? Unless it's the stainless nail file I've been clutching all this while in my hand. I wave it in the air, say, 'Certainly, it's just through there.'

And I watch him stand, hitch up his pants, shuffle to the bathroom. Why's he come here at this hour, why's he make freshening up sound like a prelude to some squalid interval? Starting to question whether I've correctly nailed his sexuality. Standing here, arranging my options. Phone someone. The front desk. The police. Run out of here. Why? Where could I go in this town to get away from Fisk? Perhaps I should just follow him in there like maybe he expects or hopes. Stabbing him in the bathroom with my nail file would be better than stabbing him out here. Easier to clean up the blood in there. Prise out those teeth from his little pink gums. Maybe I should have gone after Claude tonight. I need a drink, pour myself a gin from the minibar, cringing when I discover it's the type has a pressure pad, bills you every time you move a bottle, fuckers, so I toss it back in one, resume wondering where he's got to.

'Fisk?' I call, moving, not so steady on my feet.

'Just a minute.'

What's he doing in there? And do I really care? Drugs? Probably. Definitely. And the tightass won't share. I press my face to the bathroom door, ask, 'Fisk, you OK?'

'Sure, fine, thanks for asking.'

I try to remember when I last slept, when I showered. I sniff my arm, seeking some trace, some scent of Billy. Nothing.

'Lee?'

'What is it?'

'I think I . . .'

Alarmed now, trying to open the door, finding it's locked, thinking overdose, scandal, criminal prosecution, life languishing in a German gulag, gasping, 'Fisk, open the door.'

'OK.'

I can hear him turning the key, the barrel moving, him saying, 'Don't be angry?'

'What happened?'

The door opens slowly, revealing him, the dropped trousers, the raised shirt, the soft belly, the hair, the familiar puce instrumentation, what appears in stark contrast to the hairy chest, abdomen and legs, to be a freshly shaved groin, scrotum, which is something entirely new to my experience, and behind him, the basin full of my tipped-out toiletries.

'Do you think,' I say, 'I ought to be impressed? Jesus, do you honestly imagine I live to see this.'

And he does me the honour of turning round, spreading his cheeks so I can appreciate the masterstroke, the coup de Fisk, the short string trailing pale from his anus, more graphic proof in its own way, if it were needed, of my boundless optimism and foolishness.

'What did you do?'

'It won't come out.'

'Just pull on it, that's why the string's there.'

'It hurts.'

'It hurts? What are you talking about. Here, let me. No, wait, wait, you don't expect me to do it for you, do you. Is that what this is?'

'No, fuck no, honestly, only, please, what if it never comes out, what if it swells, stays stuck up in there, what if I die from that toxic shock syndrome.'

'Sit over there and do your stuff.'

'You think that'll work?'

'I don't know, I never heard anyone put a plug up his butt before. Where's the package? Maybe there's a number you can call, a helpline, ask them what're your options?'

'It's not funny.'

'Can't you do anything?'

'I don't think so.'

'When did you go last?'

'I don't remember.'

'Today sometime?'

'I think so. Look, I don't know.'

'Push.'

'I'm pushing.'

'Push harder.'

'I know how to do this.'

'So, do it, dump.'

'Don't you have something I could take?'

'Like what?'

'I don't know like what. A laxative, prunes, psyllium. My mother used to give us psyllium. Psyllium? I don't fucking know.'

'OK, wait here,' I say, stepping back into the room, wondering whether he's got the impression I'm his mother now, closing the door, abandoning Fisk to his fate, sacrificing toiletries, some favourite, hard-to-source, not inexpensive, cosmetics in there. Throwing things together, whatever catches my eye, seems worth salvaging, various clues, clothes, shoes, Discman, CDs, Paolo Pandolfo's Ortiz, John Cage sonatas, interludes, getting out of there, away from that gross imposition. Wondering not for the first time why men are so fixated on those things. I guess it's obvious once you think about it. And sad, for that.

★ ★ ★

Time enough to consider all that's happened since Alessia went in the hospital, since we came to Europe in the first place, since I left Vegas, since I left home, since menarche, since kindergarten, since the dope they overdosed mom with to induce my arrival did something to my head, since my daddy's sperm took an evil turn and caused me to, *I don't know why*, and besides I never set out to, or to be, you know, judgemental about any of this.

Everywhere I turn, I see people looking not so different to me. Try telling them all that's happened since whenever, try to explain my difficulties, how life won't let me be, and see how well they cope. Because who would believe it, who would understand or sympathise, who could advise me what my next step ought to be, who could encourage me one way or another. I know it's pointless so I keep my head low, keep walking, walk to the elevator, walk across the lobby, walk out into the street, seeking what I think of as *the night*, something wild, untamed, accommodating, and almost right away having a woman approach, asking to borrow my cellphone, using it to call up her own lost phone. Going along with her, walking up and down, hunting the sound of a phone, two loons, thinking the woman's nuts even when eventually we do find her phone in the gutter.

Parting from my new pal, walking further and further, observing an open-mouthed drunk in Armani, sleeping it off on the floor in the ATM lobby of a bank. Trying not to think of the man almost certainly right now in my bathroom, trapped with a tampon up his buster, about to do things to a shower curtain.

So I walk, what else can I do, only walk, keep walking, putting more and more distance between me and the Hotel Bagnasco, between me and all the rest of what's happened, the rest of my life, between myself and who I am.

Drifting, confused and exhausted, through almost indistinguishable Berlin streets in my Sandra Kuratle dress, flowery top and A-line skirt, like the events of the previous days have finally gotten to me, my hair behind me in a dark wing. Tormented, wondering where I'm going to end up. More and more of the same? Or portrayed as some sort of scandalous outré *Madame X* by vengeful ambitious Fisk?

Picturing Billy, bull-mauled, in his neat clean hospital bed, bustled by a woman I know from somewhere, wearing a floppy grey cotton top over floppy grey breasts along with a capacious blue skirt that keeps her cool, falls close to blunted shins, blue-veined, barefoot. Her eyes hanging, myxomatosis bunny hanging. Her face otherwise the shape of a prickly pear, tapering at both ends. Now I know her, where she belongs, perched on a bar-stool behind some counter, a dusty hole-in-a-wall store. What was the name of that town? Somewhere in Northern Arizona? Southern Utah? While outside, the sky begins to change, glooming. Clouds lining up along the low horizon, growing ever higher and darker. The wind playing through thin branches of stunted gaunt trees. The same wind picking at a pale beard, ruffling the dirty feathers of a maudlin black bird. A morose scavenger which appears unheralded beside him. His eyes paying no heed. Not even when the first raindrop falls smack in one of them. He never blinks. The bird hops, once, twice, looks first at one milky-blue and white eye, then at the other.

Back where I started. Rain gusting once at the glass beyond which the floored drunk appears like some figure from a museum-housed Goya I must have passed one time or another, running my eye over it, nine or so allotted seconds, urged on by a wake of other restless tourists, or was it some mildewy plate I glimpsed in one of Fisk's art books.

Looking around, searching for the creamy full moon to have it absolve me. But there's no moon, only polluting urban light. And my pulse racing in my throat, on my skin. The wind rising. Trees shedding leaves, seeds, bright coloured petals. The streets suddenly carpeted with a confetti of life. Melchior Strasse? Feeling myself uncomfortably replete, so far from home, embarked on an ever more eventful life. Wishing blindly for some cutbacks, fewer options crowding my days and nights, some mugger, some jackbooted hoodlum to take a cut-throat to my future.

Back at Heathrow to find dreary old dependable Harris loitering, creaming himself to see me, though I can't remember having booked him, going along with him, letting him take my bag, relieved I don't have to face a stranger, suffer the inevitable, pushy, rigidly formulaic spiral of recognition, judgement, heaven, hell, the same doomed reduced roller-coaster ride of all relationships.

Harris feeds me this line how since Billy's in the hospital he'd like to go out of his way to be extra attentive toward me. And I can't help it, can I, if people want to be nice to me. But no sooner does he turn the ignition than it seems we're long-term intimates, and he's midway into some narrative, a resumption of some episodic story of personal travail he's been gagging to honour me with. This first instalment features death, a rat he's just shot in the bedroom of his Tulse Hill conversion.

All I can think, all I can say, is, 'You have a gun?'

And he says, 'Yep, an air gun,' goes into numbing details of how he procured it, applied it, what the rat looked like prior to death, gnaw-gnaw, the splatter aftermath, no chance of resurrection here, no second coming of rat.

Remembering the BB guns openly on sale during the summer in Trastevere stalls, should have bought one, novelty purposes, casual homicide. Sometimes I'd like to have a gun, the stark consolation of a gun. Warmly, fondly, picturing all my nemeses, plugged, inert, and belly-up. Actually have to stop myself right on the brim of whizzing, here and now, so helpless and giddy have I turned at the homicidal possibilities of owning a gun. It's unlikely that even Harris would welcome my soiling the seat, having to mop up after me, though I know, have always known, long before Berlin and the Hotel Bagnasco, there are all sorts out there, aficionados, desperate men.

Harris, mysteriously emboldened, progresses his narrative, telling the story which Billy, allegedly, puts out, the legend he stokes, about how I sweetened our arrival in London, broke our music with the heft of my presence, that prairie allure of shrunken faded

T-shirts, washed-out combats, thriftshop skirts and dustbowl dresses, Okie pigtails, Sears-bought cosmetics, bra-less and knock-kneed, working some kind of 'luded-out, hayseed voodoo on bright-lights sophisticates.

'Let me get this straight,' I say, 'Billy told you he was my pimp?'

'No, no, that's not what he, I didn't mean to, Jesus, Lee. Look, that's not it. It wasn't Billy. Right. It wasn't even you, was it. I mean you, you're a lovely person.'

'In the flesh?'

'What?'

'Never mind.'

'It's just, fuck, Lee.'

'Stop the car.'

'What?'

'Will you do what I say and stop the fucking car.'

'Can I . . .'

'Now, Harris, now.'

'Can I tell you something, can I, look, maybe it's beside the point but I think you're, um, bloody, just insanely, uh, bloody beautiful.'

'Say that again.'

'What?'

'How you think I'm beautiful.'

'Oh.'

'See how easy it is to be nice.'

'Where are you going? Oh, fuck, don't go. Don't. No, Lee. Jesus, what's Billy going to say if I upset you? Jesus, Lee, don't go.'

So OK, what's Billy been playing at, spreading all these stories. I'm going to confront him, have it out with him. Once and for all. And in the meantime, making the essential call to who else only King, the old reliable stitcher-up of my self-inflicted wounds, reprise what it takes to get wired in this town.

Careening, bright-eyed and jittery, waste no time making my way to the hospital, clutching corner-shop carnations, a purplish heart-shaped balloon, stealing in, expecting to find Billy lying vegetative in bed, unguarded, anonymous, isolated, bandaged, attached to these myriad tubes and monitors in a darkened room, instead of which, I find, attached to him, his wife, clutching his hand, she might as well be ingesting his glory, it's all the same to me, ingesting generously, forcing me to weigh whether it's a fact guys in comas are hard all the time, seems like I heard it so stated one time, as if it were a law of nature, thermodynamics, physics, curious also whether Di ever did Dodi that way, such speculation almost on a grotty level with wondering whether Mary ever straddled a pot, chased sweaty lint bunnies from her downy perineum. Humanising stuff.

So much overtaking me here. His wide alert eyes – so much for comas. His wife's composure – so much for her plunging ahead, all bravura tongue and throat, which I could understand, catch her behaving in such a manner.

And rather than suffer any longer their mutual doe-eyed dull devotion – he knows what he's missing – stealing away, attempting to breathe, to move, quiet and decorous, along the corridor, no one paying me more than the usual attention, a few glances to confirm it's

Lee Annis, whom they've loved and envied on Jools Holland, Jo Whiley, never *TOTP*, now teeter-tottering, adorably muss-haired and wild-eyed with care, advancing brightly, profanely, across the foyer, pushing through the door and out into the night.

And now at last, thinking I'm free, *voilà tout*, and sayonara, feeling resolved, OK, and again a little foolish, hearing Nino Rota music in my head, from *otto e mezzo*, identifying me, more Guido's mistress than wife, more plump than ascetic, more Carlotta than Anouk Aimee, that silly way of walking she had, skipping, sashaying, Carlotta's Gallop.

I glimpse my reflection in the rain-flecked windows of the shallow graded ramp which I descend to board the plane. It's getting darker outside with storm clouds mustering, and runway, terminal lights appearing brighter by the second. Wearing a navy blue zipped-up tracky top, denim skirt with pink embroidered details, strappy heels the colour of new potato skins but spangly and expensive, tarty matching turquoise nails, hand and foot, crusty black eyeliner, shorn nappy hair. And I'm seated up in business thanks to Air Miles next to someone young, American, Canadian maybe, in a business suit, Italian, and designer spectacles, also Italian. He introduces himself right off as if I should know who he is or give a damn, not a boy like his name suggests but old enough to be a footballer or a race-car driver, that kind of job, my kind of man he seems to be implying, and I honestly can't place him, and if he's neither, what do I care, and I smile a reserved simple smile at him, and look straight ahead at the back

of the seat in front, the dead TV screen there, trying
to keep from being sick, and I so want to leap up and
race to the loo and slice my wrists but I manage to
restrain myself, calm my breath, sit back and close my
eyes and picture what it's like to be eight again, and
the man, what passes for a father, one of my mother's
revolving door of men-friends, baldy, barrel-chested,
reeking of K-Mart aftershave, heaves me onto the
yellowish claybank pony for the first time and smacks
Jesse's rump, and off I go, cantering into the mist, shrieking and gleeful and hanging on for all I'm worth. And
now, feeling good again, this afternoon, this instant, I
don't even feel the need to steal a hooded sideways
glance at the man alongside me, and someone else
touches my arm, and my heart flips, and for an instant
I know it's going to be Billy who couldn't let me leave
without seeing me, who couldn't let me go, and I keep
my eyes closed, picturing him crouching beside me,
leaning close, his skin all shiny sleek with rain, and
breathless with need and love and desperation, but it's
not him, it's just the big blonde cheery simpleton
stewardess with the bright painted fire-bucket mouth,
and she smiles and says something which I only half
discern, and force a grimace in response, and pull the
chalky pink tartan lap rug from under my bum and, as
directed, fix the seat belt low across my hips and pull
it taut so it wraps my bones, and watching the stewardess moving away, her low-slung backside swaying, try
to unclench my jaw and focus on my breathing, and
I'm thinking about all the people I know, have ever
known, and I'm smiling inside, believe it, and my mouth
is parched, and my bare legs are goose-bumped and

trembling with nerves, the good sort, excitement, antici-
pation, and I look at my knees, try to stare them into
compliance with my wishes, into not trembling, into
losing their bluey red and gold chequered hue, and I
press the folded lap rug there, and shiver from head to
toe, a not unpleasant prolonged rush, and the cabin
lights flicker, and the engines kick on and hum ever
louder, and the PA crackles and croaks, and a woman's
sweet-sounding voice prepares us for flight and hopefully not the worst, and I sense how everyone's in their
seat or at their post or rushing to be there, and the
captain breaks in to say air traffic has an opening and
is bumping us up the line one whole minute like it's
an eternity and honour and achievement all in one,
and I find I'm grasping the arms of my seat, whiting
my knuckles and breathing shallow, praying against my
will, since long ago I decided against praying anymore,
but right now it seems it's not enough to leave it to
God, and on we go, taxiing, and the cabin hushed, and
next to me a man, turning to check, he's still there all
right, a tepid presence, his face to the window, wondering whether it's a window or a porthole, and next we're
out at the end of the runway, and then the roar and the
race, and it's like we're forced back in our seats, and the
rush goes on for ever, as if we're never going to take
off, and on down we go until in one instant we deny
everything, every rule of God and nature, every truth,
and heave ourselves collectively into the sky, and so, I
guess, I hope, this means something, like it's a farewell
to the abyss and all of that, or else if no one hears from
me again, it was all of it, most of it, hitherto, certainly,
beautifully, hopelessly me, and the man beside me

murmurs and holds up his hand to show where I've sunk my sharp lacquered nails deep into his flesh.

Watching Gwyneth Paltrow pick at her trout, I'm guessing you're supposed to deduce that her character grasps the essentials, knows how to use the cutlery, chew with her mouth shut, but the dress raises all sorts of issues. Any moment now, whether he likes it or not, Russell Crowe is going to get a look at some parts, fabulous gummy drops adhering to her skin.

'Having second thoughts?'

'About?'

'Your wife.'

'I just realised she has reservations about every damn thing you can think of, from crop-dusting to Impressionist art, to China's civil-rights record, to why Vietnam ought to win diplomatic recognition ahead of Cuba, to the death penalty, to taking a dump alfresco.'

'She should get a hobby.'

'I told her that. Trot along to the hobby store. Pick up a useful skill like embroidery or taxidermy. Gather some roadkill off the highway. Stuff an armadillo. Enhance the home. She came back with a kid.'

'You knocking her up might have had something to do with that.'

'She's my wife.'

'That's all voodoo to me.'

'Like the thought of a baby growing inside you makes your skin crawl?'

'Like I had a hysterectomy. If you're not happy with her you should quit yapping, go ahead and ditch her.'

'How soon?'

'We get an off-the-shelf psychiatric profile, have her deemed unfit. You get the kid, she gets the road. Three, four weeks tops, wraps it up.'

'That simple?'

'You given any thought to what you might like to happen to her in the long term?' smiling at him through her smoky exhalation. 'Boy,' she says.

'Excuse me?'

'Men,' she says, looking over at a neighbouring table where an obese septuagenarian feeds strings of what seems like spinach, possibly cicoria, into his female companion's pretty, plump, painted mouth. She shakes her head, puts out her cigarette, grinding it a little longer than necessary in the glass ashtray, excuses herself, goes to visit the powder room. He pays the cheque, rises from the table, goes to wait for her at the bar, takes her by the arm as soon as she reappears, steers her outside. She leans against him for a second as if to brace herself for what lies ahead.

'How about a little walk?' he says.

She acts surprised. 'If you like,' she says.

He waves away the hovering valet, and they head off down the sidewalk toward where it's busiest, where the myriad faces have, by definition, the baffled look of losers.

'There's a lesson in this for all of us,' she whispers, looking at the crowds who drift endlessly by, their faces flushed with wonder and disbelief at the glitz, the neon, the fact that they've made it this far, 'only I haven't figured it out yet.'

'Let me know when you do.'

'It's a date,' she says, and grasps his arm tighter, snuggles close to him.

'Cold?' he asks.

She smiles, shakes her head. And standing in the midst of the heavy-girthed tourists, the white-trash optimists, the small-town honeymooners, he kisses her, driving his tongue past those thin lips until he finds hers, warm and responsive. The neon all around, running, swirling, dizzying, bleeding.

'Call me tomorrow,' she says, starting away with a wave, a sexy little smile.

Of course it can't possibly end well, so I flip, and find this museum-quality sarcophagus, and a great white, sort of Indiana Jones effigy, safari-shirted, addressing the camera, '. . . the result shows some imperfections in the passage from the lines to the planes and volumes of the figures, as can be seen with the head of the woman which is slightly inclined to the . . .'

Flipping again − despite the arid academic tone offering a chance to dazzle my neighbour with the range of my interests, the depth of my intellect, the warmth of my nature − to find a middle-aged man with the lugubrious, satiated look of one for whom no appetite has gone unsatisfied, one of the old-school, Manhattanite, rational, godless. His heavy-lidded eyes patiently regarding the young woman as she paces the limits of his darkly furnished office. She's agitated, brittle, breathless, unfocused, more displaced and disordered than he's ever seen her. Finding it difficult to keep pace with her speech, needing to slow her, he offers her water, coffee, encourages her to take a seat, reassures her he won't be long, and leaves the room.

After a few moments waiting by herself, unable to bear it any longer, she goes looking for him, following the sound of music, baroque, narcotic, finds him in the small kitchen, unmoving, apparently listening raptly to –

'Pachelbel,' he says.

They stand there, side by side, suspended, leaning awry like raggedy, skewed skyscrapers in the aftermath of a seismic calamity, listening as the music glides to polished completion.

And perhaps it all bleaches a little of her panic, asking, 'What am I doing here?'

And he says, 'You and David?'

And she shakes her head, wondering why doesn't he know what the whole world knows, that she and David were finished long ago. Realising that he's getting her to take small steps, flex barely intact behavioural features, core social functionality, evanescent manner.

'You're with someone?' he asks.

And she says, 'I don't think so.'

And he says, 'It's good to see you.'

And she says, 'It doesn't mean I'm looking.'

And he takes hold of her arms, her elbows, and says, 'You say that . . .'

And she says, 'It doesn't mean I'm not looking either.'

And he says, 'I see your picture sometimes.'

And she says, 'Do you. God!'

And he says, 'You look tired, good but tired.'

And she says, 'How's Helen?'

And he sighs, says, 'Your mother and I are not exactly . . .' releases her, turns aside . . .

Flipping back through several channels until I find, once more, '. . . the smiling mouth with curved lips, what's termed the archaic smile, the protuberant nose, the plump and round chin, several other stylistic elements such as the precision of lines, the protruding breasts, the encrustation of the eyes, lead one to appreciate just how . . .'

At LAX we glide through immigration, he with his green card, me with the crumpled old passport that bears my original, my own true name, leaving behind not only the lines of tourists queuing patiently, but the afterburn of offence, the flash aboard the plane when I realised he thought he knew enough about me to suggest I might be amenable to adjusting my schedule to accommodate him on arrival.

I still feel a little jittery, look around, half expecting to find Pearl Mundy waiting to greet me, but there are no familiar faces here, no one who might possibly recognise me apart from policemen trawling arrivals for delinquent mothers, whores and sociopaths. All the same I take hold of his arm, and with my touch it's as if a haze clears from his face, and I can't begin to worry now about what he might be reading into my behaviour. Possibly something squalid along the lines of whether I might be persuaded by the prospect of making, say, $500 for myself, cash, when the facts are I've already allowed myself to be lured by a promise of just that amount, the equivalent of little more than a couple of hundred dollars' worth of an optimum-quality bitter crystalline alkaloid to be shared in some quasi-romantic milieu. Too late for caution, I press closer to him so that even if there is someone here who knows me they won't get a clear look, a chance to identify me.

We walk to where his dust-shrouded Range Rover's parked, and kiss for the first time in the trapped heat of the squat concrete open-sided building. Only now does he explain how his home is out of bounds for a day or two, the decorators in. I know he means his wife, and think, so this is how it's going to be, and tell myself I don't care, tell myself I've heard it all before and it's not a real lie, just another part of the game, and allow him to make arrangements, check us into a motel on Fairfax, the Farmer's Daughter, where he suggests I ought to shower and then we'll go out, find something to eat. He craves Mexican. I concede I also like the idea of tacos, enchiladas, re-fried rice and beans, guacamole *and* sour cream. He insists we stay awake to resist jet-lag, and though it's worse the other way, LA–London, I acquiesce to every word, as if I've never flown before, never experienced the slow drag of altered time. He promises to take me up on Mulholland so we can view the vast expanse of city lights. And I see that he's like all the men I've known before, that now at least I know how much, or rather how little, to expect from him.

Stepping from the shower, I wipe steam from the mirror, secure the bath towel in an easy knot midway on my front, catch a glimpse through the inch-wide crack of the slightly ajar door to the other room where he stands, pulling off his shirt, slapping a hand to his tight-knit belly, looking better than I could have dreamed. And I can't help smiling as if this is the first time, feeling the almost euphoric impatience to get in there, have him hold me, press down on all the dark unwelcome thoughts that crowd me. Feeling myself prepare for him, until I notice that he's handling money, shuffling notes through his fingers. And it strikes me for just an instant that he's putting out money for me, trying to estimate how much to give me, how much to pay. And before I can take this queasy train of thought any further I notice the other man, another man's legs and feet, pale chinos, tan sock-less feet in scuffed, sun and salt-lined deck shoes. His presence some sort of anomaly in the picture I've been marshalling. I'm neither shocked nor alarmed, think-ing there must be an innocent explanation. I move even closer to the door, seeking a clearer view.

The second man's looking through my bag, the fake Kate Spade that cost $15 the last time I was in LA, when Pearl led me downtown after bargains. A bright-shirted stranger, fingering through the contents, randomly plucking out item after item, tossing aside my passport, my makeup, mascara, face powder, my moisturiser, the gold earrings, Tiffany hoops, a sparkling bracelet he evidently dismisses as tat, and which, honestly, I can't begin to confirm who purchased it for me, how much it cost him whoever he was, unpicking the elastic band which binds it and flicking through my roll of cash and setting that aside on the pillow, the most of $1,800 in hundreds, a few fifties, twenties, upending the bag, spilling out the remainder of the contents, brushing his hand over them, fanning them out on the bed, revealing them to be dross, suggesting he has no intention of putting them back the way he found them, which a hopeful view would require him to do if for no other reason than not to alarm me whenever I step from the bathroom. Now it strikes me – whoever they are, cops, reporters, bad guys, who he claimed he was on the plane – how little they care what I think. Those tokens lie on the bed, the floor, scattered like the last warning I'll ever receive.

Stepping back to recover my breath, I knock against the shower so the door rattles, and the man from the plane calls out, 'Everything OK?'

And I answer, 'Yes,' my voice faint and faltering.

I wish I had my phone in here. I could call for help. Call who? Pearl? Serge or Scott Weaver or whoever he really was? Libby Elapida? Eddie Pope? But I don't know where it is. In the other room somewhere? In my bag? Spilled out on the bed? Somewhere with those men? I have no idea who they are, apart from exactly what the word stranger means. And I remember my phone's back in London, wouldn't work here anyway.

Wondering what possessed me to hook up so impetuously with this man from the plane. As if it's all I know, the impulse to come here with him, to come to this motel, and now it's let me down like it always promised it would. If we had gone somewhere else, somewhere more exclusive, expensive, the other, higher side of Sunset, then maybe there wouldn't be so much implied jeopardy in the second stranger showing up in the room, then I could think of at least a couple of plausible explanations for his being here.

Holding my breath, I inch back toward the door as

if to check whether I've really seen the second man, as if I doubt my own eyes. And the stranger in there shows something to the man from the plane, seeking his opinion. And the man from the plane shrugs, doesn't know what it means. It's my book, *Candido*, bought to help me improve my Italian. I wish I was there right now, Rome, or on Lake Como, Capri, Ischia, with Billy, Alessia, anyone, alone, by myself. Even now, pointlessly thinking I could call Billy if I had my phone. But that was always precisely what my entire life was about – not calling Billy.

And now I'm remembering something about the shower, how in the darkness of the stall I'd noticed a window set high in the wall there, hardly more than 8x10, the size of a magazine. Trying to estimate whether I could squeeze myself through a space that tight. Realising I only have to try. I step up on the toilet rim, pull at the wire grille so it hinges up and in, and this way push at the grimy glass which hinges up and out. And I clamber, dragging myself, scraping through into the light. First an arm, then my head. One shoulder, the other. The towel snagging. Chipped paint catching, brushing off on my tired skin. Wearing nothing but a damp towel. My hair spongy, drying. And halfway through I manage to turn onto my back-side, reach high for a hand-hold, feels like crude stucco, a narrow ledge, pull myself out, backwards, hook my legs free and lower myself until I have no other choice but to let go and drop five or so feet to the concrete walkway. Where it hits me. Hits me with the force of a charging steer, or a galloping horse suddenly stop-ping, unseating me, dumping me to the ground. All of it hits me, everything I've been and done and seen, everything and everyone I've known, and it all comes up short, and bruised and rotten. I'm a twenty-eight-year-old woman, pregnant, and this is the culmination of all that time, emerging from windows, dangling, running for my life.

Making sure I still have the towel, realising if I lose this towel now I have nothing, scrambling along this back landing, down a creaking metal stairway to the service alley spotted with wheeled metal garbage units. Over to the right, the motel pool, small and blue, at street level beyond a wire-link fence. And the street, the other street, Fairfax, beyond, running parallel with the service alley, busy with late-afternoon traffic flowing both ways. And cars parked there, the dusty Range Rover. And sensing if I were to look back now I would see the bunker-shaped motel, the door to the room, all the doors and windows facing north on two levels, the particular large picture window behind which the two men wait for me, but I also know I'd lose my nerve, freeze, wait for them to come outside and get me. For an instant I wonder whether that would be so bad, might not even be a welcome outcome, some kind of ending, rather than just another intermediate stage, but that notion passes, and I realise some part of me is telling me this is not the time.

I force myself to hurry along this pot-holed alley. Passing power poles with links of sagging lines between them. Finding myself thinking in a foreign language. Trying to get up to speed with what it takes to get by in a different country. Trying not to think of the boy, the husband, whether he ever married again, whether he would have me back, whether I would go back, how this instalment alone would more than vindicate his shedding me. If word ever gets out, how will I explain a motel, and not the Chateau Marmont, the Mondrian, the Standard, as the scene of my near-demise. Praying for a prowl car to appear. Praying I don't need a prowl car. Nothing here in this alley but a few forgotten vehicles, dusty windshields, faded interiors, stale air. Hurrying barefoot over the cracked and fissured surface. Never looking back. Trying to step into the blindside of power poles, cars, seeking cover, anything to shield me from view. Every step taking me farther from the threat of discovery, pursuit, the sound of a shrill cry commanding me to stop, the chance of a hand falling roughly on my neck. Every step taking me nearer the street ahead, the greater daylight there, the blur of people, traffic, the promise of witnesses. And when I finally get there, I stand a moment checking where I am. A glimpsed wedge of hills ahead of me. Brown hills studded with greenery, shiny white houses, glass, reflections of affluence, pile upon pile.

No one pays me the least attention, none of the few pedestrians, none of the passing drivers. No one finds it strange here for a woman to walk the streets wrapped in nothing but a towel. The heat at the end of the long day, the endless summer, feels pleasant on my skin, against my eyes, in my mouth, feeling its way inside my throat, down deep into my torso, my lungs, my belly.

A blue sign suspended over traffic, confirming what I already know. This is Beverly Blvd. And for a moment I can't decide what to do. Whether to stand here and wait, or whether to keep on running, putting more and more distance between me and my pursuers, those who would harm me, contain me.

Now it seems like a good time to start running. Instinctively turning left, toward where the ocean looms. Thinking if I can reach the ocean, Pearl's house isn't far. And also, now, testing myself, finding I'm no longer able to picture Billy, Alessia, Scott Weaver, the others, not even Fisk, not even the freak in the motel, his friend, not even myself, my own flesh, my own face. All of them fading fast, deserting me as I run, racing as if the heat has gotten to me, as if I wish to desert myself. A ghostly sensation that my hair's uncut, streaming behind me. And I'm running, with my bare feet slapping against the hot pavement, the white towel clutched to my heart, the dying sun melting in my eyes.

how it ends

Ten months later, I'm in Santa Monica, trying to reverse into this shape-changing parking space, shrinking one instant, bloating the next, when a Cherokee — at least that's what I think it is, admonishing myself for failing to master these details — pulls up alongside me, the driver leaning over to check me out, raising his shades high onto his forehead, looks like Eddie Pope, it is Eddie Pope, showing slightly plumper than his recent photos.

'Hello,' he calls, 'what's up?'

'Oh,' I call back, blinking, like I'm having problems remembering who he is, 'hi, how are you?'

'What are you doing now, coming or going?'

'Why, I'm parking here, I'm . . .' not wanting to let him know I'm off shopping without any particular acquisition in mind other than the vague idea of picking up some CDs, some 16 Horsepower maybe, some Eels, some Jim White, some Johnny Dowd, so I say, 'I have some errands to run, that's all. You?'

'Oh, just passing. Thought it was you, and it was, is.'

Some third party leans on their car horn, and Eddie Pope indicates for me to stay with my car and wait for him to find me, like I have nothing better to do, and off he goes, guiding that nice substantial Cherokee round the corner, with a train of backed-up traffic flowing in his wake. Allows me an opportunity to tidy up the car, consider my appearance, salmon, short-sleeved, cashmere sweater, dark navy skirt, black boots. Thinking how his truck, inappropriately gleaming, would look so much better shrouded in a month's worth of back-country dust, red for preference. Five or so minutes pass, and I'm standing by the car when he comes strolling along, looking unhurried, comfortable in his clothes, Levi's and T-shirt, taking his hand from one pocket while pocketing his cellphone with his other. He leans in to brush his cheek against mine, takes my arm, and leads me away.

'Why don't we get some lunch,' he says.

'I don't think I . . .'

'You're not fasting are you? You look fine, really fine.'

'Thank you. No, it's simply a question of time. Right now I . . .'

'What if I promise to be snappy?'

'Snappy?'

'I'll gulp my food, and you can watch, make small-talk, fill me in on how you've been, what you've been up to.'

'You think that's something I'd like to do, watch you eat?'

'Maybe,' and he leans close so his breath caresses my face. And he whispers, with just a faint hint of mockery, 'So tell me, Lee, what's up?'

And I pull away, laughing, 'What's up yourself?'

And later, in the restaurant, he says, 'You know you almost ruined my life. I had the crappiest couple of weeks after you took off.'

'I beg your pardon?' I gasp, wondering what he might have heard, what I ever did to cause such disruption to his now famously running-like-clockwork life.

He says, 'Scott. Scott Weaver. I heard you broke his heart, you know.'

'Oh, right,' I say, relieved to hear it's so slight an offence, not even curious as to how such an insane lie got started, never mind disseminated. Though now he's peering closer at me like he's already discerned, and is troubled by, minute variations between the present Lee and the Lee he met so fleetingly a year or so ago.

He says, 'He pretty much went off the rails. When you met him he was on the verge of something, shooting this new movie. And shit, then he freaked, you know, disappeared.'

'Was that my fault?' I ask, as if my memory's clouded on that one detail.

'Maybe, maybe not. He probably needed some time to work things out, get his head straight.'

'I hope, you know, I never intended to cause him any upset, disrupt his career in any way. It was simply he was so boyish. What was it with him anyway? I spend some time with him, a couple of hours, he puts a gun to his head? I ought to come with a government warning, is that it? Look, I'd really rather not talk any more about him. It's all so long ago. Ancient history. And I don't want to suggest it was distasteful, or dreary in any way, but I have new concerns pressing all the time. My life is so hectic I can't begin to tell you. Practically, oh, most of the time I don't even know whether I'm coming or going. But no, I'm sorry, that's enough about me.'

'Tell me,' he says.

'No.'

'Why not?'

'Why not. Because, for instance, I don't even really know you, do I.'

'I'm buying you lunch, aren't I.'

'All your own idea.'

'I think that entitles me to certain confidences.'

'Well, I'm sorry but that's where we must disagree.'

'So lie. Make up some stories. Try them out on me. I won't know the difference. You'll make me happy, hearing about your adventures.'

'Lie?'

'For instance . . .'

'I know what lies are.'

'For instance, you're sitting at home some evening and you find your mind drifting, thinking, what was it with that Eddie Pope.'

'Who?'

'Eddie Pope, good-looking guy, talented, on the up-and-up.'

'Oh, him.'

'You try to figure out whether he ever had a thing for you?'

'A thing for me? Eddie Pope? No, that's impossible.'

'But you think, you think maybe there's a chance he did?'

'But I know for a fact he didn't.'

'He told you this?'

'It wouldn't have mattered whether he told me or not. Because if he had I wouldn't have reciprocated. And as he never did, it's not an issue. Are you going to finish that fish?'

'It's snapper.'

'It's yummy.'

'Tell me, Lee, you ever considered settling down?'

'Let's not get carried away here, please.'

'No, seriously.'

'Me, settle down?'

'Yes.'

'Oh, I think it's fair to say I'm much too young.'

'Too young to settle down, or too young to think about it?'

'Both.'

He smiles at me, tidies up his food, eats what he thinks edible, moves the rest to the side, lays his knife and fork together in the centre of his plate, his mouth chewing lightly, swallowing, taking a sip of water, catches me stealing a look at him, smiles some more at me. I reach for his untouched lemon slice and eat out the flesh, tearing it away from the skin, using my teeth, cheeks hollowing as I suck against the tartness, licking my fingers clean, wiping them on my napkin. He's looking at me like I'm showing signs of incontestable eccentricity.

I look away, take a deep long breath, and finally after what seems like a minute, exhale, saying, 'And another thing, what makes you think I have adventures?'

'Don't you?' he says.

I say nothing. And looking down at my lap, I find that I've twisted the linen napkin into a tightly coiled pad. I place the napkin on the table, and excuse myself, push back my chair, get to my feet. He starts to rise from his seat but I wave him back.

In the restroom I rifle through my bag, searching

for something, anything even vaguely narcotic, but can find nothing to help, not even a cigarette, not even a stale old tab of Wrigley's Extra. I lock myself in the toilet, clear my nose on toilet tissue, and working slowly from the jumble of cosmetics in my bag, start to resurface my face, resurrect the look of a youngish woman secure within the confines of her customary appearance, the shadows of a dozen howling shrinks for company.

When I emerge from the restroom, I locate Eddie Pope, still at the table, waiting patiently for me. I manage to slip out of there without his spotting me. Telling myself it's better this way.

Oddly, only now, outside in the sun, does it dawn on me that I couldn't have played it any better. I know he's going to call. One of these days. Then maybe we'll talk some more about Scott Weaver, though it doesn't much matter whether we do or not, maybe it'll go something like, 'Oh, you know, he died.'

'I heard that, yeah. It was, like, totally unexpected, right.'

'Yeah, who could have known.'

I don't get very far before I sense that something's wrong. As if I've stepped from the wrong restaurant, into the wrong street, the wrong life. Looking around, wondering who's that tailing me. He is tailing me, isn't he? He's good at this, emanates a sense that he's purely here to protect and serve, his eyes signalling, *Do not be alarmed*.

Of course I get it, I'm being shadowed by who else only the cop who shot the party-goer in Wonderland

Avenue. And being part of such a vast scheme is uniquely consoling. Sure, it's vain and pointless to struggle. And it is reassuring to know that there's someone somewhere taking an interest in little old me, wanting to see that I don't escape my share of whatever blame's going around. That's so bloody stupid. Same old, same old. If I'm not being stupid, I'm being careless. I loathe myself this instant. And immediately decide if I know I'm loathsome then maybe I'm not so stupid, not so bad, maybe there's a chance for me yet.

Looking again at the watcher, who may or may not be my delegated chastiser, or, why not, my guardian, even my saviour, and maybe it's the angle of the sun, the blur of shoppers laden obese with a panoply of bags from Gap, Banana Republic, J Crew, Abercrombie & Fitch, Borders, Discovery, but the fellow's eyes burn bright, and I feel my soul jerk, dragged unwillingly in his direction, until a rush of kids, bearing leaky envelopes of Chinese food, surround and assail him, rendering him another quotidian figure, a standard, which it finally dawns on me, I own no share of. I turn away, riven and tormented by the lack of scheme, of code, of warning, the absence of external threat, my exclusion from belonging.

Forcing myself not to hurry, I retrieve the car, drive the short distance to Fred Segal, use their lot to park, go inside, search for and locate a particular store I've been meaning to visit. Now, numbly, not for the first time, seeking some sort of amorphous comfort, consolation.

After a listless, jaded while, I say, 'Excuse me,' to the morose-looking bare-legged English girl in neatly pressed black and white, skirt and blouse, linen and dimity, and missing something, animation perhaps, 'do you have these pants in either a turquoise or an aquamarine?'

The girl says, 'I'm afraid what you see is what we're stocking at the moment.'

'But do you know whether they come in either a turquoise or like an aquamarine?'

'I really couldn't say.'

'Could you find out?'

'I only work here.'

'See, I knew that but someone else here might be able to help me because I pretty much like the cut and style, only the colour bugs me, it's so drab, olive, and what is this, charcoal, anthracite, slate?'

'No, you see, like I said before, I only work here, I don't make the tat, do I.'

'But if you troubled yourself you might be able to find out for me, mightn't you? Turquoise or aquamarine. Or as a very, very last resort, a great extreme, lilac.'

'Lilac?'

'Why not? Lilac can sometimes be interesting, even soothing at the end of a harrowing day.'

'Look, why don't you try Third Street.'

'You mean Melrose, the Fred on . . . ?'

'Third Street.'

'The Promenade?'

The girl shrugs.

'They have these same pants on Third Street?'

'You might try.'

'Thank you so much,' I say, moving to the door.

226

And the girl says, 'See you, Lee,' almost under her breath, but loud enough for me to hear, and for an instant I'm shocked, haemorrhaging poise, plummeting speedily back to appreciating so this is fame, staked out, exposed to cheap derision.

In a second I'm outside, reasoning that it's just a minor setback, heading back toward Third Street, on foot this time, stepping off the sidewalk, jaywalking, indifferent to traffic, the eyes of a watching policeman twenty yards away who frowns at the sudden squeal of brakes, the flash of legs cutting through pesky bylaws and torpid convention, the pedestrian crossing ten yards further on, and I stride out, switching to the ocean side, no longer caring whether I'm being watched, or followed; no longer concerned whether I'm drifting, or being led; indifferent to whether I'm the same as I was years before when I'd leaped into marriage, and my life for a short while was so different; untroubled by whether I'm some strange amalgam pieced together and painted by myself as much as by any greater unseen hand working to a preordained design; simply resigned to the picture I have of myself, Western type, freckled, stammering, svelte as ever; drawing my phone from my bag, touching the speed dial, clapping it to my ear, and with excessive gaiety and no little inanity, crying, 'Pearl, hi, it's me. You know those white pants you had on the other night. Yeah, tight. Well, what I want to know, that is if you don't mind sharing, is where you found that cerise string top you had on with them. It was way beyond and apt I thought. And cerise is so right for my complexion, don't you think. Yours too of course, naturally, though mauve I've always said suits you best, simply does something extra, complements your colouring. You know I'd never bullshit you . . .'

And while Pearl tells me what it seems like I wish to know, I continue to picture myself, as if I'm watching someone else, a stranger, someone alluring, self-regarding, her laughter, her presence, brightening the lot of at least some among this after-lunch crowd as they ease their way, alert, sun-blessed, along the busy street.

I notice there's a hair sprouting black from alongside my left nipple, and don't know what to do about it. It's not soft or light enough to pass off as lady-down and ignore. It's a real coarse witch's blemish. Seems like the beginning of something, or maybe the end of something. Pearl gives me a name, and a woman called Luella zaps me with this wand, this laser.

I have no clear idea why I agree to talk to the reporter – a transplanted paradigmatic New Yorker, petite, tough-talking, who brandishes a disarming ability to empathise with all that a woman of my years and free-wheeling propensities must have experienced – unless it's a need to find myself again, recover who I used to be, acknowledge the intervening haze, years of toing and froing, girl and boys, squalid affairs, excessive encounters, a little predation, a woman of queasy virtue.

I'm also aware there are plenty fake people out there going about their fake lives with fake aspirations and fake experiences, who believe they deserve a chronicler, fake or otherwise, as much as those whose lives are jammy full of truth and beauty. It may be that everyone deserves a chronicler, even if it's going to be some schnook like Marcelline – who initially over the phone betrays her prejudice, underestimates me, attempts to seduce me by sharing how she likes in her work to 'establish the coherent life and substantive character of her subjects'. All right, I think, happy to let her try, take a shot, see where it gets her.

So I accept the invitation to off-load a quarter-century's worth of incident, aberration, digression; reveal myself more thoroughly than I've ever done with all my shrinks, friends, lovers combined; divulge the often unflattering facts with such brio that the reporter soon comes to question my compos mentis. Quickly outlining my childhood; my dream of becoming a local TV weathergirl person; the loss of my parents; my shortcomings as a dancer; my unfulfilling first and only marriage; the paranoia suffusing the split; the relief of divorce; the heartache of separation from Serge; my feelings for Billy; the breakup of Anaconda; how I can understand why some people mistook us for a couple; how we used to like to play up that notion, putting out all those signs that we'd been married, divorced, lovers on and off for years; a recent nightmare featuring the ruby-eyed parboiled translucence of the latest foetus I aborted; sundry griefs and torments; adventures on the monkey bars in a dozen townships from Montpelier to West Yellowstone; my hopes and plans for the future; the few dates I've had with Eddie Pope; my never discounting marriage as an option.

Surprising how my life proves to be such a rich and

varied source of biographical trivia as much as outrage, and nothing so tawdry or frivolous as what Marcelline, the reporter, regards as my engagement with what she terms the Shirley MacLaine Syndrome, fixating on ways and means by which death may be thwarted. Of course I encourage her incredulity by advancing the case of Scott Weaver as the latest in a line of scarcely persuasive demises, a sequence which includes all the usual suspects from Marilyn to Hoffa to Elvis to Diana. I avow all this scepticism, claim that nothing, not even sight of the deceased in an open-faced casket, could persuade me other than that somehow, somewhere, Scott Weaver, for instance, lives on. Just as maybe souls and essences can be traded, swapped in mid-stream, hijacked by some light-fingered interloper, there might be more mundane ways in which to persist, not so much beyond as through death. I encourage her to investigate, ascertain the true circumstances of his death, and then she can judge for herself whether or not it was some sort of scam, nothing necessarily meta-physical, paranormal or supernatural about it, just plain old paranoiac procedures and deep cover methodology.

'His life's in shit,' I say, 'so he slips away, makes a few alterations, reemerges as someone else, someone old, someone new, no more Scott, but you, or me. How about that. Imagine he comes back as me. Imagine that. Slipping through the cracks to emerge looking like Lee Annis, taking up residence . . .' indicating my sternum, using five fingers to prod '. . . right here, for better or worse.'

Marcelline, floundering, stares open-mouthed at me, 'You're saying you used to be Scott Weaver?'

'That sounds so insane, doesn't it. I know. But why not. Or maybe not him exactly, not always some celebrity, but someone else. Someone anonymous. Someone you've never heard of. Someone humble. Someone deserving. Who knows. Can you ever really be sure it's impossible? That you're not someone else. I mean think about it. Doesn't it make you curious? Doesn't it make you feel good and hopeful? And maybe one day you'd even like to go down that road yourself, escape into someone else's life.'

She gapes at me, as if I'm a loon, from another world. And I wonder whether she's capable of piecing it together, seeing why such a nonsense appeals to me, offers the only hope of expiating so much that troubles me.

The mirror tells me I'm some way past my prime. I bet that makes a lot of people happy. The goon at this particular store on La Cienega who follows me into the street for one. Wants me to show him the contents of my pack. Like I'm some klepto seeking punishment, searching for thrills, my mother, a penis. Like I'd ever in a million years lift their Wilma Flintstone-vintage tat. What a huge mistake on his part.

Living here's so much like living in the country. Eight miles to the bank. Eight miles to the cinema. Eight miles for muffins. But overall it lacks the nuttiness of jays working pinyons, caching all those berries, to the mutual advantage of bird and tree. I suspect LA is the wrong place for me but as of now that seems to be its allure.

Sometimes I drive out in the desert, take the 395

up toward Bishop, or turn off at Lone Pine for Death Valley, and sometimes I stop the car, walk out along the road, standing directly on the broken yellow strip, looking up and down for a long while, as long as I can bear the heat, but there's nothing, nothing there, nothing moving, not even a cloud in the sky.

We hike a cab to The Eye, which Pearl promises is a mixture of food, darkness, drink, dancing, drugs, and what do you know, sex. Pearl doesn't concede it's a dyke venue until we're way inside. One look and I see there's not going to be a lot of rock in the roll. There's also a scattering of guys here only I'm not entirely convinced they're bona fide boner types. This cutie waitress in a raspberry spandex bandeau, and pelmet-level skirt, skates over, and we take the tofuburger with line-up-the-Bloody-Marys-fast route, and I clown around with the celery, chasing laughs. For once Pearl has this enormous appetite, and while I'm trying to keep from catching anyone's eye, Pearl's scanning the place like there's no get-out. Then this fluttery middle-aged woman with the fissured skin of a sun-fiend, a Slavic accent, sporty antics, comes by our table, starts preaching to Pearl about the war-crimes tribunal in the Hague, the dubious case against one Slobodan Milosevic. The day, she says, that Bush boy goes on trial for feeding his people into the Texan death chambers like so many sheep down a factory chute, is the day the tribunal shows itself other than the pawn of Mammon & Moloch, the great Western powers. Lurching to my feet, I mumble something about need-ing a whiz, wave myself permission, leave them to it.

Staying in the powder room for an age. Turning my hand, this way and that, trying to discern the snail track of scars crisscrossing my palm. The sound of someone beautifully blurging exotic cookies in a neighbouring pit. Sitting here, keeping still, until dwelling upon the partly mystifying, partly titillating graffiti, none of which appears to mention me, gets boring and repetitive. So I spoon up and pop something allows me ascend and soar a moment.

Long enough to wonder how I made it this far, crouching here in this humidified pine-scented toilet, to wonder what enables me to heave and haul around the baggage of so much life. For instance the . . . And then the . . . And . . . How I played at being a daughter, a sister, a wife, a mother. How I live with myself. How I lacked and lost so much. Humanity. Selflessness. Sense. Warmth. Even that. Seeing myself as more of an abscess of black-hole intensity than anything else. Consider the collapse of a massive star (sort of) causing an intense gravitational field. Almost hypothetical, almost invisible, owning a small diameter. Into which everything is drawn. And lost. Well, we know all about that, don't we. More white might help. Caulk up those gaps. Hurry. Until it's all gone, done, dusted. And I'm sniffling. Impatient noises from beyond the door. There are women out there of every imaginable shape and size. Reproachful women. Burdened women. Regal whores. Pastel angels. Reasoning I'd better get out of here before something novel occurs.

On my way back to the table who do I run into but my very own one and only Billy, making himself at home at the bar, and he grabs my arm, and only for this being the kind of place it is, and anyway being sort of relieved of the obligation of returning to the table and Pearl's continuing to cope a little too avidly with the attentions of the accented lady, I wouldn't be too delighted to see him, but as it is I shoot him a grown-up's smile, and he's pretty talkative, and not so abrasive as last time we met, and it's not so weird or difficult to accept his offer of a drink, and when I ask him what he's doing here, he raises his eyebrows and says research, like I should have known, and right away he asks back what I'm doing here, and I say as vacantly as possible doesn't he know I'm a hardcore committed dyke, and he says sure with a crushingly straight face, that was his first impression all right, the sudden ardours of youth and all of that, and I playfully punch his arm, and he laughs, and I'm wondering whether I should ask about his wife, her whereabouts tonight, some great fucking proof of his having signed up to maturity, never mind my own indifference, being all aloof, you know, above it, when his face tilts toward mine, giving me a full view of the inside of his mouth, and I wonder what it would be like to have him kiss me, kiss me again and again, having to ask myself is this really love? and why not? and he's drinking Becks, and orders a Corona for me, and soon as the beer comes, I thumb the slice of lime down the neck until it drowns, and while I'm sucking on the bottle I take the opportunity of having a long look at him, his floppy brown hair, his big old eyes, his face, what some magazine once described as insouciant, he says you needed that, and then he asks to see my ID, says he suspects I'm underage, and I go like foxy but underage? right he says, and I raise my arms, flash him my pale pits, saying OK you got me, I give up, and together we say in flagrante delicto, which is kind of a buzz in a moronic juvenile Orange County way, and he drops his hand on my bare shoulder for just a second, and it's like we've never met, only in another life, and like it's a plot this totally ancient song comes on, Neil Young 'Wrecking Ball', and he asks if I'd like to dance, and I don't say anything, just let him take my hand and lead me onto the floor where we dance real slow in the middle of this whole mess of heaving women, and it's just, well it's proof, I think, that the world's not entirely, you know, lose your mind shit, and Pearl and the accented woman are dancing alongside us, and Billy seems to remember Pearl, of course he never really liked her, got along with her, all the same something passes between them, a skittish look which I jump at thinking it explains his turning up here tonight, knowing where to find me, and he lets go of me for a moment, and curtsies, actually curtsies, and drawls in this real Lubbock two-stepper's voice, howdy duchess, not to Pearl, no, but to her partner, and I start tittering insanely, so he clamps his hand like a vice on my neck, and presses my face against his chest to bury my laughter just so this shrivelled woman's feelings won't get bruised or nothing, and I breathe in his scent like it's my last breath, and don't you know, it's like he never left, never cut me loose, and you'd better believe it, what I want most in the world this instant is for him to knock me up again, then The Cramps 'What's Inside a Girl' starts up, and Pearl takes Billy away from me, and I can't bear it, watching them dance and shout together, though they might as well be whispering, and then I dance with Pearl, jumping around like crazy, acting our age, ten, fifteen years ago, all it takes is a couple of dances and a few salty-lipped margaritas later I'm reeling and want to go somewhere hot and close with him, and I try to catch Pearl's eye to wave good-night but some pastel-aura'd girl has her backed up against a wall outlining something crucial, and Billy asks what's keeping me, and I let him see what I'm looking at, and without hesitation he shouts out, hey Pearl, say goodnight, and Pearl looks up past this other gal's shoulder and smiles, and that's good enough for now, as we're going out the door they're playing The Pixies 'Gigantic', and walking to the car I'm singing it, dancing round him, and again in the car on the way to his hotel, telling him he'll never find another sweet-heart like me, and later he fucks me in his room, and it's all true, and later still I go to sleep in his arms.

Call me chattels, call me prey. You want to know how it ends? Everyone wants to know how it ends. This before it even begins. This is typical. Here's how it ends. It ends on Judgement Day in abject terror and out-flung steaming viscera. Or maybe not. Listen, all that is sham, guff, fiction, spew, to keep us on the straight and narrow, to keep us in the tiresome grasp of convention. And no matter what you may under-stand, what you may have been told about me, I've never been comfortable there, in the mawkish stench of propriety. It never held me, never possessed me. Maybe I'm deluded. Maybe I've been transferring shit. It's possible. No one understands me, knows me, gets me. For all the lies and innuendoes, for all my own apparent excesses, I've always been impetuous, wayward, my own person, but not in a bad way, I would crumble to be thought of as a bad person. I'm real and factual, a mother, a woman with slush in her heart as much as the next, as needy, with magma there at the touch of the right man, viscous, carnal, incandescent, flawed as any, doesn't make me any the less a lady. Of course it's not good enough to allow things happen to you. You have to influence events, put your mark upon your time if not absolutely upon history. No matter how much you quake in your shoes, no matter how much the massed ranks of their stony-eyed retainers terrify you, no matter how much they strive to dominate and break your spirit, you have no other choice but to step up to the edge and do the needful, take control of your life. You don't want to be a victim. You want to be a hero. Or maybe even a villain. There's no great distinction between heroes and villains. Villains are as likely to be honoured and rewarded as are heroes. Not that I could ever be a villain. No matter what lies they spin about me you only have to consider my wounded, pure – well, mostly unaffected – gaze to know that villainy is beyond me. Let me tell you about LA. Let me tell you about London. Let me tell you about myself. You really want to know how it ends? I'll tell you how it ends. It ends in cream somewhere, in the South of France, or on Capri, or in the brown hills of LA. Believe it, for my sake. I do.

When I wake, Billy's on the phone, and I find myself

moaning, trying to move, trying to decide what my thoughts ought to be as to what's obviously transpired, trying to keep him in sight, even as I realise there's nothing I can do. He's tied me, stretched diagonally, to the bed. Hands together, legs together. A compass needle fixed pale and soft on steady bearings. Like it's something I ought to derive pleasure from. NE SW, I estimate. Now he moves closer and smiles at me, checks the assortment of cord which restrains me — phone and electrical, coloured, twisted: nothing to do with this room, this hotel, rather evidence of some premeditation, the laying down of essential accoutrements illustrating how he's come prepared, with just this end in mind. Oh. It makes me feel ill.

'Sure, I've been good,' he's saying, a slickness in his voice. 'That's the charm of my story, there's no sex without you. No need for you to worry.' And he holds a finger to his lips to silence me, let him finish with his caller, 'I can't wait to see you too, hon. You're the one I'm thinking of. You know you got me so long as you live.'

And as he hangs up, I manage to ask, calmly, 'Sylvia?'

And he says, 'Alessia.'

'No?' I say.

'I know,' he says. 'It's insane. Fucking choices, man. My mind. I just can't seem to make it stick. But you know something? I have to remind myself, fuck it, why deprive myself? Why be less than I can be? Why? Tell me, Lee. You know any reason why I should run against my nature?'

'Fuck you.'

'What's the problem now?'

238

'I don't want to get a fucking disease.'

'What disease? Baby, that's crazy.'

'Fuck you.'

'Here, I got to go,' he says. 'You like something to read?'

And he picks up the latest copy of *LA Weekly* and opens it to Marcelline's story, which I deliberately haven't bothered to check out. And disingenuously, for an instant, I wonder if there's something in there might have touched him off, made him less than happy. And he tosses it on the bed so I can see my photograph. That's me in rollneck sleeveless sweater, accentuated tits, long sun-starved legs, short tight skirt and heels, with the title 'SISTER LEE' in oversized Hollywood-sign lettering where my smile ought to be. Before I can start to explain or excuse the probable contents, he leans over, presses his face in mine, drives his fingers in my hair, tugs back my head, and drops one in me, his tongue ungentle, kissing, zinging me.

Oh, Billy.

Apparently, despite Marcelline's story, despite how much I made of all I did for Anaconda, despite what he just now said on the phone to Alessia, I am still his unlikely dream-girl. Which is precisely why I risked exposé and scandal, ridicule and approbation, held so little back from that Marcelline, left her to filter truth from myth, lies from pranksterism, left her to weigh the merits of such hoary legends as how I swung it for us in the early days in London, opened doors with my pussy, left her to decide how far we really took it in our rush to conceal the white-bread, uninspiring fact of our being brother and sister. Every flaky revelation was a cry to Billy, to let him know how much I crave our time together.

Now I need to figure out how to play this, how to go along with all this hotel bondage stuff, because if there's one thing I've learned during my time in the fray, it's always keep the suitor happy, satisfied and occupied, lest he grow introspective and unpersuasive. But Billy's not interested in exploiting the situation, nor in relishing the frisson he's undoubtedly garnered, nor prolonging his time with me, not even for one more second. He just grabs his bag, the battered khaki Billingham's I bought him how many Christmases ago, our first in London, heads for the door. His hanging onto that bag proving nothing to me. I worry how long he's known about Marcelline's story, and begin to appreciate how all that occurred between us last night and this morning was just a prelude to this sadistic payoff . . . hog-tied and abandoned to an uncertain future.

'Billy,' I call, straining and dragging at my binds.

But he's gone, pulling the door shut behind him. My head buzzing, thoughts scrambling, leaving me trying to decide between wishing he'd left the door ajar so someone passing in the hotel corridor might notice my predicament, and, more mundanely, hoping he hasn't hung out the *Do Not Disturb* sign, appreciating he won't raise any alarm to help me, and that housekeeping remains my best, my only chance of discovery and rescue.

In the end, the threat of public humiliation gives way to fear of asphyxiation and gangrenous extremities, until way into the afternoon something wakes me from a doze, drool cooling on my skin, the pillow clammy against my cheek, a quiet tapping on the door, and this time it opens, with no other than Marcelline slipping through into the room.

'You really are a piece of work,' she says. 'It's all lies, isn't it,' coming toward me, eyes fixed on mine. 'Lucky for me I never believed a word of it.'

'Marcelline,' I say, 'how did you . . . ?'

She makes no answer, takes her time – *I'm going nowhere* – slinks around the room, scarcely registering my situation. Certainly she's in no rush to untie me, no rush to explain how she got here, no rush to enquire how I got here, found myself in this predicament. I start to get a sense that maybe Marcelline doesn't think it's all that unusual for people to walk into someone else's hotel room and find that particular someone's sister trussed up on the bed. Maybe Marcelline even expects to be confronted by such displays. As if life here in Los Angeles, this sorcerous metropolis, corrupts and diverts us all, affords everyone the possibility of featuring in surreal and convulsive scenarios.

She moves closer, seems ready to oblige and cut me loose. Instead of which she comes out with, 'I've just had this totally interesting lunch with your Billy,' flashing me the cardkey in her hand.

'You going to untie me or what?'

'Don't you want to hear about my lunch?'

'Why?'

'He denies everything.'

'Rock'n'roll.'

'You lied to me, Lee.'

'Specifics, please.'

'About you and him, you and everything.'

'What'd you think? He'd tell you?'

'He said you have issues.'

'How original. So, I got issues. So?'

'Lay off the shit, Lee, for once.'

'You carrying?'

'That's not clever.'

'How do you think I got here, tied myself up so good? Did he tell you that, whose room this is?'

'He said he got a call, someone called him, said you were here, showed up after he'd left, showed up looking for him with some guy in tow, some guy left in a hurry, couldn't take the . . . He said you were crazy, all over the place, manipulative, seeking attention, craving affection, chasing devotion, in denial for a thousand reasons to do with your life and yours alone.'

She's sounding as if the truth's so vast, or else so miniscule — it doesn't matter which it is — so cheap, so significant, she can't absorb any of it, wouldn't wish to even if she could. Truth being something for another time and place, another race of people altogether, an entire other species.

'He couldn't make it himself,' I say, 'couldn't come and rescue me?'

'He had a flight.'

'He's gone?'

'He's, yeah, he's gone.'

'So tell me, he do you?'

'He . . . Is that what you think? No, he didn't do me. He was sweet. He was . . . It was just lunch, fact-checking.'

'After the fact?'

'What?'

'He called you?'

'He, yes, he called me.'

'And he didn't fuck you?'

'I said no.'

'You said no?'

'I mean no. No, he didn't fuck me.'

'But he wanted to, and you said no, is that what you mean?'

'No, no, that's not what I said. You're twisting my . . .'

'Hey, it's no brain-buster. Either he fucked you, tried to fuck you, or none of the above.'

'He said you'd be like this, impossible, wouldn't let it go.'

'Wouldn't let what exactly go?'

'The band, you and him, Anaconda.'

'Fuck that.'

'It's just what he said.'

'You going to see him again?'

'No.'

'No?'

'No.'

'You don't seem so sure?'

'What difference does it make?'

'That's Billy all right, irre-fucking-sistible.'

'Come on, Lee, what do you care?'

'You want the last word, is that it?'

'Huh?'

'He got you.'

'He didn't.'

'OK. So, he didn't.'

'I don't understand, what difference it makes.'

'I lied to you, he said I lied to you, and now you lied to me. You said he didn't do you, when, I don't know how many hours after he did me he did you . . .'

She laughs, this hoot, and splutters, looking at me, her eyes pleading, wishing I wasn't so hilarious, wishing I would give up sometime, let the pretence drop. Her midriff inside the tight-fitting vest rippling as she issues a final dismissive snort.

'But now you think I'm lying again,' I say. 'So it doesn't matter, does it. It's OK, I give you my blessing. Do him. Do what you like.'

'How about I bring in the photographer now?' she says.

'There's a photographer?'

That Marcelline. What a card. Thinking I want a photographer. Thinking that's what this is all about, this entire set-up. Thinking I'm publicity crazed. Thinking this is about Anaconda, a mere band, and all that goes with it, glamour, money, fame, publicity, ambition, desperation. Thinking she's paying me back in kind – unable to see the truth in my lies – exaggerating like she thinks I exaggerated during our interview, just for the sake of . . . a little mystery, how we were together, Billy and me . . . *were we?* . . . *weren't we?* . . . *did we?* . . . *didn't we?* . . . *could we?* . . . *couldn't we?*

But I can't laugh. I mean, fuck, it feels like my heart is giving out. But how could I have been so stupid. Caught out for what seems like the thousandth time. As if Billy was ever going to be the one to rescue me – more selfish even than me. What could have made me imagine that this time might be any different to all the other encounters with bastards. The same old irrepressible fantasy keeps striking at me. How I have no other choice how to view myself, my corrupt soft underbelly. What am I? A sow, wallowing in the mire of all Billy's good for is disappointing me, betraying me. A little voice telling myself there has to be more to life, to everything, telling myself I'll know better next time. Now I need to get out of this bind.

Marcelline, finding it hard to stop laughing, asking whether I have a knife. Telling her if I had a knife I wouldn't need her help.

Still finding it difficult to come to terms. This betrayal is more complete, more instantaneous, more final. Who would have believed it. This what? This love? This death of love? Marcelline's eyes jiggy with the thrill of it, apparently imagining she's next in line to take up that particular baton. The survivor's uncloaked *schadenfreude*. How death vivifies all of us.

Where Marcelline's concerned I'm probably no more than Billy's wacky sister, a small price to pay for Billy's attention, maybe even his devotion. I ought to warn her. I really ought to.

I'm trembling, worrying why I'm so jinxed. This my first, my best, my only chance, scuttled, because I failed to hook him. He preferred to run off back to blandness, and in the process let me appreciate how he's renouncing me for ever, or until he changes his mind. It would have been better, more of an achievement, if I'd killed him, gotten a gun from somewhere, used energetic coitus, fucked him terminally. Now, what else, unless I marry, Eddie Pope or God, either or, take your

245

pick, both available, I'm certain to end my days in some
department store, some office, shuffling petty affairs,
greasy logistics, running from legions of would-be
heroes. Unless Marcelline's pulling a stunt here.

I say, 'You're sure he's gone?'

'Sure, I'm sure.'

'You saw him on the plane?'

'Yeah, no, not exactly.'

'Then you don't know?'

'He's gone, Lee, gone.'

'Fuck.'

'Maybe it's for the best.'

'How do I get out of here? Can you give me a
ride?'

Following Marcelline to her car, walking barefoot in
the hot sun, the pinecones popping, raining their seed,
hard stones cracking as they strike all around me on
the sticky asphalt lot, bombarding me as I walk, watchful of the brown wrack of split pine needles, aware of
sweat already blossoming on my neck, arms, thighs,
symptomatic of the corruption of my entire enterprise.

Something about the sunny smell of California, the
bright burst of crimson bougainvillea against the hotel
wall, conjuring this picture of my mother while she
was dying, asking for something nice to smell. For half
an hour I was so weary, so out of it, so mired in sick-
room drudgery, I couldn't understand what she meant
by something nice to smell. Then, just as I remembered there was such a thing as perfume, expensive
designer scent, that kind of unaffordable deal, Billy
walked in, bringing her flowers. These snow-white

dwarf tulips. A dozen or so clutched in his hand. Unwrapped. Freshly cut. Lord knows where he found them. Certainly made her happy, made her smile. Made me weep. For her, for him, for us.

Struggling to unravel Billy's purpose in sending Marcelline to release me. Why her? Why this big-haired, flat-chested, prissy-knickers? Why not someone else? Why not a maid? Why not Pearl? Did he imagine by sending her to find me that any doubt in her mind about us would be dispelled, that the worst she could possibly imagine was that somehow we had colluded in dressing the scene to suggest we were involved, sick and entangled? A sort of implied narrative – the only kind of narrative I am at ease with – like something you glimpse in the pages of *Vogue Paris*, a Guy Bourdin picture-spread featuring mysterious women wearing little more than Harry Winston diamonds, like a still from a movie which leaves you trying to fathom what has just occurred, what is about to happen next. Yet, all that he told her, his story, his schedule, his checking out, my turning up here, his flight, his everything, is so full of holes, even Marcelline must see, if she ever stops to think. But she'll never see it any other way. Because he took the trouble to seduce her. Because he sent her to me. Because she will always believe no one would ever endanger themselves to such a degree. Especially when such a prize as herself is on the line. So the joke's on her. And fuck him.

Marcelline drives me back to Elysian Park. Thirty minutes of inadequate air-conditioning, small-talk, likes, tastes, desires. And drops me off on the street outside my basement apartment with a smiley promise never to call. There's my Guatemalan neighbour from the next-door duplex, weeding, with her faithful little terrier, Pico, gnawing on a rubber bone. I incline to bestow a little wave but he's turned away, is looking down the street, showing me his chocolate and tan tail, and the blue-dressed, round-hipped woman is momentarily focused on the comings and goings at the gay legation across the street. I juggle shoes, jacket, purse, manage to insert the key and unlock the gate, savour the clunk of the sprung bolt, push against the grille, walk through, glance over my shoulder to check the mailbox set into the wall, swing the gate shut behind me, and go barefoot down the concrete steps toward the yard, the enclosed, neglected garden. The silence pressing thick about me, the cool shade of eucalyptus that I share with a couple of small green lizards, ants beneath a possible fig tree, feeding on those fallen fruit which in all the months that I've lived here, I've never had identified.

If you are lost in your life? If there is nothing else in the world? If you wake alone in your bed? If your future has been taken from you? If you've been buried alive?

The more I struggle to reach the surface, the more I feel a greater force pressing against me, crushing. I consider all the usual resources, the analgesics of sex and drugs and shopping, and pack up my life and head for Rome.

Here I am. Unable to sleep. Thinking of desert nights.

Blood-warm silken air running in my mouth, on exposed skin. The garden filled with the determined chatter of insects, new-fledged cicadas, the steady thrum of faraway traffic. The leased rectangle of so-called lawn flooded with expensive hose-water, a rippled chocolate mud, set on this built-over hillside. Not quite patrician enough. Not quite Monte Parioli. The occasional shriek of a scooter on the street above. The murmur of pedestrians, slow moving, up and down, down and up, nursing ice-cream, leading dogs, children, grandparents. Snatches of conversation slipping through the open windows, abetted by the faulty intercom at the gate, always broadcasting the throaty native accent I cannot master. The initial slick and bare terror of finding myself here by myself, my future all around me. Weeping, kohl-darkened eyes plastered shut, huddling, rocking, hair falling tapered about enfolded knees, trying not to picture what alternatives my mother might have dreamed for me and my life.

And when I venture out, I find myself astonished then flipped into engagement by the chattering crowds at the high end of my street, packed into the small park located on the summit at Muse. The warm nights of this new summer keeping everyone out of doors. Couples on benches beneath trees. Hundreds at tables in the Casina delle Muse overlooking the Tevere, the valley. A smaller crowd at the Caffe Parnaso. And in between, the crackling explosive racket of the little arcade, with children pounding, banging, shooting, shouting. And occasionally, cheerful Chinese and Filipino maids are to be seen, leading around and around their tortoise-paced, ninety-year-old, bird-frail charges by liver-spotted wrists.

Nothing changes. It goes on. One thing leads to another, and that's all there is.

Down on the Corso, standing inside the blue light of Messaggerie, listening to the music while leafing through magazines, searching for news of Billy.

The carabinieri officer at Piazza Bligny smiling at me, day after day. A cavalryman in black uniform, shiny boots, twin red stripes on his pants, plain silver spurs.

Wearing these heels, these trousers, and gold woven haltertop. Walking to meet the politician at Monte-citorio. Stared at by tourists and locals alike who seem to decipher the nature of my assignation from my hair, these clothes, this face. Hurrying to get there by nine. Promised a tour of parliament, to be followed by dinner, some frenzy. The Gucci revealing my neck, my shoulders, my arms, my back, my skin.